Acclaim for Jim Shepard's

Like You'd Understand, Anyway

A *Time* and *Esquire* Best Book of the Year

"[Shepard] knows more about pacing and primal emotions than almost any best-selling author out there. His new stories . . . [are] as perfectly tuned as the best work of Michael Chabon and David Mitchell."   —*New York*

"A collection that knocks me dumb. . . . [Shepard] gives us our world in this little book. We'd be fools to ignore the offer."
                    —Benjamin Alsup, *Esquire*

"The characters Shepard has brought to life contain multitudes, incredible contradictions. . . . What's most remarkable about these stories, in the end, is how gently Shepard wraps the most extremely foreign and obscure events around emotional dilemmas common to all of us."   —*The Boston Globe*

"Wildly inventive."   —*Time*

"Fathers misunderstanding sons. Brothers clashing with brothers. Men undertaking dangerous exploits in pursuit of theories that are patently absurd. Jim Shepard casts a cool yet ultimately sympathetic eye on those who perpetrate such follies and, in doing so, reveals their humanity."   —*The Hartford Courant*

"Ranges daringly across time, bounding from ancient history to the present—and back."   —*New York Sun*

"The stories themselves are triumphs: darkly funny, deeply intelligent, and unforgettable. . . . A profound and disturbing book, full of dark delights. A book to re-read and to treasure."
—*Chronogram*

"A gem. . . . [Shepard] manages astonishing diversity."
—*Time Out Chicago*

Jim Shepard

Like You'd Understand, Anyway

Jim Shepard is the author of six novels and two previous
collections of stories. He teaches at Williams College in
Williamstown, Massachusetts.

Like You'd Understand, Anyway

STORIES

Jim Shepard

Vintage Contemporaries
Vintage Books
A Division of Random House, Inc.
New York

FIRST VINTAGE CONTEMPORARIES EDITION, AUGUST 2008

Stories in this collection originally appeared in the following publications: "The Zero Meter Diving Team" in *Bomb* (Fall 2007), "Proto-Scorpions of the Silurian" on failbetter.com (Summer 2005), "The First South Central Australian Expedition" in *Granta* (Fall 2006), "Trample the Dead, Hurtle the Weak" and "Sans Farine" in *Harper's* (September 2005 and November 2006), "Hadrian's Wall" in *McSweeney's* (Fall 2004), "Pleasure Boating in Lituya Bay" in *Ploughshares* (Spring 2007), "Courtesy for Beginners" in *A Public Space* (Summer 2007), "Ancestral Legacies" in *Seed* (Summer 2004), "Eros 7" in *Tin House* (Winter 2007), "My Aeschylus" in *The Virginia Quarterly Review* (Fall 2006).

The Library of Congress has cataloged the Knopf edition as follows:
Shepard, Jim.
Like you'd understand, anyway : stories / Jim Shepard.—1st ed.
p. cm.
I. Title.
PS3569.H39384L55 2007
813'.54—dc22 2007003639

Vintage ISBN: 978-0-307-27760-2

Book design by Virginia Tan

www.vintagebooks.com

Printed in the United States of America
10 9 8 7 6 5 4 3 2 1

For my brother, John

Contents

Acknowledgments

Without crucial contributions from the following sources, many of the stories in this book would not have existed, or would have existed in a much paltrier form: Don J. Miller's "The Alaska Earthquake of July 10, 1958" and "Giant Waves in Lituya Bay Alaska"; Howard Ulrich's and Vi Haynes' "Night of Terror"; Elliott B. Roberts' "History of a Tsunami"; Lawrence Elliott's "There's a Tidal Wave Loose in Here!"; Antoine de Baecque's *Glory and Terror*; Regina Janes' *Losing Our Heads*; Olivier Blanc's *Last Letters*; Peter Vansittart's *Voices of the Revolution*; Stanley Loomis's *Paris in the Terror*; Rodney Allen's *Threshold of Terror*; Daniel Arasse's *The Guillotine and the Terror*; Daniel Gerould's *Guillotine: Its Legacy and Lore*; Barbara Levy's *Legacy of Death*; Simon Schama's *Citizens*; J. Mills Whitham's *Men and Women of the French Revolution*; Bettyann Holtzmann Kevles's *Almost Heaven*; Rex Hall and David Shayler's *The Rocket Men*; Nina Lugovskaya's *The Diary of a Soviet Schoolgirl*; Jamie Doran and Piers Bizony's *Starman*; Cathy Young's *Growing Up in Moscow*; Philip Clark's *The Soviet Manned Space Program*; John Herington's *Aeschylus*; W. K. Pritchett's *The Greek State at War*; James Davidson's *Courtesans and Fishcakes*; Victor David Hanson's *The Western Way of War*; Bertha Carr Rider's *Ancient Greek Houses*; D. J. Conacher's *Aeschylus: The Earlier Plays and Related Studies*; Michael M. Sage's *Warfare in Ancient Greece*; R. E. Wycherley's *The Stones of Athens*; George Sfikas's *Wild Flowers of Greece*; Richard Lattimore's *Greek Lyrics*; Anthony Podlecki's *The Political Background of Aeschylean Tragedy*; Robert

Acknowledgments

Flaceliere's *Daily Life in Greece at the Time of Pericles;* Nicholas Sekunda's *Marathon 490 B.C.;* Steven Pressfield's *Gates of Fire;* George Derwent Thomson's *Aeschylus and Athens;* Robert Holmes Beck's *Aeschylus: Playwright, Educator;* Thomas G. Rosenmeyer's *The Art of Aeschylus;* and, of course, Aeschylus's surviving works, in translations by Richmond Lattimore, Seth G. Benardete, David Grene, Janet Lembke, C. J. Herington, Frederic Raphael, and Kenneth McLeish. Also: Richard C. Davis' *The Central Australia Expedition 1844–1846: The Journals of Charles Sturt;* Jan Kociumbas's *The Oxford History of Australia 1770–1860;* Bernard Smith and Alwyn Wheeler's *The Art of the First Fleet and Other Early Australian Drawings;* Tim Flannery's *The Explorers;* Ken Gelder and Jane Jacobs' *Uncanny Australia;* Alan Moorehead's *Cooper's Creek;* V. M. Chernousenko's *Chernobyl, Insight from the Inside;* Iurii Shcherbak's *Chernobyl, A Documentary Story;* Grigori Medvedev's *The Truth about Chernobyl;* Alla Yaroshinskaya's *Chernobyl: the Forbidden Truth;* Alan Bowman's *Life and Letters on the Roman Frontier;* Nic Fields' *Hadrian's Wall A.D. 122–410;* G. R. Watson's *The Roman Soldier;* John David Breeze's *Hadrian's Wall;* Mingtao Zhang's *The Roof of the World;* Clare Harris and Tsering Shakya's *Seeing Lhasa;* Reinhold Messner's *My Quest for the Yeti;* Michel Peissel's *Tibet: The Secret Continent;* and Thubten Jigme Norbu and Colin Turnbull's *Tibet.*

I'm also grateful for the support provided by the John Simon Guggenheim Memorial Foundation, the inspiration provided by F. Andrus Burr, Paul Park, and David Wright, the expertise provided by Colin Adams, Charles Fuqua, Michael MacDonald, Rebecca Ohm, Rich Remsberg, Matthew Swanson, Robbi Behr, David Dethier, and Mike Loverink of Air Excursions, the incisive editorial intelligence of Gary Fisketjon and Liz Van Hoose, the invaluable, tireless, and long-term contributions, as readers and friends, of Steve Wright, Lisa Wright, Gary Zebrun, and Mike Tanaka, and finally, in the category of those who have read pretty much everything, the unending aesthetic and emotional support provided by Sandra Leong and Ron Hansen, and—as always—Karen Shepard.

Like You'd Understand, Anyway

The Zero Meter Diving Team

Guilt, Guilt, Guilt

Here's what it's like to bear up under the burden of so much guilt: everywhere you drag yourself you leave a trail. Late at night, you gaze back and view an upsetting record of where you've been. At the medical center where they brought my brothers, I stood banging my head against a corner of a crash cart. When one of the nurses saw me, I said, "There, that's better. That kills the thoughts before they grow."

Hullabaloo

I am Boris Yakovlevich Prushinsky, chief engineer of the Department of Nuclear Energy, and my younger brother, Mikhail Vasilyevich, was a senior turbine engineer serving reactor Unit No. 4 at the Chernobyl power station, on duty the night of 26 April 1986. Our half brother Petya and his friend were that same night outside the reactor's cooling tower on the Pripyat River, fishing, downwind. So you can see that our family was right in the thick of what followed. We were not—how shall we put it?—very *lucky* that way. But then, like their country, the Prushinskys have always been first to protest that no one should waste any pity on *them*. Because the Prushinskys have always made their *own* luck.

3

The All-Prushinsky Zero Meter Diving Team

My father owns one photo of Mikhail, Petya, and myself together. It was taken by our mother. She was no photographer. The three of us are arranged by height on our dock over the river. We seem to be smelling something unpleasant. It's from the summer our father was determined to teach us proper diving form. He'd followed the Olympics from Mexico City on our radio, and the exploits of the East German platform divers had filled him with ambition for his boys. But our dock had been too low, and so he'd called it the Zero Meter Diving Platform. The bottom where we dove was marshy and shallow and frightened us. "What are you frightened of?" he said to us. "*I'm* not frightened. Boris, are *you* frightened?" "*I'm* not frightened," I told him, though my brothers knew I was. I was ten and imagined myself his ally. Petya was five. Mikhail was seven. Both are weeping in the photo, their hands on their thighs.

Sometimes at night when our mother was still alive our father would walk the ridge above us, to see the moon on the river, he said. He would shout into the darkness: he was *Victor Grigoryevich Prushinsky, director of the Physico-Energy Institute.* While she was alive, that was the way our mother—Mikhail's and my mother—introduced him. Petya's mother didn't introduce him to anyone. Officially, Petya was our full brother, but at home our father called him Half-life. He said it was a physicist's joke.

"Give your brother your potatoes," he would order Petya. And poor little Petya would shovel his remaining potatoes onto Mikhail's plate. During their fights, Mikhail would say to him things like "Your hair seems *different* than ours. Don't you think?"

So there was a murderousness to our play. We went on rampages around the dacha, chopping at each other with sticks and clearing swaths in the lilacs and wildflowers in mock battles. And our father would thrash us. He used an ash switch. Four strokes for me, then three for Mikhail, and I was expected to apply the fourth. Then three for Petya, and Mikhail was expected to apply the fourth. Our faces were terrible to behold. We always applied the final stroke as though we wanted to outdo the first three.

When calm, he quoted to us Strugatsky's dictum that *reason* was the ability to use the powers of the surrounding world without ruining that world. Striped with welts and lying on our bellies on our beds, we tinted his formulation with our own colorations of fury and misery. Twenty-five years later, that same formulation would appear in my report to the nuclear power secretary of the Central Committee concerning the catastrophic events at the power station at Chernobyl.

Loss

Our mother died of the flu when I was eleven. Petya lost his only protector and grew more disheveled and strange and full of difference. Mikhail for a full year carried himself as though he'd been petrified by a loud noise. Later we joked that she'd concocted the flu to get away, and that she was off on a beach in the Black Sea. But every night we peeped at one another across the dark floor between our beds, vacant and alone.

In the mornings I took to cupping Mikhail's fist with my palms when he was thumb-sucking, as though I were praying. It brought us nose to nose and made me shudder with an enraged tenderness. Petya sucked his thumb as well, interested.

That Warm Night in April

What is there to say about the power station, or the river on which it sits? The Pripyat just a few kilometers downstream drains into the Dnieper, having snaked through land as level as a soccer pitch with a current the color of tea from the peat bogs nearby. In the deeper parts, it's cold year round. For long stretches it dips and loops around stands of young pines.

Mikhail was pleased with the area when he settled there. He was a young tyro, the coming thing, at twenty-eight a senior turbine engineer. There were three secondary schools, a young people's club, festive covered markets, a two-screen cinema, and a Children's World department store. Plenty of good walking trails and fishing. Petya followed him. Petya usually followed him from assignment to assignment, getting odd jobs, getting drunk, getting thrown in jail, getting bailed out of trouble by his brother. Or half brother.

"Why doesn't he ever follow *you*?" Mikhail asked me the night Petya showed up on his doorstep yet again. Mikhail didn't often call. It was a bad connection that sounded like wasps in the telephone line. Petya was already asleep in the dining room. He'd walked the last twenty versts after having hitched a ride on a cement truck.

They found him a little apartment in town and a job on the construction site for the spent fuel depository. As for a residence permit: for that, Mikhail told me on the phone, they'd rely on their big-shot brother.

I was ready to help out. We both treated Petya as though he had to be taught to swallow. "Let *me* do that," we'd tell him, before he'd even commenced what he was going to attempt. Whatever went wrong in our lives, we'd think they *still* weren't as fucked-up as Petya's.

Mikhail's shift came on duty at midnight, an hour and twenty-five minutes before the explosion. Most of the shift members did not survive until morning.

Petya, I was told later, was fishing that night with another layabout, a friend. They'd chosen a little sandbar near the feeder channel across from the turbine hall, where the water released from the heat exchangers into the cooling-pond was twenty degrees warmer. In spring it filled with hatchlings. There was no moon and it was balmy for April, and starry above the black shapes of the cooling towers.

Earthenware Pots

As chief engineer of the Department of Nuclear Energy, I was a mongrel: half technocrat, half bureaucrat. We knew there were problems in both design and operating procedures, but what industry didn't have problems? Our method was to get rid of them by keeping silent. Nepotism ruled the day. "Fat lot of good it's done *me*," Mikhail often joked. If you tried to bring a claim against someone for incompetence or negligence, his allies hectored you, all indignation on his behalf. Everyone ended up shouting, no one got to the bottom of the problem, and you became a saboteur: someone seeking to undermine the achievement of the quotas.

People said I owed my position to my father, and Mikhail owed his position to me. ("More than they know," he said grimly, when I told him that.) At various congresses, I ran my concerns by my father. In response he gave me that look Mikhail called the Dick Shriveler. "Why's your dick big around him in the first place?" Petya once asked when he'd overheard us.

We all lived under the doctrine of ubiquitous success. Negative information was reserved for the most senior leaders, with censored versions available for those lower down. Nothing instructive about precautions or emergency procedures could be organized, since such initiatives undermined the official position concerning the complete safety of the nuclear industry. For thirty years, accidents went unreported, so the lessons derived from these accidents remained with those who'd experienced them. It was as if no accidents had occurred.

So who gave a shit if the Ministry of Energy was riddled through with incompetents or filled with the finest theorists? Whenever we came across a particular idiocy, in terms of staffing, we quoted to one another the old saying: "It doesn't take gods to bake earthenware pots." The year before, the chief engineer during the start-up procedures at Balakovo had fucked up, and fourteen men had been boiled alive. The bodies had been retrieved and laid before him in a row.

I'd resisted his hiring. That, for me, constituted enough to quiet my conscience. And when Mikhail submitted an official protest about sanctioned shortcuts in one of his unit's training procedures, I forwarded his paperwork on with a separate note of support.

Pastorale

The town slept. The countryside slept. The chief engineer of the Department of Nuclear Energy in his enviable Moscow apartment slept. It was a clear night in April, one of the most beautiful of the year. Meadows rippled like silvery lakes in the starlight. Pripyat was sleeping, Ukraine was sleeping, the country was sleeping. The chief engineer's brother, Mikhail, was awake, hunting sugar for his coffee. His half brother, Petya, was awake, soaking his feet and baiting a hook. In the number 4 reactor the staff, Mikhail included, was running a test to see how long the turbines would keep spinning and producing power in the event of an electrical failure at the plant. It was a dangerous test, but it had been done before. To do it they had to disable some of the critical control systems, including the automatic shutdown mechanisms.

They shut down the emergency core cooling system. Their thinking apparently had been to prevent cold water from entering the hot reactor after the test and causing a heat shock. But who knows what was going through their minds? Only men with no understanding of what goes on inside a reactor could have done such a thing. And once they'd done that, all their standard operating procedures took them even more quickly down the road to disaster.

The test was half standard operating procedure, half seat-of-the-pants initiative. Testimony, perhaps, to the poignancy of their longing to make things safer.

Did Mikhail know better? His main responsibility was the turbines, but even so even he probably knew better. Did he suspect his colleagues' imbecility? One night as a boy after a beating he hauled himself off his bed and pissed into our father's boots, already wet from the river. He'd never suspect, Mikhail told us. Mikhail lived a large portion of his life in that state of mind in which you take a risk and deny the risk at the same time, out of rage. No one in his control room knew nearly enough, and whose fault was that? "Akimov has your sense of humor," he told me once about his boss. It didn't sound like good news for Akimov's crew.

Minutes after they began, the flow of coolant water dropped and the power began to increase. Akimov and his team moved to shut down the reactor. But they'd waited too long and the design of the control rods was such that, for the first part of the lowering, they actually caused an *increase* in reactivity.

South Seas

On the evening of 1 May 1986 in Clinic No. 6 in Moscow I made the acquaintance of two young people: another senior turbine engineer and an electrical engineer. They had beds on either side of Mikhail's. The ward overflowed with customers. A trainee was collecting watches and wedding rings in plastic bags. Everyone was on some kind of drip but there weren't enough bowls and bins, so people were vomiting onto the floor. The smell was stunning. Nurses with trays skidded around corners.

Mikhail was a dark brown: the color of mahogany. Even his gums. When he saw my face he grinned and croaked, "South Seas!" A doctor changing his intravenous line explained without looking up that they called it a nuclear tan.

I was there partially in an official capacity, to investigate what had happened at the last moments.

Mikhail said, "Are you *weeping*? The investigator is *weeping!*" But his comrades in the nearby beds were unsympathetic. He interrupted his story in order to throw up in a bin between the beds.

He'd been in the information processing complex, a room a few levels below the control room. Two shocks had concussed the entire building and the lights had flashed off. The building had seemed to tip into the air and part of the ceiling had collapsed. Steam in billows and jets had erupted from the floor. He'd heard someone shouting, "This is an emergency!" and had pitched himself out into the hall. There was a strobe effect from the short circuits. The air smelled of ozone and caused a tickling sensation in the throat. The walls immediately above him were gone and he could see a bright purple light crackling between the ends of a broken high-voltage cable. He could see fire, black ash falling in flakes, and red-hot blocks and fragments of something burning into the linoleum of the floor.

He worked his way up to the control room, where everyone was in a panic. Akimov was calling the heads of departments and sections, asking for help. You could see the realization of what he'd helped to do hitting him. According to the panels, the control rods were stuck halfway down. Two trainees, kids just out of school, were standing around frightened, and he sent them off to *lower the control rods by hand.*

"The investigator is *weeping!*" my brother said triumphantly, again.

"This is a great tragedy," I told him, as though chiding him. The other engineers gazed over from their beds.

"Oh, yes," he said, as though someone had offered him tea. "Tragedy tragedy tragedy."

When it became clear that he wasn't going to go on, I asked him to tell me more.

"We have no protection systems—nothing!" he remembered Perevozchenko saying. Their lungs felt scalded. Their bronchioles and alveoli were being flooded with radionuclides. Akimov had sent him to ascertain the amount of damage to the central hall. He'd made his way to the ventilation center, where he could see that the top of the building had been blown off. From somewhere behind him he could hear radioactive water pouring down the debris. Steel reinforcing beams corkscrewed in various directions. His eyes stung. It felt as though something was being boiled in his chest. There was an acid taste to the steam and a buzz of static on his skin. He learned later that the radiation field was so powerful it was ionizing the air.

"Take that down, investigator," Mikhail said. He tried to drink a little water.

The Maximum Permissible Dose

At 1:23:58 the concentration of hydrogen in the explosive mixture reached the stage of detonation, and the two explosions Mikhail had felt in the information processing complex destroyed the reactor and the reactor building of Unit 4. A radioactive plume extended to an altitude of thirty-six thousand feet. Fifty tons of nuclear fuel evaporated into it. Another seventy tons spewed out onto the reactor grounds, mixing with the structural debris. The radioactivity of the ejected fuel reached twenty thousand roentgens per hour. The maximum permissible dose, according to our regulations for a nuclear power plant operator, is five roentgens per year.

Some Rich Asshole's Just Lost His Job

Petya said the explosions made the ground shake and the water surface ripple in all directions. Pieces of concrete and steel started landing in the pond around them. They could hear the hissing as the pieces cooled. For a while they watched the cloud billow out and grow above the reactor. By then the fire was above the edge of the building. Through a crack in one of the containment walls they could see a dark blue light. "Some rich asshole's just lost his job," he remembered remarking to his friend. I assume he meant someone other than his eldest brother.

And by then they'd both begun to feel dreadful. Their eyes streamed tears as they reeled about, so sluggish and disoriented it took them an hour to traverse the half kilometer to the medical station. By the time they arrived, it resembled a war zone.

The Individual Citizen in the Vanguard

How much difference could an individual bureaucrat really make in our system? That was a popular topic for our drinking bouts. For the epic bouts, we seemed to require a Topic. The accepted wisdom, which tempered our cynicism enough to smooth the way for our complacency, was that with clever and persistent and assiduous work and some luck, the great creeping hulk that was our society *could* be nudged in this or that direction. But one had to be patient, and work within the system, and respect the system's sheer *size*.

Because, you see, our schools directed all their efforts to inculcating industriousness (somewhat successfully), obedience (fairly successfully), and toadyism (very successfully). Each graduation produced a new crop of little yes-people. Our children learned criticism from their families, and from the street.

The Individual Citizen Still in the Vanguard

By four in the afternoon the day after the explosion, the members of the government commission began to gather, having flown in from everywhere. I'd been telephoned at five that morning by the head of the Party Congress. He was already exhausted. The station managers were assuring him that the reactor itself was largely undamaged and radioactivity levels within normal limits. There was apparently massive damage, however, and they couldn't control the fires. When I told him, rubbing my face and holding the phone, that that made no sense, his response was, "Yes. Well." I was to be on a military transport by eight-thirty. Mikhail, I knew, would be on duty, but when I phoned up Petya, there was no answer.

On the drive in from the airport, we slowed to traverse roads flooded with a white foam along the shoulders. The decontamination trucks we passed made us quiet. When we found our voices, we argued about whether the reactor had been exposed. The design people were skeptical, insisting that this variant was so well conceived that even if the idiots in charge had wanted to blow it up, they couldn't have.

But all that talk petered out when we assembled on the roof of the Town Committee office and could see over the apartment buildings to Unit 4. Its wall was open and flames were burning straight up from behind it. The air smelled the way metal tastes. We could hear the children down in the courtyard having their hour of physical training. "Which way is the wind blowing?" someone asked, and we all looked at the flags on the young people's club.

We moved back to the Town Committee office and shut the windows and shouted and squabbled for an hour, with contradictory information arriving every moment. *Where is Mikhail?* a voice in my head inquired repetitively. We had no idea what to do. As my mother used to say, it's only thunder when it bangs over your head. It wasn't possible, we were told, to accurately gauge the radiation levels, because no one had dosimeters with the right scales. The ones here went up to a thousand microroentgens per second, which was 3.6 roentgens per hour. So all of the instruments were off the scale wherever you went. But when Moscow demanded the radiation levels, they were told 3.6 roentgens an hour. Since that's what the machines were reading.

The station had had one dosimeter capable of reading higher

levels, the assistant to the nuclear power sector reported. But it had been buried by the blast.

Everyone was hoping that the bad news would announce itself. And that the responsibility and blame would somehow be spread imperceptibly over everyone equally. This is the only way to account for our watchmaker's pace, at a time when each minute's delay caused the criminal exposure of all those citizens—all those children—still going about their ordinary day outside.

The deputy chief operational engineer of the number 4 unit was managing to sustain two mutually exclusive realities in his head: first, the reactor was intact, and we needed to keep feeding water into it to prevent its overheating; and second, there was graphite and fuel all over the ground. Where could it have come from?

No one working at the station, we were told, was wearing protective clothing. The workers were drinking vodka, they said, to decontaminate. Everyone had lost track of everyone. It was the Russian story.

The Game of I Know Nothing Played Long Enough

The teachers in the schools heard about the accident through their relatives, who had heard from friends overseas—routine measurements outside Swedish power stations having already flagged an enormous spike in radioactivity—but when they inquired whether the students should be sent home, or their schedule in any way amended, the second secretary of the Regional Committee told them to carry on as planned. The Party's primary concern at that point seemed to be to establish that an accident on such a scale could not happen at such a plant. We had adequate stores of potassium iodide pills, which would at least have prevented thyroid absorption of iodine-131. We were forbidden as yet to authorize their distribution.

So throughout the afternoon children played in the streets.

Mothers hung laundry. It was a beautiful day. Radioactivity collected in the hair and clothes. Groups walked and bicycled to the bridge near the Yanov station to get a close look into the reactor. They watched the beautiful shining cloud over the power plant dissipate in their direction. They were bathed in a flood of deadly X-rays emanating directly from the nuclear core.

The fire brigade that had first responded to the alarm had lasted fifteen minutes on the roof before becoming entirely incapacitated. There followed a round-the-clock rotation of firemen, and by now twelve brigades, pulled from all over the region, had been decimated. The station's roof, where the firefighters stood directing their hoses, was like the door of a blast furnace. We learned later that from there the reactor core was generating thirty thousand roentgens per hour.

What about helicopters? someone suggested. What about them? someone else asked. They could be used to dump sand onto the reactor, the first speaker theorized. This idea was ridiculed and then entertained. Lead was proposed. We ended up back with sand. Rope was needed to tie the sacks. None was available. Someone found red calico gathered for the May Day festival, and all sorts of very important people began tearing it into strips. Young people were requisitioned to fill the sacks with sand.

I left, explaining I was going to look at the site myself. I found Mikhail. He was already dark brown by that point. I was told that he was one of those selected for removal by special flight to the clinic in Moscow. His skin color had been the main criterion, since the doctors had no way at that point of measuring the dose he'd received. He was on morphine and unconscious the entire time I was there. As a boy he'd never slept enough, and all of his face's sadness emerged whenever he finally did doze. There in the hospital bed, he was so still and dark that it looked like someone had carved his life mask from a rich tropical wood. At some point I told an orderly I'd be back and went to find Petya.

While hunting his apartment address I asked whomever I encountered if they had children. If they did I gave them potassium iodide pills and told them to have their children take them now, with a little water, just in case.

I found Petya's apartment but no Petya. A busybody neighbor with one front tooth hadn't seen him since the day before but asked many questions. By then I had to return to the meeting. The group had barely noticed I was gone. No progress had been made, though outside the building teenagers were filling sandbags with sand.

All of Them: Heroes of the Soviet Union

By late afternoon the worst of the prevaricators had acknowledged the need to prepare for evacuation. In the meantime untold numbers of workers had been sent into the heart of the radiation field to direct cooling water onto the nonexistent reactor. The helicopters had begun their dumping, and the rotors, arriving and departing, stirred up sandstorms of radioactive dust. The crews had to hover for three to five minutes directly over the reactor to drop their loads. Most managed only two trips before becoming unfit for service.

Word finally came through that Petya too had been sent to the medical center. By the time I got over there he'd been delivered to the airport for emergency transport to Moscow. When I asked how he'd gotten such a dose, no one had any idea.

At ten a.m. on Sunday the town was finally advised to shut its windows and not let its children outside. Four hours later the evacuation began.

Citizens were told to collect their papers and indispensable items, along with food for three days, and to gather at the sites posted. Some may have known they were never coming back. Most didn't even take warm clothes.

The entire town climbed onto buses and was carried away. Many getting on were already intensely radioactive. The buses were washed with decontaminant once they were far enough out of town. Eleven hundred buses: the column stretched for eighteen kilometers. It was a miserable sight. The convoy kicked up rolling billows of dust. In some places it enveloped families still waiting to be picked up, their children groping for their toys at the roadside.

That night when the commission meeting was over, I went my own way. Even the streetlights were out. I felt my way along with small steps. I was in the middle of town and might as well have been on the dark side of the moon. Naturally, I thought, Petya had somehow been there, on the river. Whenever the shit cart tipped over, there was Petya, underneath.

The Zero Meter Diving Team

It turned out Petya was installed on the floor below Mikhail's in Moscow's Clinic No. 6. When I asked an administrator if some sort of triage was going on, she said, "Are you a relative?" When I said I was, she said, "Then no."

He was hooked up to two different drips. He didn't look so bad. He was his normal color, maybe a little pale. His hair was in more riot than usual.

"Boris Yakovlevich!" he said. He seemed happy to see me.

At long last he'd gotten his chance to lie down, he joked. His laziness had always been a matter of contention between us.

"Has Father been by to see me?" he asked. "I've been out of it for stretches."

I told him I didn't know.

"Has he been to see Mikhail?" he asked.

I told him I didn't know. He asked how his brother was holding up. I told him I was going to visit Mikhail directly afterward and would report back.

"Are you feeling sorry for me?" he asked after a pause. A passing nurse seemed surprised by the question.

"Of course I am," I told him.

"With you sometimes it's hard to tell," he said.

"What can I do for you?" I asked after another pause.

"I have what they call a 'period of intestinal syndrome,' " he said glumly. "Which means I have the shits thirty times a day." And these things in his mouth and throat, he added, which was why he couldn't eat or drink. He asked after the state of the reactor, as though he were one of the engineers. Then he explained how he'd ended up near the reactor in the first place. He described his new Pripyat apartment and said he hoped to save up for a motorcycle. Then he announced he was going to sleep.

"Get me something to read," he said when I got up to leave. "Except I can't read. Never mind."

The next floor up, the surviving patients were sequestered alone in sterile rooms. Mikhail was naked and covered in a yellow cream. Soaked dressings filled low bins in the hall. Huge lamps surrounded the bed to keep him warm.

"Father's been to see me," he said instead of hello.

He said that four samples of bone marrow had been extracted and no one had told him anything since. Most of the pain was in his mouth and stomach. When he asked for a drink, I offered some mango juice I'd brought with me. He said it was just the thing he wanted. He was fed up with mineral water. He shouted at a passing doctor that the noise of her heels was giving him diarrhea.

"When we got outside, graphite was scattered all around," he said, as if we'd been in the middle of discussing the accident. "Someone touched a piece of it and his arm flew up like he'd been burned."

"So you knew what it was?" I asked.

I assumed I wasn't allowed to touch him because of the cream. He was always the boy I'd most resented and the boy I'd most wanted to be. I'd been the cold one, but he'd been the one who'd made himself, when he'd had to be, solitary and unreachable.

An orderly wheeled in a tray of ointments, tinctures, creams, and gauzes. He performed a counterfeit of patience while he waited for me to leave.

"Have you had enough of everything?" I asked Mikhail. "Is there anything I can bring?"

"I've had the maximum permissible dose of my brother Boris," he said. "Now I need to recuperate." But then he went on to tell me that Akimov had died. "As long as he could talk, he kept saying he did everything right and didn't understand how it had happened." He finished the juice. "That's interesting, isn't it?"

Mikhail had always said about me that I was one of those people who took a purely functional interest in whomever I was talking to. Father had overheard him once when we were adults and had laughed approvingly.

"Someone's going to have to look after Petya," he said, his eyes closed, some minutes later. I'd thought he'd fallen asleep. As far as I knew, he wasn't aware that his brother was on the floor below him.

"I have to get on with this," the orderly finally remarked.

When I told him to shut up, he shrugged.

There Is No Return. Farewell. Pripyat, 28 April 1986

Two years later, at four in the morning, my father and I drove into the Zone. The headlamps dissolved picturesquely into the pre-dawn mist, but my father's driver refused to slow down. It was like being in a road rally. The driver sat on a lead sheet he'd cadged from an X-ray technician. For his balls, he explained when he saw me looking at it. Armored troop carriers with special spotlights were parked here and there working as chemical defense detachments. The soldiers wore black suits and special slippers.

Even through the misty darkness we could see that nature was blooming. The sun rose. We passed pear trees gone to riot and chaotic banks of wildflowers. A crush of lilacs overwhelmed a mile marker.

Mikhail had died after two bone marrow transplants. He'd

lasted three weeks. The attending nurse reported final complaints involving dry mouth, his salivary glands having been destroyed. But I assumed that that was Mikhail being brave, because the condition of his skin had left him in agony for the final two weeks. On some of my visits he couldn't speak at all, but only kept his eyes and mouth tightly closed, and listened. I was in Georgia at the start-up of a new plant the day he died. He was buried, like the others in his condition, in a lead-lined coffin that was soldered shut.

Petya was by then an invalid on a pension Father and I had arranged for him. He was twenty-five. He found it difficult to get up to his floor, since his building had no elevator, but otherwise, he told me when I occasionally called, he was happy. He had his smokes and his tape player and could lay about all day with no one to nag him, no one to tell him that he had better amount to something.

"It's a shame," my father mused on the ride in. "*What* is?" I asked, wild with rage at the both of us. But he looked at me with disapproval and dropped the subject.

At Pripyat a sawhorse was set up as a checkpoint, manned by an officer and two soldiers. The soldiers had holes poked in their respirators for cigarettes. They'd been expecting my father, and he was whisked off to be shown something even I wasn't to be allowed to see. His driver stuck his feet out the car's open window and began snoring, head thrown back. I wandered away from the central square and looked into a building that had been facing away from the reactor. I walked its peeling and echoing hallways and gaped into empty offices at notepads and pens scattered across floors. In one there was a half-unwrapped child's dress in a gift box, the tulle eaten away by age or insects.

Across the street in front of the school, a tree was growing up from beneath the sidewalk. I climbed through an open window and crossed the classroom without touching anything. I passed through a solarium with an empty swimming pool. A kindergarten with little gas masks in a crate. Much had been looted and tossed about, including a surprising number of toys. At the front of one room over the teacher's desk someone had written on a red chalkboard, *There Is No Return. Farewell. Pripyat, 28 April 1986.*

Self-Improvement

The territory exposed to the radioactivity, we now knew, was larger than one hundred thousand square kilometers. Many of those who'd worked at Chernobyl were dead. Many were still alive and suffering. The children in particular suffered from exotic ailments, like cancer of the mouth. The director of the Institute of Biophysics in Moscow announced that there hadn't been one documented case of radiation sickness among civilians. Citizens who applied to the Ministry of Health for some kind of treatment were accused of radiophobia. Radionuclides in large amounts continued to drain into the reservoirs and aquifers in the contaminated territories. It was estimated that humans could begin repopulating the area in about six hundred years, give or take three hundred years. My father said three hundred years. He was an optimist. Nobody knew, even approximately, how many people had died.

The reactor was encased in a sarcophagus, an immense terraced pyramid of concrete and steel, built under the most lethal possible circumstances and, we'd been informed, already disintegrating. Cracks allowed rain to enter and dust to escape. Small animals and birds passed in and out of the facility.

I left the schoolyard and walked a short way down a lane overhung with young pines. Out in the fields, vehicles had been abandoned as far as the eye could see: fire engines, armored personnel carriers, cranes, backhoes, ambulances, cement mixers, trucks. It was the world's largest junkyard. Most had been scavenged for parts, however radioactive. Each step off the road added a thousand microroentgens to my dosimeter reading.

The week after Mikhail died, I wrote my father a letter. I quoted him other people's moral outrage. I sent him a clipping decrying the abscess of complacency and self-flattery, corruption and protectionism, narrow-mindedness and self-serving privilege that had created the catastrophe. I retyped for him some graffiti I'd seen painted on the side of an abandoned backhoe: that the negligence and incompetence of some should not be concealed by the patriotism of others. I typed it again: *the negligence and incompetence of some should not be concealed by the patriotism of others.* Whoever had written it was more eloquent than I would ever be. I was writing to myself. I received no better answer from him than I'd received from myself.

Science Requires Victims

My father and I served on the panel charged with appointing the commission set up to investigate the causes of the accident. The roster we put forward was top-heavy with those who designed nuclear plants, neglecting entirely the engineers who operated them. So who was blamed, in the commission's final report? The operators. Nearly all of whom were dead. One was removed from hospital and imprisoned.

During his arrest it was said he quoted Petrosyants's infamous remark from the Moscow press conference the week after the disaster: "Science requires victims."

"Still feeling like the crusader?" my father had asked the day we turned in our report. It had been the last time I'd seen him. "Why not?" I'd answered. Afterward I'd gotten drunk for three days. I'd pulled out the original blueprints. I'd sat up nights with the drawings of the control rods, their design flaws like a hidden pattern I could no longer unsee.

But then, such late-night sentimentalities always operate more as consolation than insight.

I could still be someone I could live with, I found myself thinking on the third night. All it would take was change.

A red fox, its little jaws agape, sauntered across the road a few meters away. It was said that the animals had lost their skittishness around man, since man was no longer about. There'd been a problem with the dogs left behind going feral and radioactive, until a special detachment of soldiers was bused in to shoot them all.

Around a curve I came upon the highway that had been used for the evacuation. The asphalt was still a powdery blue from the dried decontaminant solution. The sky was sullen and empty. A rail fence ran along the fields to my left. While I stood there, a rumble gathered and approached, and from a stand of poplars a herd of horses burst forth, sweeping by at full gallop. They were followed a few minutes later by a panicked and brindled colt, kicking its legs this way and that, stirring up blue and brown dust.

"Was I ever the brother you hoped I would be?" I asked Mikhail toward the end of my next-to-last visit. His eyes and mouth were squeezed shut. He seemed more repelled by himself than by me, and he nodded. All the way home from the hospital that night, I saw it in my mind's eye: my brother, nodding.

Proto-Scorpions of the Silurian

It's a crappy rainy morning in Bridgeport, Connecticut, and I'm home from seventh grade with a sore throat and my parents and brother are fighting and I'm trying every so often to stay out of it. Jonathan Winters is on *Merv Griffin,* doing his improv thing with a stick.

My father's beside himself because he thinks my mother threw out the *Newsweek* he's been saving to show my brother. It had war casualties on the cover. "You couldn't find your ass with both hands and a banjo," he tells her, though she's not looking.

"Go take a shit for yourself," she tells him on her way through to the living room. He slams drawers in the kitchen. When he gets like this he stops seeing what's in them. We have to double-check everywhere he's looked to find anything. All of this is probably going to make my brother go off and we all know it, but none of us can stop.

He was institutionalized at sixteen and released eight months later. It was at Yale–New Haven, a teaching hospital, and they either didn't have much of an idea of what to do with him, or they were totally at a loss, depending on who you talked to.

"God forbid we should go somewhere," my mother says from the living room. She's smoking and keeping to herself. "What we need to do instead is show each other magazines."

"Maybe *you* should go somewhere," my father tells her.

My brother and I are playing 500 rummy. He's kicking my ass.

For a while I was kicking his. He's quiet like he's trying to concentrate. He hates when my father goes out of his way to do something for him. He pats his hair, which is falling out because of the medication, the way you check your pockets for something before you leave the house. His eyes are getting scarier, distracted and unfocused.

He takes a break to make a tuna sandwich. White bread, no mayonnaise: he forks it out of the can and tries to spread it around. The tuna doesn't cooperate. He clears his throat a lot. My mother's still talking to herself. I try a joke. He gets that look you get when bile backs up. He's at this point eighteen or nineteen and has, as he puts it, his whole fucking life ahead of him.

I ask my father why he's home from work today. "What're you, a cop?" he goes.

I'm flipping my cards and debating whether to look at my brother's while he makes the sandwich. I'm also poking through a book I took out from the library. It has a giant scorpion on the cover, and you have to take something out and do a report, every week. It always takes forever to find something that's even halfway interesting. I get good grades, which is what I do instead of talking to people. My parents think I'm going to college. My father says when people ask that it's the one thing this family hasn't fucked up.

Prearcturus gigas it says was over a meter long. I try pronouncing the name under my breath.

"*You're* all right," my brother says, eyeing me.

That turns out to be a scorpion three feet long. There's a life-size picture of the fossil's pedipalps—movable things near the mouth that help shovel the prey in—next to a photo of ones from the largest scorpion today. It's like hunting knives next to fingernail parings.

My father starts rooting through the garbage under the sink, swearing. My mother calls it saying the rosary. "Don't go through the garbage," she tells him. "It's not in the garbage." Nobody's watching the TV in the den.

Scorpions apparently went nuts during the Carboniferous period, which was way before the dinosaurs. According to what the book calls the fossil record. But our science teacher says the fossil record's a joke. That it's like saying we can figure out who lived in the U.S. by going through twelve dumpsters. Sitting there at the table, waiting, I come across these things from before the Carboniferous that weren't even scorpions. Proto-scorpions. They have like no eyes, no claws. Who knows. They may just be lousy fossils.

My father starts shaking the plastic garbage can upside down into the sink. We can smell it from where we are. "I have no idea what you're doing," my brother tells him. My mother says he better not be making a mess.

"*There*, you son of a bitch," my father goes, pulling out the magazine.

"What do you want from me?" my brother says when he holds it up. "A dance?"

After a minute my father starts cleaning everything up, dropping stuff back into the can's liner. I start winning at rummy.

"Fucking Cincinnati Kid," my brother goes, watching me tote up.

"I'm the kid with all the answers," I tell him. You can see him wondering how I meant that and then figuring it's not worth finding out.

"So here's the article I was talking about," my father tells him. There's a muffin wrapper stuck to it.

"Very nice," my brother goes. He's rearranging the suits in his hand. He's starting to look worse. He doesn't do almost anything but work out, and his arms when he flexes them rip the T-shirt sleeves.

"I'm out," I tell him again and fan the cards out between us. I catch him with another big hand.

He sits there with his eyes on me, setting one molar on another. While he does the math I page around some more in the book. There's a drawing of something that looks like a shingle with some antennae. It looks like I'm showing off, beating him while reading a book. But it's somewhere to put my eyes, so I can't bring myself to shut it.

"You playing cards or reading?" my father wants to know. He can see my brother's face.

"The *library,*" my mother says from the other room. "That's the only place anybody in this family goes."

"Where're we gonna go? It's a fucking *downpour,*" my brother tells her.

She doesn't answer. My father wipes his sponge around the rim of the sink, finishing the cleanup.

I'm given a dream hand—a run and a half—right off his deal. And the card I need after that is the first one he discards. I think about not saying anything. Then I go ahead. "I'm out again," I tell him, putting my cards down to show him.

He pulls his hands back to his lap and sits there. Then he turns the whole table over. At its highest point the whole thing's up over my head. A few minutes after it hits, the neighbor across the street calls to see if everything's all right.

Later when everything's quiet I'm still in the kitchen. There's a divot in the linoleum where the table edge came down. I'm in the corner with my back to the cabinets. My brother's in his room. My mother's in hers. My father hurt his back wrestling my brother up the stairs. He's got the heating pad on it. One end of the pad's tucked into his belt so it looks like he's plugged into the wall.

There's tuna in my sock. My throat's still sore. There's not enough self-pity to go around. "Is he your brother or *not?*" my father's asking me.

"Yeah," I tell him.

"So you wanta *help* him?" he wants to know.

"Yeah," I tell him, tearing up.

"Well then why *don't* you help him?" he wants to know.

Because there's what we want, and what we do, I'd figured out, even then.

"You want to help him?" he asks me again.

"Not really," I tell him, sitting there. Not really, I tell myself, now.

Hadrian's Wall

Who hasn't heard by now of that long chain of events, from the invasion by the Emperor Claudius to the revolt of Boudicca and the Iceni in the reign of Nero to the seven campaigning seasons of Agricola, which moved our presence ever northward to where it stands today? From the beginning, information on our campaigns has never ceased being gathered from all parts of the province, so it's easy to see how historians and scribes of the generation before me have extended the subject's horizons.

In my father's day, before my morning lessons began, I would recite for my tutor the story of the way the son of all deified emperors, the Emperor Caesar Trajan Hadrian Augustus, on whom the necessity of keeping the empire within its limits had been bestowed by divine command, had scattered the Britons and recovered the province of Britannia and added a frontier between either shore of Ocean for eighty miles. The army of the province built the Wall under the direction of Aulus Platorius Nepos, pro-praetorian legate of Augustus. I would finish our lesson by reminding my tutor that my father had worked on that wall, and my tutor would remind me that I had already reminded him.

The line chosen for the Wall lay a little to the north of an existing line of forts along the Stanegate, the northernmost road. The Wall was composed of three separate defensive features: the first a ditch to the north, the second a wide, stone curtain wall with turrets, milecastles, and forts strung along its length, and the third a large earthwork to the south. Their construction took three legions five years.

I have memories of playing in the freshly dug material from the bottom of the ditch. I found worms.

The ditch is V-shaped with a square-cut ankle-breaker channel at the bottom. Material from the ditch was thrown to the north of it during construction to form a mound that would further expose the attacking enemy. The turrets, milecastles, and forts were built with the Wall serving as their north faces. Double-portal gates placed front and rear at the milecastles and forts provide the only ways through.

The countryside where we're stationed is naked and wind-swept. The grass on the long ridges is thin and sere. Sparse rushes accentuate the hollows and give shelter to small gray birds.

The milecastles are situated at intervals of a mile, and between them, the turrets, each in sight of its neighbor, ensure mutual protection and total surveillance. The forts are separated by the distance that can be marched in half a day.

Here then is the aggregate strength of the Twentieth Cohort of Tungrians whose commander is Julius Verecundus: 752 men, including 6 centurions, of which 46 have been detached for service as guards with the governor of the province, under the leadership of Ferox, legate of the Ninth Legion. Of which 337 with 2 centurions have been detached for temporary service at Coria. Of which 45 with 1 centurion are in garrison in a milecastle six miles to the west. Of which 31 are unfit for service, comprising 15 sick, 6 wounded, and 10 suffering from inflammation of the eyes. Leaving 293 with 3 centurions present and fit for active service.

I am Felicius Victor, son of the centurion Annius Equester, and I serve in the Twentieth Cohort as scribe for special services for the administration of the entire legion. All day, every day, I'm sad. Over the heather the wet wind blows continuously. The rain comes pattering out of the sky. My bowels fail me regularly and my barracksmates come and go on the bench of our latrine while I huddle there on the cold stone. In the days before his constant visits, my father signed each of his letters *Now in whatever way you wish, fulfill what I expect of you.*

My messmates torment me with pranks. Most recently they sent off four great boxes of papyrus and birch bark for which I'm responsible in two wagonloads of hides bound for Isurium. I would have gone to get them back by now except that I do not care to injure the animals while the roads are bad. My only friend is my own counsel, kept here in this account. I enter what I can at day's end while the others play at Twelve Points or Robber Soldiers. I sit on my clerk's stool scratching and scratching at numbers, while even over the wind the bone-click of dice in the hollow of the dice box clatters and plocks from the barracks. Winners shout their good fortune. Field mice peer in at me before continuing on their way.

Our unit was raised in Gallia Belgica according to the time-honored logic concerning auxiliaries that local loyalties are less dangerous when the unit's not allowed to serve in its native region. Since spring, sickness and nuisance raids have forced the brigading of different cohorts together in order to keep ourselves at fighting muster.

Scattered tribes from the north appear on the crests of the low hills opposite us and try to puzzle out our dispositions. The wind whips through what little clothing they wear, mainly what looks like muddy flags between their legs. We call them *Brittunculi,* or "filthy little Britons."

Even with their spies they don't fully grasp how many of the turrets and milecastles go undermanned. Periodically our detachments stream swiftly through the sparsely guarded gates and we misleadingly exhibit strength in numbers.

The governor of our province has characterized us as shepherds guarding the flock of empire. During punitive raids all males capable of bearing arms are butchered. Women and children are caravanned to the rear as slaves. Those elderly who don't attempt to interfere are beaten and robbed. Occasionally their homes are torched.

Everyone in our cohort misses our homeland except me. I would have been a goat in a sheep pen there, and here I contribute so little to our martial spirit that my barracks nickname is Porridge. When with some peevishness I asked why, I was dangled over a well until I agreed that Porridge was a superior name.

Every man is given a daily ration of barley. When things are going badly and there's nothing else to eat and no time to bake flatbread, we grind it up to make a porridge.

I was a firebrand as a brat, a world-beater. I was rambunctious. I was always losing a tooth to someone's fist. My father was then an auxilia conscripted in his twenty-first year in Tungria. Later, after his twenty-five year discharge, he was granted citizenship and the tria nomina: forename, family name, and surname. I was born in the settlement beside the cavalry fort at Cilurnum. My mother worked in a gambling establishment with an inscription above the door that read DRINK, HAVE SEX, AND WASH. My father called Cilurnum a roaring, rioting, cock-fighting, wolf-baiting, horse-riding town, and admired the cavalry. My mother became his camp wife and gave him three children: a sickly girl who died at birth, Chrauttius, and me. Chrauttius was older and stronger and beat me regularly until he died of pinkeye before coming of age. Our father was on a punitive raid against the Caledonii when it happened. He returned with a great suppurating wound across his bicep and had a fever for three days. When my mother wasn't at work in the gambling establishment, she attended him with an affectionate irritation. She dressed and bound his wound with such vigor that neighbors were required to hold him down while she flushed the cut with alcohol. His bellows filled our ears. When he was recovered he brooded about his elder son. "Look at him," he said to my mother, indicating me.

"Look at him yourself," she told him back.

He had a particular way he favored of being pleasured which required someone to hold his legs down while the woman sat astride him. Usually my mother's sister assisted, but during his fever she feared for her own children, so I was conscripted to sit on his knees. I'd been on the earth for eight summers at that point, and I was frightened. At first I faced my mother but when she asked me to turn the other way, I held my father's ankles and pitched and bucked before he kicked me onto the floor.

At the start of my eighteenth summer I armed myself with a letter of introduction from him to one of his friends still serving with the Tungrian cohort. My father's command of the language was by no means perfect, and since my mother had had the foresight to secure me a tutor for Latin and figures, I helped him with it. *Annius to Priscus, his old messmate, greetings. I recommend to you a worthy man* . . . and so on. I've since read thousands.

I then presented myself for my interview held on the authority of the governor. Though I had no citizenship, an exception was made for the son of a serving soldier, and I was given the domicile *castris* and enrolled in the tribe of *Pollia.* Three different examiners were required to sign off on a provisional acceptance before I received my advance of pay and was posted to my unit. Attention was paid to my height, physical capacity, mental alertness, and most especially my skill in writing and arithmetic. A number of offices in the legion required men of good education, since the details of duties, parade states, and pay were entered daily in the ledgers, with as much care, I was told, as were revenue records by the civil authorities.

Thus I was posted to my century, and my name entered on the rolls. I trained for two summers in marching, physical stamina, swimming, weapons, and field service, so that when I finished I might sit at my stool and generate mounds of papyrus and birchbark, like an insanely busy and ceaselessly twitching insect.

I have a cold in my nose.

We're so undermanned that during outbreaks of additional sickness, detachments from the Ninth Legion are dispatched for short periods to reinforce our windblown little tract. And there are other auxilaries manning the wall on either side of us. Asturians, Batavians, and Sabines to our east, and Frisiavones, Dalmatians, and Nervii to the west.

My father's agitating to be put back on active duty. He's discovered the considerable difference between the standard of living possible on an officer's pay as opposed to a veteran's retirement pension. He's tried to grow figs and sweet chestnuts on his little farm, with a spectacular lack of success. He claims he's as healthy as ever and beats his chest with his fist and forearm to prove it. He's not. The recruiting officers laugh in his face. Old friends beg to be left alone. He's asked me to intercede for him, as he interceded for me. He believes I have special influence with the garrison commander. "Oh, let him join up and march around until he falls over," my mother tells me, exasperated.

Every day he rides his little wagon four miles each way to visit my clerk's stool and inquire about his marching orders. The last phrase is his little joke. It's not clear to me when he acquired his sense of humor. Even when the weather is inclement he presents himself, soaked and shivering, with his same crooked smile. His arms and chest have been diminished by age. "This is my son," he tells the other clerk each day: another joke. "Who? This man?" the other clerk answers every time. There's never anyone else in our little chamber.

Sometimes I've gone to the latrine when he arrives, so he waits, silent, while the other clerk labors.

Upon hearing that I still haven't spoken to the garrison commander, he'll stand about, warming himself at our peat fire while we continue our work. Each time he speaks, he refashions his irritation into patience. "I've brought you sandals," he might say after a while. Or, "Your mother sends regards."

"Your bowels never worked well," he'll commiserate if I've been gone an especially long time.

On a particularly filthy spring day dark with rain, he's in no hurry to head home. Streams of mud slurry past our door. The occasional messenger splashes by, but otherwise everyone but Wall sentries is under cover. The peat fire barely warms itself. The other clerk and I continually blow on our hands, and the papyrus cracks from the chill if one presses too hard. While I work surreptitiously

34

on a letter to the supplymaster in Isurium, requesting that our boxes of papyrus be restored to us, my father recounts for us bits of his experiences working on the Wall. The other clerk gazes at me in silent supplication.

"We're quite a bit behind here," I finally remind my father.

"You think *this* is work?" he says.

"Oh, god," the other clerk mutters. The rain hisses down in wavering sheets.

"I'm just waiting for it to let up," my father explains. He gazes shyly at some wet thatch. He smells faintly of potash. He reknots a rope cincture at his waist, his knuckles showing signs of the chilblains. His stance is that of someone who sees illness and hard use approaching.

"Were you really there from the very beginning?" I ask. The other clerk looks up at me from his work, his mouth open.

My father doesn't reply. He seems to be spying great sadness somewhere out in the rain.

When I point out that without that wall there'd be Britons on this very spot at this very moment, the other clerk gazes around. Water's braiding in at two corners and puddling. Someone's bucket of moldy lentils sits on a shelf. "And they'd be welcome to it," he says.

The Wall was begun in the spring of his second year in the service, my father tells us, as the emperor's response to yet another revolt the season before. The emperor had been vexed that the Britons couldn't be kept under control. My father reminds us that it was Domitius Corbulo's adage that the pick and the shovel were the weapons with which to beat the enemy.

"What a wise, wise man was he," the other clerk remarks wearily.

Nepos had come from a governorship of Germania Inferior. Three legions—the Second Augusta, the Sixth Victrix pia fidelis, and the Twentieth Valeria Victrix—had been summoned from their bases and organized into work parties. The complement of each had included surveyors, ditchdiggers, architects, roof tile makers, plumbers, stonecutters, lime burners, and woodcutters. My father had been assigned to the lime burners.

Three hundred men working ten hours a day in good weather extended the Wall a sixth of a mile. He worked five years, with the construction season running from April to October, since frosts interfered with the way the mortar set.

The other clerk sighs, and my father looks around for the source of the sound.

Everything was harvested locally except iron and lead for clamps and fittings. The lime came from limestone burnt on the spot in kilns at very high temperatures. The proportion of sand to lime in a good mortar mix was three to one for pit sand, two to one for river sand.

"Now I've written *two to one*," the other clerk moans. He rises from his stool and crushes the square on which he's been working.

"Water for the lime and mortar was actually one of the biggest problems," my father goes on. "It was brought in continuously in barrels piled onto gigantic oxcarts. Two entire cohorts were assigned just to the transport of water."

The other clerk and I scratch and scratch at our tablets.

As for the timber, if oak was unavailable, then alder, birch, elm, or hazel was used.

While I work, a memory vision revisits me from after my brother's death: my father standing on my mother's wrist by way of encouraging her to explain something she'd said.

Locals had been conscripted for the heavy laboring and carting, he tells us, but everyone pitched in when a problem arose. He outlines the difficulties of ditchdigging through boulder clay. Centurions checked the work with ten-foot rods to insure that no one through laziness had dug less than his share or gone off line.

The rain finally lets up a bit. Our room brightens. A little freshness blows through the damp. My father rubs his forearms and thanks us for our hospitality. The other clerk and I nod at him, and he nods back. He wishes us good fortune for the day. "And you as well," the other clerk answers. My father acknowledges the response, flaps out his cloak, cinches it near his neck with a fist and steps out into the rain. After he's gone a minute or two, it redoubles in force.

On my half day of rest I make the journey on foot to their little farmstead. When I arrive I discover that my father's gone to visit me. He never keeps track of my rest days. A cold sun is out and my mother entertains me in their little garden. She sets out garlic paste and radishes, damsons and dill. My father's trained vines to grow on anything that will hold them. There's also a new addition: a small shrine erected to Viradecthis, set on an altar. It's a crude marble of Minerva that he's altered with a miniature Tungrian headdress.

I ask if he's now participating in the cult. My mother shrugs and says it could be worse. One of her neighbors' sons has come back from his travels a Christian. Worships a fish.

She asks after my health, recommending goat cheese in porridge for my bowels. She asks after gossip, though it always saddens her that I have so little. How did her fierce little wonder boy grow into such a pale little herring?

She smiles and lays a hand on my knee. "You have a good position," she reminds me proudly. And I do.

It would appear from my father's belongings that a campaign is about to begin. His scabbards are neatly arrayed next to his polishing tin. The rest of his kit is spread on a bench to dry in the sun. His marching sandals have been laid out to be reshod with iron studs. A horsefly negotiates one of the studs.

She tells me that periodically he claims he'll go back to Gallia Belgica, where the climate is more forgiving to both his figs and his aches. Having returned from service in Britannia as a retired centurion would make him a large fish in that pond. But he has no friends there, and his family's dead, and there's ill feeling bound to be stirred up by the relatives of a previous wife who died of overwork and exposure.

Besides, there's much that the unit could do with an old hand, she complains he's always telling her. Sentry duty alone: some of the knotheads taking turns on that wall would miss entire baggage trains headed their way.

She asks, as she always does, about my daily duties. She enjoys hearing about my exemptions. A soldier's daily duties include muster, training, parades, inspections, sentry duty, cleaning our centurions' kits, latrine and bathhouse duty, firewood and fodder collection. My skills exempt me from the latter four.

She wants to know if my messmates still play their tricks on me. I tell her they don't, and that they haven't in a long while. I regret having told her in the first place.

When I leave she presents me with a wool tunic woven with decorations. I wear it on the walk back.

During training, recruits who failed to reach an adequate standard with a particular weapon received their rations in barley instead of wheat, the wheat ration not restored until they demonstrated proficiency. While I was quickly adequate with the sword, I was not with the pilum and could hit nothing no matter how close I brought myself to the target. My father even tried to take a hand in the training. My instructor called me the most hopeless sparrow he'd ever seen when it came to missile weapons. For three weeks I ate only barley and have had the shits ever since. On the one and only raid in which I've taken part, I threw my pilum immediately, to get it over with. It stuck in a cattle pen.

Night falls on the long trek back to the barracks. I strike out across the countryside, following the river instead of the road, the sparse grasses thrashing lightly at my ankles. At a bend I stop to drink like a dog on all fours and hear the rattletrap of my father's little wagon heading toward the bridge above me. When he crosses it his head bobs against the night sky. He's singing one of his old unit's songs. He's guiding himself by the light of the moon. It takes him a long while to disappear down the road.

By any standards our army is one of the most economical institutions ever invented. The effective reduction and domination of vast tracts of frontier by what amounts to no more than a few thousand men requires an efficiency of communication that enables the strategic occupation of key points in networks of roads and forts. Without runners we have only watchfires, and without scribes we have no runners.

In my isolation and sadness I've continued my history of our time here. So that I might have posterity as a companion as well.

More rain. Our feet have not been warm for two weeks. We are each and every one of us preoccupied with food. We trade bacon lard, hard biscuits, sour wine, and wheat. When it's available, we trade meat: ox, sheep, pig, goat, roe deer, boar, hare, and fowl. We trade local fruit and vegetables. Barley, bean, dill, coriander, poppy, hazelnut, raspberry, bramble, strawberry, bilberry, celery. Apples, pears, cherries, grapes, elderberries, damsons and pomegranates, sweet chestnuts, walnuts, and beechnuts. Cabbages, broad beans, horse beans, radishes, garlic, and lentils. Each group of messmates has its own shared salt, vinegar, honey, and fish sauces. Eight men to a table, with one taking on the cooking for all. On the days I cook, I'm spoken to. On the days I don't, I'm not. The other clerk runs a gambling pool and is therefore more valued.

The muster reports worsen with the rain. Eleven additional men are down with roundworm. One of the granaries turns out to be contaminated with weevils.

For two nights one of the turrets—off on its own on a lonely outcropping here at the world's end, the Wall running out into the blackness on each side—contains only one garrisoned sentry. No one else can be spared. He's instructed to light torches, knock about on both floors, and speak every so often as though carrying on a conversation.

It's on this basis that one might answer the puzzling question: how is it that our occupation can be so successful with so few troops? The military presence is by such methods made to seem stronger and more pervasive than it actually is. We remind ourselves that our detachments can appear swiftly, our cavalry forts never far away.

This tactic could also be understood to illuminate the relationship between the core of the empire and its periphery. Rome has conquered the world by turning brother against brother, father against son; the empire's outer borders can be controlled and organized using troops raised from areas that have just themselves been peripheral. Frontiers absorbed and then flung outward against newer frontiers. Spaniards used to conquer Gaul, Gauls to conquer Tungrians, Tungrians to conquer Britannia. That's been Rome's genius all along: turning brother against brother and father against son. Since what could have been easier than that?

Peace on a frontier, I've come to suspect, is always relative. For the past two years of my service our units have devoted their time between small punitive raids to preventing livestock rustling and showing the flag. But over the last few days we've noted our scouts—lightly armed auxiliaries in fast-horsed little detachments—pounding in and out of our sally ports at all hours. Rumors have begun to fly around the barracks. Having no friends, I hear none of them. When I ask at the evening meal, having cooked dinner, I'm told that the Britons are after our porridge.

My night sentry duty comes around. I watch it creep toward me on the duty lists the other clerk and I update each morning so no one's unjustly burdened or given exemption. The night my turn arrives, it's moonless. The three companions listed to serve with me are all laid low with whipworm.

At the appointed hour I return to the barracks to don my mail shirt and scabbard. As I'm heading out with my helmet under my arm, one of my messmates calls wearily from across the room, "That's mine." At the duty barracks I'm handed a lantern that barely lights my feet and a small fasces with which to start the warning fire. All of this goes in a sack slung over my shoulder on a short pole which I'll carry the mile and a half through the dark along the Wall to the turret. Before I leave, the duty officer ties to the back of my scabbard a rawhide lead with two old hobnailed sandals on the end of it, so I'll sound like a relieving party and not a lone sentry.

"Talk," he advises as I step out into the night. "Bang a few things together."

The flagstone paving along the Wall's battlement is silver in the starlight. With the extra sandals and my kit sack I sound like a junk dealer clanking along through the darkness. Every so often I stop to listen. Night sounds reverberate around the hills.

I'm relieving a pair of men, neither of whom seem happy to see me. They leave me an upper story lit by torches. Two pila with rusted striking blades stand in a corner. A few old cloaks hang on pegs over some battered oval shields. A mouse skitters from one of the shields to the opposite doorway. There's an open hearth for heat in the story below, invisible from the heath. Up here two windows afford a view but with the glare from the torches I'm better off observing from outside. The moonlessness won't grant much opportunity to track time.

After a few minutes I find I haven't the heart to make noise or clatter about. I untie the rawhide lead and pitch the sandals down below. I don't bother with the hearth and in a short time the lower story goes dark. The upper still has its two torches and is nicely dry, though a cold breeze comes through the windows. I alternate time inside with time on the Wall. It takes minutes to get used to seeing by starlight when I go back out.

Some rocks fall and roll somewhere off in the distance. I keep watch for any movement in that direction for some minutes, without success.

My father liked to refer to himself as stag-hearted. He was speaking principally of his stamina on foot and with women. "Do you miss your brother?" he asked me on one of those winter fortnights he spent hanging about the place. It was only a few years after my brother's death. I still wasn't big enough to hold the weight of my father's sword at arm's length.

I remember I shook my head. I remember he was unsurprised. I remember that some time later my mother entered the room and asked us what was wrong now.

"We're mournful about his brother," my father finally told her.

He was such a surprising brother, I always think, with his strange temper and his gifts for cruelty and whittling and his fascination with divination. He carved me an entire armored galley with a working anchor. He predicted his own death and told me I'd recognize the signs of mine when it was imminent. I was never greatly angered by his beatings but once became so enraged by something I can't fully remember now, involving a lie he told our mother, that I prayed for the sickness which later came and killed him.

"I prayed for you to get sick," I told him on his deathbed. We were alone and his eyes were running so that he could barely see. The pallet beneath his head was yellow with the discharge. He returned my look with amusement, as if to say, *Of course.*

Halfway through the night a bird's shriek startles me. I chew a hard biscuit to keep myself alert. The rain's a light mist and I can smell something fresh. My mother's wool tunic is heavy and wet under the mail.

When I'm in the upper story taking a drink, a sound I thought was the water ladle continues for a moment when I hold the ladle still in its tin bucket. The sound's from outside. I wait a few seconds before easing out the door, crouching down behind the embrasure to listen and allow my eyes to adjust. I hold a hand out to see if it's steady. The closest milecastle is a point of light over a roll of hills. My heart's pitching around in its little cage.

Barely audible and musical clinks of metal on stone extend off to my left down below. No other sounds.

The watchfire bundle is inside to prevent its becoming damp. In the event of danger it's to be dumped into a roofed and perforated iron urn mounted on the outer turret wall and open-faced in the direction of the milecastle. The bundle's been soaked in tar to light instantly. The watchfire requires the certainty of an actual raid, not just a reconnaissance. You don't get a troop horse up in the middle of the night for a few boys playing about on dares.

There's the faint whiplike sound of a scaling rope off in the darkness away from the turret. I raise my head incrementally to see over the stone lip of the embrasure and have the impression that a series of moving objects have just stopped. I squint, then widen my eyes. I'm breathing into the stone. After a moment, pieces of the darkness detach and move forward.

When I wheel around and shove open the turret door a face, bulge-eyed, smash-toothed, smeared with black and brown and blue, lunges at me and misses, and a boy pitches off the Wall into the darkness below with a shriek.

Behind him in the turret, shadows sweep the cloak pegs between me and my watchfire bundle. A hand snatches up my sword.

So I jump, the impact rattling my teeth when I land. When I get to my feet, something hits me flush in the face. On the ground I hear two more muffled blows, though I don't seem to feel them. I'm facedown. Pain pierces inward from any mouth movement and teeth loll and slip atop my tongue. I'm kicked around. When my septum contacts the turf a drunkenness of agony flashes from ear to ear.

When it recedes there are harsh, muted sounds. One of my ears has filled with liquid. There's commotion for a while, and then it's gone. In the silence that follows I make out the agitated murmur of the detachment mustering and then setting out.

I test various aspects of the pain with various movements. Lifting my head causes spiralling shapes to arrive and depart. Fluids pour across my eyes. At some point, silently weeping, I stop registering sensations.

In the morning I discover they'd been pouring over the Wall on both sides of me, the knotted ropes trailing down like vines.

Everyone is gone. Smoke is already high in the sky from both the milecastle and the fort. When I stand I teeter. When I look about me only one eye is working. The boy from the turret door is dead not far from me, having landed on rock. That his weapon is still beside him suggests he was overlooked.

The rain's stopped and the sun's out. My mother's wool tunic is encrusted and stiff. I walk the Wall throwing back over those ropes closest to my turret, blearily making my dereliction of duty less grotesque. It requires a few hours to walk across the heather past the milecastle, and then on to the fort. Since I can't move my jaw, I presume it's broken. Two of the fort's walls have been breached but apparently the attack was repulsed. Legionaries and auxiliaries are already at work on a temporary timber rampart. Minor officers are shouting and cursing. The *Brittunculi* bodies are being dragged into piles. The Tungrians' bodies probably have already been rolled onto pallets and carried into the fort.

My head is bound. A headache doesn't allow me to raise it. My first two days are spent in the infirmary. My assumption about my jaw turns out to be correct. I ask if my eye will be saved and am told that's a good question. A vinegar and mustard poultice is applied. Two messmates come by to visit a third dying from a stomach wound. They regard me with contempt tinged with pity. Over the course of a day I drink a little water. My father visits once while I'm asleep, I'm informed. I ask after those I know. The clerk who shared my little room died of burns from the barracks fire. He survived the night but not the morning. Somehow the location of the raid was a complete surprise, despite the rumors.

It takes all of six days for four cohorts of the Ninth Legion, with its contingents of light and heavy horse, supported by two of the tattered cohorts of the Tungrians, to prepare its response. The Romans suffer casualties as though no one else ever has. There are no speeches, no exhortations, among either the legions or the auxiliaries. The barracks ground is noisy only with industry. The

Romans, hastily camped within our walls, go about their business as if sworn to silence. Only butchery will allow them to speak.

I live on a little porridge sipped through a straw. No one comments on the joke. On the fifth day I report my ready status to my muster officer. He looks me up and down before moving his attention to other business. "All right, then," he says.

On the sixth day of our muster my father appears over my pallet, the first thing I see when I wake in the barracks. He's wearing his decorations on a harness over his mail, and the horsehair crest of his helmet sets some of our kitchenware, hanging from the rafters, to rocking. He's called himself up to active duty and no one's seen fit to argue with him.

It's only barely light. He tells me he's glad for my health and my mother sends her regards and good wishes and that he'll see me outside.

At the third trumpet signal the stragglers rush to take their positions in the ranks. A great quiet falls over the assembled units, and the sun peeks across the top of the east parapet. The herald standing to the right of a general we've never seen before asks three times in the formal manner whether we are ready for war. Three times we shout, *We are ready.*

We march all day, our advance covered by cavalry. The sun moves from astride our right shoulder to astride our left. By nightfall we've arrived at a large settlement with shallow earthen embankments and rickety palisades. Are these the men, or the families of the men, responsible for the raid? None of us care.

Their men are mustering themselves hurriedly into battle order before the settlement, unwilling to wait for the siege. They wear long trousers and have animals painted on their bare chests: Caledonii. Is this their tribal territory? I have no idea.

We are drawn up on the legion's left. At the crucial time, we know, the cavalry will appear from behind the settlement, sealing the matter. On this day, with my father somewhere lost in the melee off to my right, we will all of us together become the avenging right arm of the empire. We will execute what will be reported back to the provincial capital as a successful punitive raid. I will myself record the chronicle with my one good eye. I will write, *When we broke through the walls and into the settlement we killed every living thing. The women, the children, the dogs, the goats were cut in half and dismembered. While the killing was at its height pillaging was forbidden. When the killing was ended the trumpets sounded the recall. Individuals were selected from each maniple to carry out the pillaging. The rest of the force remained alert to a counterattack from beyond the settlement. The settlement was put to the torch. The settlement was razed to the ground. The building stones were scattered. The fields were sown with salt.* My comrades-in-arms will think no more of me than before. My father and I will continue to probe and distress our threadbare connections. And what my mother will say about her marriage, weeping with bitterness in a sun-suffused haze a full summer later, will bring back to me my last view of the site after the Twentieth Tungrians and the Ninth Legion had finished with it, pecked over by crows and studded with the occasional shattered pilum: "We honor nothing by being the way we are. We make a desolation and we call it peace."

Trample the Dead, Hurdle the Weak

Guy's hurt? Fuck 'im. Guy can't get up, play's still going? Run his ass over. Whistle's blown? Stretcher bearer time. Grab a blow and let the Sisters of Mercy do their thing.

"Faggots," Wainwright says whenever the trainers come out for someone. He means the trainers.

We're not talking games, here. We're talking summer practice, two-a-days, guys keeling over in the heat. When more than one guy has the dry heaves we call it *Hee Haw* because of the sound.

"That shit's not funny," somebody'll say when they see us laughing. Some fat shit, holding his knees, blowing chow. "Dude for the Vikings *died*."

We have it written in chalk and boxed on a corner of the blackboard that doesn't get erased: TRAMPLE THE DEAD, HURDLE THE WEAK. When the coaches first wrote it, they spelled it E-L, both times. "Dumb fucks," Wainwright said when he saw it. He rubbed it out with his arm and wrote it right.

"Who's been screwing with my inspirational slogans?" our defensive coordinator wanted to know.

"*I* been," Wainwright told him. It was after the afternoon half of a two-a-day and those of us not on fluids or hurling were on the rug, our legs spread out, because it felt cooler than the benches or we couldn't get up to the benches. "Just streamlining the spelling, Coach."

"You better be careful you don't get on my list, Wainwright," Coach told him.

"I'm on everybody's list, Coach," Wainwright told him back.

Wainwright's a blue chipper's blue chipper. The top prospects in all of the regular and online rating services are always quarterbacks or running backs or wide receivers. He's been the cover of *Street & Smith's High School Edition* two years running at linebacker. "L.T. never made the cover," I tell him.

"I don't think they had one for high school back then," he tells me.

We argue on the way home from practice as to whether L.T. really wanted to *kill* people out there.

It's a hundred degrees with eighty percent humidity. Wainwright sweats right down the center of his chest, like he's wearing big stripes. Girls line the road we take home, just so they can say they saw him.

We want to cause panic on the field one hundred percent of the time. As far as we can tell, when it came to that, L.T. came the closest. We put him up there in the ninetieth percentile.

"You know how when you get licorice and you double it to get more in your mouth at once?" he said. "That's what he did to Theisman's thigh."

L.T. was also the snot bubble guy. He said his favorite hits were the ones that popped a snot bubble out of the ball carrier's nose.

I met Wainwright my first day of varsity practice. I came out of the locker room and hadn't buckled my chin strap, and already there was an altercation. Wainwright and this fucking giant were locked up and pulling each other's face masks around. The giant I knew, everybody knew: Junior Cooley, our All-State offensive tackle. He benched 350 pounds. His helmet on his head looked like a bucket on a bush.

They avoided each other for a play or two, and then on a screen pass Junior swung upfield looking for someone to block and Wainwright was already in the air and en route. They hit each other so hard *I* could feel it. The little ear pads came out of Junior's helmet. The ball carrier and some of the pursuit all piled into the body. Everybody made those *oooh* sounds.

Wainwright pulled himself from the pile, his helmet a little askew. Junior's face mask bolts were snapped and the blood from his nose had fanned upward to cover his forehead. Wainwright put a hand on each side of Junior's helmet and got in close and waited for Junior to focus, and told him, "Remember: the next play could be your last, but your *education'll* never be taken away."

He says he motivates through intimidation and positive reinforcement.

He runs full tilt, adjusts full tilt, arrives at full tilt. He hits like someone falling down an elevator shaft. "Friggin' *seismic*," I heard the defensive line coach murmur once. What the coaches love about him is that no matter what, he gets to where he needs to go. And always arrives on time, in a hurry, and in a shitty mood.

Between games he likes to mingle with the regular students. Sprats, he calls them.

Most of us played for serious youth football or Pop Warner programs but even so this was eye-opening, this level of hitting. Whenever you'd hear a pop or a real collision on the field, a coach would murmur, "Welcome to the big time." They didn't even need to be looking.

"Those of you who want to play, strap on your hats," Big Coach said at our team meeting, day one. We call our defensive coordinator Coach and the head coach Big Coach. "Because we're gonna be flying around and cracking heads."

An hour or so after Junior's reorientation Wainwright and I converged on a hit and his forearm shiver glanced off the ball-carrier's helmet and whacked mine. My helmet opened a divot in my forehead. I was bleeding like someone was pouring water over my head.

Wainwright liked my stitches afterwards. He called me The Lid for the way my scalp looked.

I had to miss two or three practices until I figured out how to keep one of my mom's maxipads over my stitches with a headband.

Here's the thing: Wainwright and me are pretty sure that my dad's kid is this All-State running back for Port Neches-Groves down around Beaumont. We saw the kid's picture in the *Street & Smith's* last year and he looked just like me. We checked him out on the Web site and Wainwright was like *cackling* when the kid's face popped up. "You, only smarter" was the way he put it. Plus my aunt made my mom cry once just by mentioning Beaumont. Plus she wouldn't answer when I asked about it. "Don't talk stupid," she said. "I don't know any other way *to* talk," I told her.

We wouldn't play a school from Beaumont unless both schools got pretty deep into the state tournament. But that could happen. They're district champs, and we're us.

Wainwright and me both got brother issues. When I point that out to him, he goes, "Yeah, except yours are uninteresting." His brother's now with the Jaguars, getting paid serious money to hurt people every Sunday. He's third on their depth chart, but still. If you don't count Mystery Boy out at Port Neches-Groves, my family hasn't amounted to much. My regular brother's five years older than me and his main claim to fame is that he taught me how to play by kicking my ass up and down the field. I played a lot of games with him when I was crying so hard I could barely see the ball. "Be a Spartan," he'd say in front of our friends after he'd leveled me, to keep me from running home to my mother. "Be a Spartan." "I'll *kill* you," I'd usually scream, when I finally could, and then I'd try.

"Get off me," he'd tell me when I'd go after his Adam's apple or eyes.

Our dad left when I was two and my brother was seven. My mom says she never heard from him again but we think she's lying. I ask my brother what he was like and he says, "What do you *think*? He was a dick."

When I keep after him he'll say to Mom, "Mom. Wasn't Dad a dick?"

"Stop it," Mom'll tell him.

I Googled his name and came up with a guy who wrote science fiction who I couldn't tell where he lived and a guy who sold boats in Michigan. I don't think either guy is him.

There's nobody with his name in the Beaumont area, according to the phone book. But get this: the kid's name is Corey. Our name's Royce.

"Look at that: it's a fucking antonym," I said when I realized.

"That's *anagram,* you fucking clown," Wainwright said back.

But it *was.* I called all three Coreys the operator gave me. Of course there were two unlisted, too. It was probably one of those.

Because we're a regional high school, we pull in talent from all over. Big Coach calls us by our hometowns if he doesn't remember our names. I'm Paducah. The weakside guy alongside Wainwright is Cee Vee. Wainwright's Wainwright.

We got a Web site with home page graphics of about eight of us swarming a guy from Childress, our big rival. The Web site's called HumDuckLand, and above that it says *Show 'Em You Got the HumDuck.*

On the sidebar there's News, Team Info, Spirit Groups, History, Merchandise, and Tickets. Click on Spirit Groups and you pull up categories for Cheerleaders, the Pepettes, the LHS Band, and the Majorettes. Under History you find HumDuck Origins, Team Records, Past Coaches, Traditions, and Ex-Players.

"Why don't you just drive over to Beaumont if you want to meet this kid?" Wainwright asked me on the way home from practice. Yellow jackets did figure eights over his head. They liked his shampoo.

"I wanna meet him on the *field*," I told him. Though I thought about actually driving there. That I would if I had to. But Wainwright wants a piece of him too. Partly because he thinks it's cold, what my dad did, if he did it. And partly because he's tired of hearing that the kid's unstoppable. "Un*stop*pable," he said, the first time he heard it, like he'd just smelled barbecue.

They're 8-o thanks mostly to that kid. So maybe they got it in themselves to step up to where we're going to be. It'd be a bigger deal for them than for us. Every year we're something: State Final-

ists, Regional Finalists, Regional Semi-Finalists, Bi-District Finalists. Our 1996 team won the Texas State Championship. Our JVs
are divided into Team White and Team Blue, thirty-man rosters
that each play different schedules, so what we call our baby boys
can get some work. White plays at five, Blue at seven, Varsity at
nine. Our stadium holds 18,400 but is being upgraded. JVs are
mostly sophomores, though every so often there's a Wainwright or
a me that moves up early. Everybody keeps an eye on everybody
else.

Media Day is the second Friday in August. The coaches stand
around in their white T-shirts and blue shorts giving us grief like
they're sweet guys because all the beat reporters are there.

Our home unies are dark blue—jerseys, pants, helmets. The
coaches think it psyches out opponents that we practice in those
in the heat. "How do they know we don't just practice in white?"
Wainwright asked them once. They let it go. That same day he just
stood looking at them at the end of a 104-degree ballbreaker of a
scrimmage and said, "They don't have *any idea* how serious this
is." When he saw me looking at him he said, "And neither do you."

At Homecoming all the Kings and Queens are photographed
with the team. They're in team-color tuxes and gowns. "You think
this kid Corey is Homecoming King?" I asked Wainwright after
that same scrimmage.

"You have *no idea* who I am, do you?" he asked me back.

"So who *are* you?" I asked him. But he was heading for the
showers. A lot of our conversations ended like that.

I was scared shitless when I first came out, and not of the coaches.
Like all freshmen I was shipped over to JV, Team White, and I was
so nervous the first day I had the shits for thirty minutes and was
late for my first real practice. I was in the stall bent over and miserable and thinking, *No way you can compete at this level.* I had my
chin on my knees. In tiny letters at the bottom of the door, someone had scratched *Shit shit shit.*

I called my brother from the pay phone near the furnace room. He'd started three of his four years for LHS. I remember I said something like, I might be in a little over my head here. I was having trouble not blubbering. He told me not to worry that much yet, that everything would come to me. "Hey, *leave* if you wanta leave," he finally said when I wouldn't let it go. "What you gonna do back *here*?" Meaning my mom's house, where we lived. I didn't have an answer for him. I still had all my dad's tools in my bedroom. I didn't know how to use most of them and they didn't need to be in my bedroom. "What's up with the socket wrench?" Wainwright asked me the one time he hung out there.

First practice Big Coach saw me, he said he thought my neck was too small for this level. Then a year or so later he said, "Son, you got some big feet there." He seemed to like me more because of it. You heard a lot of stupid shit over the course of a summer practice schedule.

They moved me to defense pretty much when I arrived. I didn't have the foot speed. Apparently heart didn't matter. So I went after any running back on the field. If they wouldn't let me be a running back, I'd punish the guys who were. And that was *before* I found out about this kid Corey. The coaching staff loved it, until they didn't. "He's on our side, son," Big Coach called out to me after a headhunter hit in practice. It got a laugh from the other coaches.

First day was picture day. They gave me number 47. I sat there thinking how great this was. Then I looked around and saw two more number 47s.

I came in at 140 pounds and ate and pumped my way up to 155. I got myself out of JV my sophomore year, halfway through our scrimmage with Quanah. On the second half kickoff I did a surface-to-air thing with their lead guy on the wedge and blew him back into their ballcarrier, who went ass over shoulder pads and fumbled. I opened my eyes and there was the ball and I rolled over and pulled it in. I was on the Web site under both *Hit of the Week* and *HumDuck of the Week*. The HumDuck face was superimposed over my helmet. It looked like some Donald Duckish freak was trying to kill someone.

The next practice I was working out with the varsity. Thank God the offense was working on its option, because I had no idea what our coverages were at that point.

Some varsities are all seniors. That's how rare it is.

Wainwright had already moved up. Half the crowds at our scrimmages were there to see him. I was pretty much in a state of panic about being left behind.

Around here, Big Coach likes to remind us, we live under the shade of trees we didn't plant and drink from wells we didn't dig. There's a shitload of tradition, is what he means.

Wainwright's the main upholder of that tradition as far as everybody else is concerned. Players for other teams: they're wearing another color and they're on his field. He takes it personally.

I try to ride that wave but there are mean dogs and mad dogs, and it's not that easy to make the leap.

Our sophomore year we were trailing Childress early and their halfback had already ripped off four or five ten-yard runs against us. "You boys don't *tackle* all that well," their center said when we were all unpiling. Later he tried to pull on a trap and I held him up and Wainwright caught him at full speed with his head turned. We stayed over him while the trainers worked on him. "You boys don't stay *conscious* all that well," Wainwright told him when he came to.

Now that Wainwright and me're juniors, we're on a mission. He wants to kill everybody in sight starting with whoever's in front of him and I want to kill everybody in sight starting with that kid Corey. Nobody wants to practice with us. We both have a thing for our fullback. The kid's father comes to every single one of his practices to watch his son get that big ass up in the air and put his head down and go. So Wainwright and me meet him in the hole and blow him up, time after time. We just decleat him. Guys'll be getting back up and he'll be putting a shoe back on.

His dad tried to talk to us after one practice, but the coaches broke it up.

We have other ways of passing time too, like throwing golf balls out of the stadium when standing on the fifty-yard line.

It's got to be five hundred miles to Beaumont. It's all the way over by Louisiana.

Midseason sophomore year I tore my MCL. It sounded like someone cracking walnuts in my knee. Wainwright was flying by when it happened and imitated the sound I made for weeks afterwards. I'd done this whimpering thing before I could stop myself. "Oooo, it *hurts*," he said in this falsetto whenever he saw me gimping around. They scoped it out, supposedly, but something fucked up and it kept catching and locking, and swelled up. I stumped around for a week or two looking for sympathy and then late one afternoon during this ice storm—it was like *black* outside—Coach saw me doing nothing in the locker room and asked if I wanted to play the next week. Shit yeah, I told him. I stumped back and forth to show him I was All Heart. "Let me see you run, then," he said. I looked around the locker room. "Outside," he said. I went out in shorts and quarter-inch cleats for the ice. Once I got out into the sleet I poked my head back in. "It's fucking *slippery*, Coach," I said. I demonstrated by skating my foot around even with the cleats. The cement steps were like a hockey rink.

"You don't *haveta* play," he said. "And watch your language."

Bite me, I thought. I ran like a fucking gazelle. I was never colder in my life. Ice built up on one side of my face from the wind.

I swear more than most people on the team. A lotta Christians around here. We moved from Rahway, New Jersey, when I was in seventh grade.

Anyway, my knee was fine after that.

"I gotta be ready for Port Neches-Groves," I told Wainwright during my rehab.

"Long as you're ready," he said. "I don't care who you're ready for."

I spent a lot of time at home doing leg lifts with gallon jugs filled with sand on either side of my ankle.

"Gotta work," my brother would chuckle from the other room.

"Why?" I'd go. "You don't."

Which he'd also think was funny. He said he wanted to test the welfare state. That's what he tells relatives when they ask if he's found anything yet.

My mom's brothers and sisters are the ones who ask. My dad only had one brother, and we don't know where he is, either.

"What about Wal-Mart?" my mom'll say. "They're hiring."

"I could be a greeter," my brother'll say. "Welcome to fucking Wal-Mart."

My mom doesn't think he should work for Wal-Mart. She thinks he should go to college out of state, maybe back up north. She says he has a God-given brain. He would've had scholarships to Kent State and Utah State, but he tanked on his grades his senior year. He comes to the games partway through the first half and sits on the opponent's side. He takes credit for my being All-State. He's probably right. By the time I got to Pop Warner, when kids my own age would hit me, I'd be like: please.

Wainwright's brother, meanwhile, recovered a big fumble against the Ravens on opening day. His family gets the NFL package so they can watch his games. Every time Wainwright gets another award, his dad tells him, "Well, if you turn out to be a tenth of the player your brother is, I'll be happy."

"I think you're a tenth now," I told him once we were alone, the first time I heard his dad say that. He didn't say anything back. Later that night he took a couple of his parents' tropical fish out into the driveway and fungoed them into the neighbor's yard with his old wiffle bat.

We lost our conference championship to Childress last year when I got beat deep halfway through the second half and neither team scored again. I was only helping out on a two-deep coverage, but still. They went on to the 5A Finals. This year their stadium cups feature a photo of their wide receiver running down the side-lines with a number 47 chasing him. Number 47 is me.

Port Neches-Groves lost in the Bi-District round anyway, which made me feel a little better.

Big Coach and Childress's coach have a bet going every year and the winner gets this butt-ugly hassock that has our colors, blue and white, on one side, and their colors, orange and brown, on the other. The two booster groups made it together. All fall Big Coach has been yelling at us that he wants to be able to put his feet up again after a hard day of motivating sad sacks in the heat.

And Wainwright and me have decided that we're not losing as juniors. Anybody who's not on board for that—anybody who dogs it in practice, or shies away from going for a ball over the middle, or is a pussy about being hurt—hears from us. One guy we cornered in the showers. He kept crying and calling us faggots but he got the message.

Our offense blows but our defense gets more and more awesome.

Our first nine games we've given up 55 points—a little over 6 a game—and that's because Big Spring, who we opened with, scored 18 on us off turnovers. Besides Wainwright and me we got Nunez and Swearington and Stribling and that's just in our front seven. And we're all maniacs. Our nickel back tackled his great aunt when he was five years old. She walked through the front hall to give him a hug and he took her out. He says she bounced back strong.

But here's the thing: I'm sleeping less and less. I can't sit still. Something's fucking me up from the inside.

"What do you mean?" my mom says when I tell her something weird's going on.

"I don't know," I tell her.

"Is it something physical?" she says. "You wanna go to a doctor?"

"It's mental," my brother calls from the TV room.

"You're not helping," my mom calls back.

"I have no idea where your father is," she tells me. "I'd tell you if I did."

I'm just keyed up early, is Wainwright's opinion. Even so, he gives me that look, the one the kid we cornered in the showers probably saw.

In the Floydada game, he did something in a pileup that made me ask if he was nuts when we were coming off the field and he ignored me the rest of the game. I kept to myself after that. I didn't hear from him and he didn't hear from me. *I don't need you*, I thought. But then it was like whatever control I had went away.

I e-mail the guy who sells boats in Michigan: *This is my name. Are you my dad?*

I have to e-mail him again before he e-mails back *Heck No*.

"Don't you wonder if he's living in Beaumont?" I ask my brother.

"You know what I heard?" my brother says back. "I heard that that kid is such a great running back because his father loves him so much."

Before every practice we're supposed to come up with what Big Coach calls a Fact from History or Science. His father was a superintendent of schools and he's big on people knowing something. Mine on Thursday practice the week before Childress week is that according to surveys, ten percent more young people in America this year have felt like they were going to go nuts than ten years ago.

"Where'd you get *this*?" Big Coach wants to know, fingering my scrap of paper.

I show him: Dr. Joseph Mercola, author of *Total Health Program*.

Port Neches-Groves's Web site's mailbag link is going all spastic all week because the entire starting backfield—Corey and Cody Clark, the quarterback, and Michael Thibodeaux, the fullback— are all hurt and Clark and Thibodeaux out at least a week and smart money says that that's the end of the line with powerhouse Port Arthur coming up.

"What's the matter with *you*?" my brother asks when he finds me in his room, squatting on the floor. I'm naked. It's three in the morning.

I couldn't sleep, I tell him.

"What, you think you're gonna be more *fucked-up* than me, too?" he goes. He says it like if he *could* kill me, he would.

I just squat there, shocked by his voice.

"You wanta feel sorry for somebody? Feel sorry for *me*," he says. When I look at him his eyes are all teared up.

"What's wrong?" my mom wants to know when she comes downstairs to make coffee. We're both in the kitchen. I put on some sweatpants and a shirt when I got too cold. The sun's up and the dog's out.

She sees me shivering and turns up the heat. "Nobody *answers* anymore?" she wants to know. "Maybe I should shout all the time?" she asks, when nobody says anything.

She leaves the room and comes back with a desk drawer she upends over my plate. Pencil stubs, old photographs, rubber bands, tacks. "Your father's stuff," she tells me, exasperated. "Knock yourself out."

Nobody in the photos is him. There's a bill from 1987 for some dry cleaning.

I even go to the school nurse. "I feel like—" I tell her when it's my turn. That's as far as I get. It's not like if I *found* him anything would be any better.

"Tryin' to get outta practice?" Wainwright asks me later in the hall. He has eyes in the back of his head. He dips a shoulder towards me and I flinch.

I come free on a blitz in practice that afternoon and I'm about to decapitate our starting QB when our fullback puts his helmet into my sternum. "Who blacks out on a *chest* hit?" Wainwright asks when I come to. I'm somewhere where everything's white. He says I'm black and blue from my throat to my stomach. He pulls back the sheet and hospital gown and shows me with a hand mirror.

"Thank God," my mom says to herself when she sees me. She had to come from work. My brother's not with her. It's killing her, I can tell.

Can I play with a bruised sternum? The doctor's on the fence about it. He says we can wait and see. Big Coach says it's my call. I rest all weekend and I'm held out of practice Monday and Tuesday. Wednesday I can go and watch, anyway. Already it's like I'm not even on the team. For an hour nobody's on the same page and Coach stands there doing a slow burn until finally he tells the defense that since they're not thinking maybe it's because they're not getting enough blood to their heads. He makes them all do handstands until he tells them to stop. Wainwright's is like a statue. He points his toes.

This goes on for five minutes, kids' feet and legs teetering. People pull over on River Road to watch. Various kids, trying to hold their handstands, laugh. When they do, Coach crosses to where they are and pushes them over with his foot.

When practice breaks up I'm still over by the fence. Wainwright heads in with two of the other linebackers. I hang there on the chain link like the crowd on Media Day.

On Thursday somebody tapes photos in the urinals of Childress's stars on offense and defense.

Friday morning I wake up crying. *This is it,* I tell myself, but that's not why I'm crying. My mother makes coffee and nobody says anything before I go to school. My brother looks like if the whole house blew up, that'd be okay too. My hand is jerking so much that I try only once to drink my coffee and then dump the mug in the sink.

The school hallways are all hung with blue and white banners. The tape's come off the cinderblock on one and the first letter's drooped over on itself, so instead of BEAT CHILDRESS the thing reads EAT CHILDRESS. A custodian passes me with a ladder.

There's a pep rally we're all supposed to go to but I skip it and hide out in the library. I can hear the marching band's percussion section whaling away.

"Good luck tonight," one of the librarians says. She doesn't seem surprised I'm not at the rally.

I stick myself off in the stacks, looking back and forth through the same book. Who cries on the morning of a big game? I hold my hands in my lap as best I can.

When I was six or seven, my brother took me into the woods behind our house. I think those woods are gone now but I haven't been back to check. He broke sticks on trees. Every stick he picked up he laced into tree trunks until it broke. Sometimes it took a while. Sometimes the splinters went whizzing by my face. We walked for half the afternoon and then we stopped. I took my sneakers off because there was a rock in one. I could hear traffic, a highway, somewhere. He whacked more sticks into trees while I sat there. "It's just me and you now," he finally said, though I knew that. He meant about our dad. He was only eleven or twelve himself. "You're not gonna leave me here, are you?" I said. I asked because of the way he was talking.

Even then I knew he couldn't help me and I couldn't help him. And he looked like he knew what I was thinking. "You're not going to *leave* me?" I asked again, but he just got up and headed home.

I had to hustle to keep up. "You mean like we gotta stick together?" I remember asking. "No. We don't have to do nothin'," he said back. And in nightmares I had after that he took me out on a dock and the dock became a rug and there'd be this bell going off in the distance.

The library's computers have our team Web site on their monitors to show spirit. This year's slogan at the top is *Declaring War in 04*. I check out the Port Neches-Groves site on the net. Their news headline is *Indians Shorthanded for Biggest Game of the Year*.

For our on-field introductions there's some kind of mylar tent or tunnel leading past the north bleachers into the end zone. The nonstarters form two lines leading into it for us to run through. It's like going through a human funnel that empties onto the field. We end up at the 50 yard line in a big pile, bouncing, bouncing, bouncing. Guys're throwing themselves on the top and flipping and ending up in the middle on the bottom. From the seedings it's clear we'll have to win four straight, including this one, for me to meet that kid Corey in the 5A semifinals. Childress wins the toss and the defense huddles up around Coach and he gets on his hands and knees in the grass and scrabbles around whacking our shoes with his hands. He goes all the way around the huddle doing it to everybody. "Check your *feet* see if you're *ready,*" we hear him shouting over the crowd. Wainwright's just outside the huddle. He already thinks his feet are ready.

First series Childress goes 73 yards in 11 plays and has a first and goal at the 3. We stuff them twice and they overthrow their tight end and so that fast it's Thrilling Goal-Line Stand time: fourth and inches, and they're going for it.

Wainwright's standing there, weight on one leg, hands on his hips like he's waiting for a fat guy to catch a bus. Somewhere east of us down near the Gulf of Mexico, Corey's getting down in his three-point stance, nowhere near one hundred percent. Guys are waiting on the other side of the line like horses at a starting gate with a baby in the middle of the track. All over Texas, kids are getting ready to cripple and be crippled, and parents are doing their bit or downing a drink or missing out entirely because they've got things to do, too.

Childress runs a flanker reverse, of all things, and I get caught going the wrong way and chopped at the ankles by somebody. I hit the ground and something spears me and launches off my back, taking my wind with it: Wainwright's cleats. He catches the flanker high and clotheslines him.

What's it mean to say you want to do something if you don't do it? It took our family two days to drive down here from New Jersey. The first night, all our stuff in the back, they thought I was asleep, and started talking about my dad again. My mom got defensive. She said he always *meant* well.

"What good does *that* do us?" I asked.

"Look who's up," my brother said.

"Everybody's worried about what he didn't do for us," my mother said. "What about what we didn't do for ourselves?"

It shut us up for a while. "Sounds like we got the right dad after all, then," my brother finally said. And we left it at that.

The stands go nuts. Our defense mobs itself in celebration. I still can't breathe. Some of my ribs must be cracked. My sternum feels like it did in the hospital. My arms and legs and head are okay, but everything else wants to die. Wainwright squats next to me and shrugs off some glad-handers, his eyes unreadable under his helmet shadow. The Sisters of Mercy hustle towards me with their stretcher. If I can walk or be carried I'm going to be there for Corey in four weeks. I'm going to be there so his father can see. I'm going to be there so his father can see and say, *Who is that kid? That kid's amazing. That kid's a terror.*

Ancestral Legacies

This is the roof of the world. An immense, sequestered place, the highest of the high plateaus, many times the size of the Reich. I'm still sick. The porters still gesticulate and exchange private jokes when they assume my attention is elsewhere. Beger's bad ankle is still swollen. Somewhere I've misplaced my certainty.

The day was brutally hot and now no one can get warm. We sit around the fire like terns thunderstruck by the cold. Ahead of us the hardpan goes on for two thousand kilometers before it encounters a tree. It feels like the back of the beyond, the place where rumors lose their way. This is the second week of the trek, and every aspect of what's surrounded us has been featureless.

Beger lies on his side wrapped in a blanket. The boot on his good foot is too near the fire. We watch its sole sizzle as though we're dumbfounded by speech. Above us the starlessness comes and goes. When the wind dies, there's no sound. One of the pack animals coughs up something with a ragged, liquid snort.

We're feeding the fire with pats of yak dung. So even it is hushed. It's a feeble, smelly warmth.

We're without information or curiosity. Neither of us speculate. Confronted with what surrounds us, our powers of imagination have dissipated.

The world is empty. The world in every direction is empty. After sunup the sky comes down like an edict. The blue is so intense that birds fly low to the ground, intimidated.

In Lharigo I was chased away from a nomad encampment.

Children threw stones. Dogs gamboled unpleasantly about my heels. Women waved small ceramic pots of flour to exorcise my evil spirit.

Beger received the same greeting when he straggled in an hour or so later. "I don't think we should ask about the yeti," he said, grimacing at his forearm. A dog had shredded his sleeve.

My name is Ernst Schäfer and I sit with my assistant, Beger, and seven sherpas with uncertain work habits only a very small part of the way across the Chang Tang, the frozen desert between the Trans-Himalayas and the Kunlun Mountains.

The sherpas, already convinced of our slow-wittedness, tell stories of the yeti—women the yeti have abducted, yaks killed in a single blow, shattered sheep pens, and always the ubiquitous footprints. How can you tell when a yak's been killed in a single blow? Beger wants to know. In response they snigger at him and pass around a small pot of dried cream and a sack of what they call *tsampa,* a kind of roasted barley. Beger is offered none of either. They're really a very dirty people.

Gulam, the sherpas' leader, intones as though telling ghost stories to a child, "They come into the village and take what they want." The other porters parody the terrified expressions of the eyewitnesses.

"When the facts run dry, they start inventing," Beger complains, gingerly unlacing his boot. "They lie to us on principle."

His foot does not look good. My guess would be an infection from a leech at the beginning of the trip.

Beger and I are the entirety of Operation Tibet, which was a closely guarded secret when we began and, now that we're a flyspeck in the darkness on the other side of the moon, has no doubt become even more so. We are what's known back at the offices of the Reichsführer SS as the Schäfer Unit. This has been the cause of much bitter amusement on Beger's part. Whenever we hit a snag or find ourselves powerless before native intransigence or a pack of goats that won't clear the track, leaving us half-frozen and shivering and peering miserably down into an icy abyss, Beger will say, "Don't they see that we're the Schäfer Unit?"

"I think they do," I'll tell him.

Our purpose, as far as the Reichschancellery understands, is twofold. First, we're to explore prehistoric and linguistic issues related to locating the core of the Nordic-Aryan legacy. The language is the Reichsführer's. And second, the two of us are to incite the Tibetan army against British troops. The plan involves our rendezvousing with emissaries from our new ally, the Bolsheviks. With their help, I'm to become a German Lawrence of the Himalayas. The Bolshevik emissaries are nowhere to be found. There is no Tibetan army, and there are no British troops.

This kind of foolishness carries very little water with me. Before I was assigned to Ancestral Legacy, an odd bureaucratic backwater recently flooded with funding, I was an ornithologist of international renown, as well as an expert in zoology, botany, agriculture, and ethnology. Not to mention one of the foremost Tibetan specialists of this age. So, as I told Beger, while I've been continually impressed with Reichsführer Himmler's political gifts, I've been able to contain my awe when it comes to his scientific theories. His theories are the donkey cart we've used to land us where we want to be: here on this high plateau with sufficient funding and no oversight, in search of the yeti.

Beger's interests in the yeti lie in his having made a name for himself with a precocious monograph on the importance of the forehead in racial analysis. He studied anthropology at the institute in Berlin-Dahlem with Fischer and Abel, and he's convinced the yeti are an early hominid. He can imagine to what uses a yeti skull could be put in his research. And naturally he's devoted to science, so in the normal course of events he can work up a useful curiosity about most phenomena. Plus there's the invigorating fact that service in the Schäfer Unit has excused him from active military duty. His service to the Fatherland is supposed to be his ongoing evaluation of the Tibetan material we're intended to gather.

We haven't gathered much. He did some desultory poking around with one of the sherpas as translator before we left Lharigo. But for the most part I've led us to areas considered desolate even by Tibetan standards: areas of the yeti, or of nothing at all.

The ideal age for a man on an expedition like this is between thirty-one and thirty-five. I'm thirty-seven. A man much younger, like Beger, who's twenty-five, possesses the necessary vigor in abundance but not the discipline and focus of mind so crucial to patient inquiry.

And lately his powers of observation have been curtailed sharply by a postadolescent self-absorption. He's miserable about his foot and miserable that we're so out of touch with the world. He has two brothers serving in the war with Poland, a bit of news we learned about from a week-old Italian newspaper.

Of course we knew something was up before we left.

One brother is a Stuka pilot, the other a sapper in the Wehrmacht. I do a poor job keeping track of which is which.

This part of the Chang Tang is far from even the rarely used trade routes. Gulam has led us here because his uncle and brother insist that yeti roam these regions at night in search of food. During the day, with nothing stirring in any direction, the notion seems absurd, but we do well to remind ourselves that over the centuries the Tibetans have learned to survive in an environment that presents an unyielding stone face to outsiders.

We have more than Gulam's assertions on which to base our decision: two days into the trek we encountered a veritable square dance of footprints baked into a previously marshy depression near a water source. The footprints were six inches deep and two and a half feet long. A separate and enormous big toe was clearly visible on each.

"What was this, a meeting hall?" Beger remarked, unsure where to begin with his measuring tape.

. . .

One sherpa stands watch while the others sleep. Beger's head is under the blanket, and because his complaints have stopped I assume he's asleep as well. Eventually he pulls his boot from the fire.

Each night, my shivering prevents me from listening as intently as I would like. I have not found a solution to this problem. The previous night I walked off half a kilometer into the darkness, keeping a fix on the wavering glow of the fire. The exercise warmed me a little, and as soon as I stopped moving, small, brittle sounds rose up around me. Nocturnal rodents or insects, perhaps, going about their business. Gazing off at a tiny glow of warmth in the distance: that must be, I realized, the yeti's experience.

When I wake, the fire's gone out. The sherpa standing watch is on his back, snoring. There's a whistling—at a high, high pitch—impossibly far off.

When Alexander had conquered the entire known world—when he'd finally subjugated even the Indus Valley and pushed his phalanxes up to the precipices and chasms of the Kashmir—he's said to have sent a small expedition off to engage the yeti, maddeningly visible on the higher elevations. The expedition perished and the yeti eluded him. Pliny the Elder, who would later fall victim to his own thirst for knowledge while attempting to record natural processes during the eruption of Mount Vesuvius, insisted that in the Land of the Satyrs—the mountains that lay to the east of India—lived creatures that were extremely swift and could run on two feet or four. They bore a human shape and because of their agility and strength could be caught only when infirm or old.

Aelianus, historian of the Emperor Septimus, wrote of *his* legions' frustration with the same satyrs, whom he described as shaggy-haired and startlingly accurate with stones. As far back as 1832, Britain's first representative to Nepal described an unknown creature that moved erectly, was covered in long, dark hair, and had no tail.

But of course it wasn't until a scientist—the renowned Tibetan specialist L. A. Waddell—reported sightings that Western interest was piqued. And when in 1921 Howard-Bury reported the animals on the north side of Everest at nineteen thousand feet, a journalist rendered the yeti's Tibetan name as *abominable snowman:* a mistranslation that torments us to this day. "And no wild goose chases after abominable snowmen," the Reichsführer warned me during our last personal interview before my departure.

"What do they eat?" Beger asks once we're under way the next morning. He's taken to riding one of the pack animals for part of the day to rest his foot. Undifferentiated flatness stretches as far as the eye can see. Occasionally some brittle yellow grass. And this is the late summer, when the vegetation is at its best.

"Glacier rats," Gulam calls from the front the column, two animals ahead. "Some rabbits. Maybe a marmot."

Our column is stopped for the rest of the morning by winds we heard approaching while they were still hours off. When they scoured across the last few hundred yards we could see the hardpan come alive in a line. Now that they've arrived we can lean at an angle into them without falling forward. A piece of clothing is ripped from one of our bundles and spirited off into the distance. Eventually the animals are gathered in a circle and made to sit while we take shelter in the center. Beger and I wrap our heads against the blowing grit. We can hear the porters playing *bakchen,* a game like dominos.

Our plan is to go at least seventeen hundred kilometers into the heart of the Chang Tang. The Tibetan name is synonymous with hardship and desolation. The entire plateau possesses no plants other than artemisia, wild nettles, a few dwarf willows I'm assured are still a thousand kilometers away, and these arid and burnt-looking needlegrasses now aflutter in the gale. Only two nomadic and elusive tribes inhabit its rim. Gulam's second in command is along principally to work his magic to prevent hail. Within minutes a clear sky here can cloud over with horrendous and lethal hailstorms. In one of the first European accounts of the plateau, an entry lists the loss of five men, each of their names followed by the phrase *Dead by Hail.*

As quickly as the wind comes, it's gone. We stand again, and what we shake off glitters in the sun. The ground feels frozen—the bone-dry hardpan rests on permafrost—and yet the sun is hot and there's no trace of snow. We estimate our altitude to be sixteen thousand feet. Our hearts pound every day, as a matter of course, from the thinness of the air and the excitement.

We get under way again. Within the hour, there's some distress from the porters. They've lost their tea maker, and I refuse to allow them to go back for it.

Beger is back on foot, keeping up nicely, with a little hop-step he's developed. He asks my opinion of the Polish air force.

"Are you thinking of Ewald?" I ask.

"Alfred," he says. "Ewald's the sapper."

"Of course," I tell him. "Ewald's the sapper." After giving the matter thought, I dismiss his worries. One of the few details the Italian news account was able to provide concerned the massive nature of our initial attacks on the Poles' airfields. "And I've seen the Poles' airfields," I remind him. "They're the Tibetans of Europe."

He laughs, pleased, and repeats the phrase.

I overheard him and some of his cronies in a wine cellar near the university the night before we left. He was unaware I was occupying the next high-backed booth. "He's like a father to you," one of the cronies had joked.

"Yes, the kind effortlessly surpassed," he'd responded. When the laughter subsided he referred to my book, published the year before, and quoted the opening sentence.

"All right, you lot, keep it down," the serving girl had scolded the gathering with a mock sternness from her station behind the bar.

Say what you will about the National Socialists' ideologies, but they're all essentially ideologies of human inequality. Of which a half hour in any Tibetan village would provide ample proof: between the walls and the woodpiles in every courtyard are the proudly displayed chest-high mounds of horse manure; beside the manure will always be someone as apparently simpleminded as he is elderly, pounding butter tea in a knee-high cylinder. For days afterward you'll smell of frozen garlic and rancid fat.

Families are helpful panoplies of any number of degenerate diagnostic characteristics, as if arrayed for the scientist's perusal. Even the most masculine of the porters we have here with us partake at times of the nature of the child, or the female, or the senile Caucasian. During the planning of our trek, for example, Gulam could not be instructed to use my fountain pen. Instead he took it in his fist and tapped out a shape on the paper as if he was working with a chisel.

These are people whose methods of going about the day have remained unchanged since the Stone Age. And yet they were for a time in the ancient world the uncontested masters of Central Asia.

My theory is that the altitude, combined with the intensity of ultraviolet rays and the cold, hugely reduces the likelihood of bacterial reproduction. Otherwise these people would have long since died off, given their lack of commitment to even the most elementary hygiene.

. . .

71

Another long week of walking and riding. Beger cries out periodically when he turns his foot in his boot. The porters have tried a different poultice.

At twilight we come to the edge of a great salt lake, a startling robin's egg blue in the blinding sun. Dried salts of varying widths band the shoreline. Three of the porters explore with Gulam while the others start a fire and erect a communal tent. Some sort of animal sinew is employed for the guy ropes.

Beger is of the opinion that we have a much better chance of finding the yeti in the higher elevations, where most of the sightings have been recorded.

"The conventional wisdom," I tell him.

He responds with an unpleasant smile before turning away. The lobes of his ears below his fur hat are a merry red from the sun. "Here, what's to prevent them from seeing us coming kilometers and kilometers away?" he asks.

"By all accounts they have no fear of people," I remind him. "And of course they'd have as much warning in the mountains as they would here."

He glumly drops the subject.

"Our only alternative is to choose whom to trust and then to trust them," I tell him.

He snorts.

Gulam returns pleased. A short way down the shoreline are fresh footprints and the crushed bones of something.

"Maybe they're using this as a salt lick," Beger says from inside the tent.

After dark a yak is set out as a lure. Staked to the ground fifty yards or so from the camp, it bleats and grunts its frustration at being separated from its fellows. I clean and ready our rifles. They're formidable, if a little balky when left untended, but their heft is reassuring. The yak bleats all night long. The next day we travel twenty or so kilometers around the shoreline and repeat the procedure.

The guns travel in specially sewn oilskin pouches for protection against the grit. Beger tries soaking his foot in the salt water while we watch the sun set. Up to this point, in terms of birds, I've noticed only a few small snow finches and the occasional sand grouse.

The sun's rays lance over mountain ridges that remain un-imaginably distant. The salt around us turns orange in the light.

From that first childhood moment in which I could see over my windowsill, I dreamed of far horizons. At the age of seven I found a translation of Sir Charles Bell's *Grammar of Colloquial Tibetan*. The first two phrases I learned were "the elephant gun is on the yak" and "all monks are too lazy." Few foreigners have explored Tibet as comprehensively as I have. I've traversed eleven thousand kilometers on quests botanical and zoological. I've suf-fered missionaries, British colonial officers, unwashed philoso-phers, and the mineral ingratitude of the natives themselves. With Tibet, everyone grasps a different aspect, but no one comprehends the entirety. It's more than a country. It's an island looking down on the rest of the planet.

Our third morning at the lake, the yak is still bleating, the wind still blowing. Outside the tent it's very cold. I watch two of the porters rig up an ingenious little sling for their food pouches.

I'm interested in the racial origins of inventiveness. The gene for nomadism is clearly hereditary, given that racial groups like the Comanche, the Gypsies, and the Tibetans are all nomadic; what, then, of the gene for resourcefulness of a certain kind, or inventiveness? Might that not be an area in which such peoples are our equal, if not superior?

Beger, when I raise the notion, is intrigued by the idea, within limits.

This is a golden time for anthropologists, especially within the Reich. Lenz was certainly correct to remark that we're presently governed by the first widely influential leader to recognize that the central mission of politics is race hygiene. All of us in the sciences have profited by such a regime, even if we've also had to accommodate ourselves to a good deal of foolishness and boorishness. It is, we all agree, crucial to delineate precisely and objectively the hierarchical boundaries between the classes and the races, because scientific precision reassures the ordinary citizen that the law will protect his own security.

We've all done our bit. Ancestral Legacy devoted many man-hours of work to the drafting of the Marriage Health Law, especially to the definitions of hereditary degeneracy in its various manifestations. And before this mission I myself had begun branching out into the more positive aspects of eugenics: conceiving new methods to increase the birthrate of the superior populations. It's a national opportunity. And there's simply too much funding there to ignore.

The new poultice seems to have made Beger worse. He soldiers on but remarks more than once with a sheepish smile that he's feeling a little green. We stop for a midday meal, and I tend to his foot myself. The smell once his boot is off is eye-watering.

"We may have to go back," I tell him, unwrapping the mess.

He can't even bring himself to disagree, though he's stricken at the prospect of having let us down.

Gulam's hail magician, who also dabbles in medicine, is called over to examine the foot. He seems briskly untroubled by what he sees and returns half an hour later with some kind of paste in a wooden bowl. He applies the paste with his fingers and leaves me to rewrap the foot.

The next morning the tethered yak is gone. The tether is snapped. Footprints surround the spot and trail away to the salt lake, where they disappear. I ask who was on watch but the porters refuse to acknowledge any accusation in my question. The yeti are, after all, magical animals.

The incident does seem to have affected morale, however. A certain listlessness or wariness is evident in the manner in which the group goes about its business of packing up and preparing to get under way. "We will all be killed," one of the porters says *sotto voce* to Gulam, believing me out of earshot. He sounds matter-of-fact.

I take advantage of a small snow squall nearby to hold up the column, gather the porters round and deliver a scientific lecture on the origins of snowstorms. I want them to register that a white man's rationality can have more power than all of the mountain spirits whirling in their heads. They seem impressed enough with the information they've been given. I ask if there are questions, and they all stare back at me silently. I give the word for the column to proceed.

We strike out, finally, from the shores of the lake, heading back into the endless plains. The change depresses Beger's spirits further. "How much longer like this?" he asks the porter closest to him on the pack animal.

"Until the rocks grow beards," the porter jokes.

Two or three of them still mutter every so often about the loss of their tea maker. But they are of a race that can make do in any number of ways, I remind myself. This is a people who can burn sheep dung hot enough to melt metal.

Truth be told, our friend Reichsführer Himmler has had some very strange ideas. He wants to prove that the Nordic race descended directly from the skies. His theory of glacial cosmogony insists that all cosmic energy erupts from the collision between ice and fire, and nowhere is that clash more primeval, of course, than here, where the land is closest to the upper sky. Hence the entire department of Ancestral Legacy, with its charge to study the originary area, spirit, deeds, and legacy of the Indo-Germanic race. The whole thing is mostly unscientific. He's sent us off in search of a proto-Gangetic Indo-European language, which would be evidence that Tibet was once inhabited by a Caucasian race, perhaps ancestors of the Scythians. I had a number of talks with him in which I sought to guide him back to firmer theoretical ground, all without success. There is a certain futility to resisting one of the Reichsführer's pet projects.

In the middle of the night I'm awakened by that same high whistling. Surrounded by snores, I wrestle myself hurriedly into my outer garments and emerge from the tent, shining my pocket torch about. The porter on watch is gazing disinterestedly off into the darkness. When I shine my beam in the direction of our tethered yak, it's swallowed in the gloom. I investigate. The tethered yak is gone. The porter claims to have heard nothing.

The entire next day Beger seems half-asleep. Every so often a porter's casual hand nudges him back upright on his pack animal.

During the evening meal that night their barley beer tastes slightly strange. Beger is already asleep and I find that I too can hardly keep my eyes open. I give Gulam instructions about tethering the next yak closer to camp and then close my eyes for a moment's rest. The next morning I wake very late, my mouth an old stewpot. The sun outside the tent is blinding. The yak is tethered nearby, as I requested. The porters and the other pack animals are gone.

Beger exhibits surprisingly little reaction to the news. They left water and food, as well as the guns. I have my compass. But with only the two of us, we're at least three weeks from help, I tell him.

"At least," he agrees, his face turned to the tent wall.

We seem unable to rouse ourselves quickly, and thus get started distressingly late in the day. The yak periodically rebels at being ridden, so we make only a handful of kilometers before having to stop for the night. We manage three days of this before that yak disappears as well. This time even the tether is gone.

"Somewhere some yeti are having a feast," Beger says to himself when I inform him. He spends the day out of the sun in the dispirited half teepee of the tent. Without help, I've only been able to erect it in a semicollapsed way.

What a creature, I think, with real wonder. Sitting at the tent's entrance and tracking the dust storms and whirligigs on the horizon, I remind myself that I've done what I set out to do: validated, to my own satisfaction, my belief. Before me, science had to settle for the same trio of consolation prizes: footprints, dens, fecal matter. I'm going to be like Du Chaillu, the Frenchman who was the first to shoot a gorilla: an animal that for two thousand years Europeans believed to be mythical. And I'm not simply discovering another animal. On the scrolls that serve as meditation aids in the monasteries, the yeti are positioned between the animals and mankind. I've been mocked for devoting my life to a legend. But legends have moved whole nations and held them together.

Beger turns feverish in the night. I minister to him with water and cool compresses. He cries silently and gives himself over to being held. He sweats through his undergarments, and when I peel them off, we both can see a red line running from his ankle up to the lymph nodes in his groin.

I get him redressed and resettled. His ankle I leave alone.

I doze beside him, dreaming of river crossings, the frigid water roiling and rushing and spray that tastes of minerals. In Shigatse the breeze smelled of juniper trees and tasted of dust. A spotted white bull lolled about in the middle of the street. In one village where we were welcomed, children bathed in our honor. We bedded down in furs on the ground, and the fleas and my fears that we wouldn't find enough petrol the next day kept me awake. That day on a high pass we saw across a half-mile gorge the giant goat known as the takin. It was snub-nosed and fearsome across the shoulders, and reputed to have pushed travelers off narrow and precipitous tracks. But its hair, in the sun, was a stunning gold. *The golden fleece,* I thought. *The golden fleece.*

. . .

I wake in the darkness, my hand hunting for my torch. We're both wheezing from the thinness of the air. Holding my breath, I cover Beger's mouth and nose with my palm and listen. There's a strong wind; under it, a far-off whistling. Something smells. I give Beger a shake but it fails to rouse him. I think of the yak outside the night before, its eyes shut against the wind, snow speckling its black fur.

In June the sherpas observe the Mani Rimbu—"All Will Be Well"—a celebration during which they venerate their nature gods. At the climax a gruesomely costumed effigy of a yeti appears. A missionary whose garden had been torn to pieces told me when I came to investigate, "These creatures are God's children, the same as us."

The whistling comes from the other side of the tent. The one wall that's fully erect shudders and buffets against its pole.

I try to listen. Beger wheezes, his breathing further obstructed by blankets. Bruno: his first name is Bruno.

During our initial interview Gulam told me of a face-to-face encounter near his uncle's corral. The thing's face and palms were black. Its nostrils frightening in ways he couldn't make clear. He'd been petrified by the yellow of its eyes. It had hissed and then scrambled away, toting a yak calf under its arm.

A shriek, a bellow, sounds above the tent. I switch on the torch and jerk its beam to the opening. The face in the darkness bares its teeth. The faces behind it jostle forward.

Pleasure Boating in Lituya Bay

Two and a half weeks after I was born, on July 9th, 1958, the plates that make up the Fairweather Range in the Alaskan panhandle apparently slipped twenty-one feet on either side of the Fair-weather fault, the northern end of a major league instability that runs the length of North America. The thinking now is that the southwest side and bottom of the inlets at the head of Lituya Bay jolted upward and to the northwest, and the northeast shore and head of the bay jolted downward and to the southeast. One way or the other, the result registered 8.3 on the Richter scale.

The bay is T-shaped and seven miles long and two wide at the stem, and according to those who were there it went from a glassy smoothness to a full churn, a giant's Jacuzzi. Next to it, mountains twelve to fifteen thousand feet high twisted into themselves and lurched in contrary directions. In Juneau, 122 miles to the south-east, people who'd turned in early were pitched from their beds. The shock waves wiped out bottom-dwelling marine life through-out the panhandle. In Seattle, a thousand miles away, the Univer-sity of Washington's seismograph needle was jarred completely off its graph. And meanwhile, back at the head of the bay, a spur of mountain and glacier the size of a half-mile-wide city park—forty million cubic yards in volume—broke off and dropped three thousand feet down the northeast cliff into the water.

This is all by way of saying that it was one of the greatest spasms, when it came to the release of destructive energy, in his-tory. It happened around 10:16 p.m. At that latitude and time of year, still light out. There were three small boats anchored in the south end of the bay.

The rumbling from the earthquake generated vibrations that the occupants of the boats could feel on their skin like electric shock. The impact of the rockfall that followed made a sound like Canada exploding. There were two women, three men, and a seven-year-old boy in the three boats. They looked up to see a wave breaking *over* the seventeen-hundred-foot-high southwest bank of Gilbert Inlet and heading for the opposite slope. What they were looking at was the largest wave ever recorded by human beings. It scythed off three-hundred-year-old pines and cedars and spruce, some of them with trunks three or four feet thick, along a trimline of 1,720 feet. That's a wave crest 500 feet higher than the Empire State Building.

Fill your bathtub. Hold a football at shoulder height and drop it into the water. Imagine the height of the tub above the waterline to be two thousand feet. Scale the height of the initial splash up proportionately.

When I was two years old, my mother decided she'd had enough of my father and hunted down an old high school girlfriend who'd wandered so far west she'd taken a job teaching in a grammar school in Hawaii. The school was in a little town called Pepeekeo. All of this was told to me later by my mother's older sister. My mother and I moved in with the friend, who lived in a little beach cottage on the north shore of the island near an old mill, Pepeekeo Mill. We were about twelve miles north of Hilo. This was in 1960.

The friend's name was Chuck. Her real name was Charlotte something, but everyone apparently called her Chuck. My aunt had a photo she showed me of me playing in the sand with some breakers in the background. I'm wearing something that looks like overalls put on backward. Chuck's drinking beer from a can.

And one morning Chuck woke my mother and me up and

asked if we wanted to see a tidal wave. I don't remember any of this. I was in pajamas and my mother put a robe on me and we trotted down the beach and looked around the point to the north. I told my mother I was scared and she said we'd go back to the house if the water got too high. We saw the ocean suck itself out to sea smoothly and quietly, and the muck of the sand and some flipping and turning white-bellied fish that had been left behind. Then we saw it come back, without any surf or real noise, like the tide coming in in time-lapse photography. It came past the high-tide mark and just up to our toes. Then it receded again. "Some wave," my mother told me. She lifted me up so I could see the end of it. Some older boys who lived on Mamalahoa Highway sprinted past us, chasing the water. They got way out, the mud spraying up behind their heels. And the water came back again, this time even smaller. The boys, as far out as they were, were still only up to their waists. We could hear how happy they sounded. Chuck told us the show was over, and we headed up the beach to the house. My mother wanted me to walk, but I wanted her to carry me. We heard a noise and when we turned we saw the third wave. It was already the size of the lighthouse out at Wailea. They'd gotten me into the cottage and halfway up the stairs to the second floor when the walls blew in. My mother managed to slide me onto a corner of the roof that was spinning half a foot above the water. Chuck went under and didn't come up again. My mother was carried out to sea, still hanging on to me and the roof chunk. She'd broken her hip and bitten through her lower lip. We were picked up later that day by a little boat near Honohina.

She was never the same after that, my aunt told me. This was maybe by way of explaining why I'd been put up for adoption a few months later. My mother had gone to teach somewhere in Alaska. Somewhere away from the coast, my aunt added with a smile. She pretended she didn't know exactly where. I'd been left with the Franciscan Sisters at the Catholic orphanage in Kahili. On the day of my graduation, one of the sisters who'd taken an interest in me grabbed both of my shoulders and shook me and said, "What is it you *want*? What's the *matter* with you?" They weren't bad questions, as far as I was concerned.

I saw my aunt that once, the year before college. My fiancée, many years later, asked if we were going to invite her to the wedding, and then later that night said, "I guess you're not going to answer, huh?"

Who decides when the time's right to have kids? Who decides how many kids to have? Who decides how they're going to be brought up? Who decides when the parents are going to stop having sex and stop listening to one another? Who decides when everyone's not just going to walk out on everyone else? These are all group decisions. Mutual decisions. Decisions that a couple makes *in consultation with one another.*

I'm stressing that because it doesn't always work that way.

My wife's goal oriented. Sometimes I can see her *To Do* list on her face when she looks at me. It makes me think she doesn't want me anymore, and the idea is so paralyzing and maddening that I lose track of myself: I just step in place and forget where I am for a minute or two. "What're you doing?" she asked once, outside a restaurant.

And of course I can't tell her. Because then what do I do with whatever follows?

We have one kid, Donald, named for the single greatest man my wife has ever known. That would be her father. Donald's seven. When he's in a good mood he finds me in the house and wraps his arms around me, his chin on my hip. When he's in a bad mood I have to turn off the TV to get him to answer. He has a good arm and good hand-eye coordination but he gets easily frustrated. "Who's *that* sound like?" my wife always says when I point it out.

He loses everything. He loses stuff even if you physically put it in his hands when he's on his way home. Gloves, hats, knapsacks, lunch money, a bicycle, homework, pencils, pens, his dog, his friends, his way. Sometimes he doesn't worry about it; sometimes he's distraught. If he starts out not worrying about it, sometimes I make him distraught. When I tell these stories, I'm Mr. Glass Half Empty. Which is all by way of getting around to what my wife calls the central subject, which is my ingratitude. Do I always have to start with the negatives? Don't I think he *knows* when I talk about him that way?

"She says you're too harsh," is the way my father-in-law put it. At the time he was sitting on my front porch and sucking down my beer. He said he thought of it as a kind of mean-spiritedness.

I had no comeback for him at the time. "You weren't very nice to my parents," my wife mentioned when they left.

Friends commiserate with her on the phone.

My father-in-law's a circuit court judge. I run a seaplane charter out of Ketchikan. Wild Wings Aviation. My wife snorts when I answer the phone that way. My father-in-law tells her, who knows, maybe I'll make a go of it. And if the thing does go under, I can always fly geologists around for one of the energy companies.

Even knowing what I make, he says that.

Number one on her *To Do* list is another kid. She says Donald very much wants a little brother. I haven't really heard him address the subject. She wants to know what *I* want. She asks with her mouth set, like she's already figured the odds that I'm going to let her down. It makes me what she calls unresponsive.

She's been on me about it for a year, now. And two months ago, after three straight days of our being polite to one another—Good morning. How'd you sleep?—and avoiding brushing even shoulders when passing through doorways, I made an appointment with a Dr. Calvin at Bartlett Regional about a vasectomy. "Normally, couples come in together," he told me at the initial consult.

"This whole thing's been pretty hard on her," I told him.

Apparently it's an outpatient thing, and if I opt for the simpler procedure I could be out of his office and home in forty-five minutes. He quoted me a thousand dollars, but not much out of pocket, because our health insurance should cover most of it. I was told to go off and give it some thought and get back in touch if and when I was ready to schedule it. I called back two days later and lined it up for the Saturday before Memorial Day. "That'll give you some time to rest up afterwards," the girl who did the scheduling pointed out.

"He *had* a pretty big trauma when he was a baby," my wife reminded her mom a few weeks ago. They didn't realize I was at the kitchen window. "A couple of traumas, actually." She said it like she understood that it was going to be a perennial on her *To Do* list.

So for the last two months I've gone around the house like a demolition expert who's already wired the entire thing to blow and keeps rechecking the charges and connections.

It was actually flying some geologists around that got me going on Lituya Bay in the first place. I flew in a couple of guys from Exxon-Mobil who taught me more than I wanted to know about Tertiary rocks and why they always got people salivating when it came to hunting up petroleum. But one of the guys also told the story of what happened there in 1958. He was the one who didn't want to camp in the bay. His buddy made serious fun of him. The next time I flew them in I'd done my research, and we talked about what a crazy place it was. I was staying overnight with them, because they could pay for it, and they had to be out at like dawn the next morning.

However you measure things like that, it has to be one of the most dangerous bodies of water on earth. It feels freakish even when you first see it. Most tidal inlets are not nearly so deep—I think at its center it's seven hundred feet—but at the entrance there's barely enough draft for a small boat. So at high and low tides the water moves through the bottleneck like a blast from a fire hose. That twilight we watched a piece of driftwood *stay ahead* of a tern that was gliding with the wind. The whole bay is huge but the entrance is only eighty yards wide and broken up by boulders. Stuff coming in on the high tide might as well be on the world's largest water slide, and when the tide running out hits the ocean swells, it's as if surf's up on the north shore of Hawaii from both directions at once. We were two hundred yards away and had to shout over the noise. The Frenchman who discovered the bay lost twenty-one men and three boats at the entrance. The Tlingits lost so many people over the course of their time here that they named it Channel of the Water-Eyes, "water eyes" being their term for the drowned.

But the scared guy had me motor him up to the head of the bay and showed me the other problem, the one I'd already read about: stupefyingly large and highly fractured rocks standing at vertiginous angles over deep water in an active fault zone, as he put it. On top of that, their having absorbed heavy rainfall and constant freezing and thawing. The earthquakes on this fault were as violent as anywhere else in the world, and they'd be shaking unstable cliffs over a deep and tightly enclosed body of water.

"Yeah yeah yeah," his buddy said, passing around beef jerky from the backseat. I was putt-putting the seaplane back and forth as our water taxi at the top of the bay's T. Forested cliff faces went straight up five to six thousand feet all around us. I don't know how trees that size even grew like that.

"You have any kids?" the scared guy asked out of nowhere. I said yeah. He said he did too and started hunting up a photo.

"Well, what's a body to do when millions of tons avalanche into it?" his buddy in the back asked.

The scared guy couldn't find the photo. He looked at his wallet like what else was new. "Make waves," he said. "Gi-normous waves."

While we crossed from shore to shore they pointed out some of the trimlines I'd read about. The experts figure their dates by cutting down trees and looking at the growth rings, and some of the lines go back as far as the middle of the 1800s. They look like rows of plantings in a field, except we're talking about fifty-degree slopes and trees eighty to ninety feet high. There are five lines, and their heights are the heights of the waves: one from 1854 at 395 feet; one twenty years later at 80 feet; one twenty-five years after that at 200 feet; one from 1936 at 490 feet; and one from 1958 at 1,720 feet.

That's five events in the last hundred years, or one every twenty. It's not hard to do the math, in terms of whether or not the bay's currently overdue.

In fact, that night we did the math, after lights-out in our little three-man tent. The scared guy's buddy was skeptical. He was still eating, having moved on to something called Moose Munch. We could hear the rustling of the bag and the crunching in the dark. Given that the waves occurred every twenty years, he said, the odds of one occurring on any single day in the bay were about eight thousand to one. There was a plunk down by the shore when something jumped. After we were quiet for a minute, he joked, "That's one of the first signs."

The odds were way smaller than that, the scared guy finally answered. He asked his buddy to think about how much unstable slope they'd already seen from the air. All of that had been exposed by the last wave. And it had now been exposed almost fifty years, he said. There were open fractures that were already visible.

So what did *he* think the odds were? his buddy wanted to know.

Double-digits, the scared guy said. The low double-digits.

"If I thought they were in the double-digits, I wouldn't be here," his buddy said.

"Yeah, well," the scared guy said. "What about you?" he asked me. It took me a minute to realize it, since we were lying in the dark.

"What about me?" I said.

"You ever notice anything out here?" he asked. "Any evidence of recent rockfalls or slides? Changes in the gravel deltas at the feet of the glaciers?"

"I only get out here once a year, if that," I told him. "It's not a big destination for people." I started going over in my head what I remembered, which was nothing.

"That's 'cause they're smart," the scared guy said.

"That's 'cause there's nothing here," his buddy answered.

"Well, there's a reason for that," the scared guy said. He told us he'd come across two censuses of the Tlingit tribes living in the bay from when the Russians owned the area. The populations had been listed as 241 in 1853 and zero a year later.

"Good night," his buddy told him.

"Good night," the scared guy said.

"What was that? You feel that?" his buddy asked him.

"Aw, shut up," the scared guy said.

What's this thing about putting people to *use*? What's that all about? What happened to just loving being *around* someone? Once, when I'd gotten Donald up off his butt to make him throw the baseball around with me, I asked that out loud. I only knew I'd done it when he said, "*I* don't know." Then he asked if we could quit now.

"Did you ever really think you'd find someone that you weren't in some ways cynical about?" my wife asked the night we'd decided we were in love. I was flying for somebody else, and we were lying under the wing of the Piper that we'd run up onto a beach. I'd been God's lonely man for however many years—twelve in the orphanage, four in high school, four in college, a hundred after that—and she was someone I wanted to pour myself down into. I was having trouble communicating how unusual that was.

That morning she'd watched me load a family I didn't like into a twin-engine, and I'd done this shoulder shake I do before something unpleasant. And she'd caught me, and her expression had given me a lift that carried me through the afternoon. Back in my room that night, she made a list of other things I did or thought, any one of which was proof she paid more attention than anyone else ever had before. She held parts of me like she had never seen anything so beautiful. At three or four in the morning she used her arms to tent herself up over me and asked, "Don't we have to sleep?" and then answered her own question.

Around noon we woke up spooning, and when I held on when she tried to head to the bathroom, we slid down the sheets to the floor. She finally lost me by crawling on all fours to the door.

"Well, she's as happy as *I've* ever seen her," her father told me at the rehearsal dinner. Twenty-three people had been invited and twenty-one were her family and friends.

"It's *so nice* to see her like this," her mother told me at the same dinner.

When I toasted her, she teared up. When she toasted me, she said only, "I never thought I would feel like this," and then sat down.

We honeymooned in San Francisco. Here's what that was like for me: I still root for that city's teams.

I've always been interested in the unprecedented. I just never got to experience it very often.

Her family is Juneau society, to the extent that such a thing exists. One brother's the arts editor for the *Juneau Empire;* another works for Bauer & Gates Real Estate, selling half-million dollar wilderness vacation homes to second-tier Hollywood stars. Another, go figure, is a lawyer. On holidays they give each other things like Arctic Cats. Happy birthday: here's a new 650 4x4. The real estate brother was 11-1 as a starter and team MVP for JDHS the year they won the state finals. The parents serve on every board there is. Their daughter when she turned sixteen was named queen of the Spring Salmon Derby. She still has the tiara with the leaping sockeye.

They didn't stand in the way of our romance. That's what her dad told anyone who asked. Our wedding announcement said that the bride-elect was the daughter of Donald and Nila Bell and that she'd graduated from the University of Alaska summa cum laude and was a first-year account executive for Sitka Communications

Systems. It said that the groom-elect was a meat cutter for the Super Bear Supermarket. I'd done that before I'd gotten my pilot's license, back when I'd first gotten to town, and the guy doing the announcement had fucked up.

"You don't think he could have *checked* something like that?" my wife wanted to know after she saw the paper. She was so upset on my behalf that I couldn't really complain.

It's not like I never had any advantages. I got a full ride, or nearly a full ride, at Saint Mary's in Moraga, near Oakland. I liked science and what math I took, though I never really, as one teacher put it, *found* myself while I was there. A friend offered me a summer job as one of his family's set-net fishermen my junior year, and I liked it enough to go back. The friend's family got me some supermarket work to tide me over in the winter, and it turned out that meat cutting paid more than boning fish. "What do you *want* to do?" a girl at the checkout asked me one day, like if she heard me bitch about it once more she was going to pull all her hair out, so that afternoon I signed up at Fly Alaska and Bigfoot Air, and I got my commercial and multiengine, and two years later had my float rating. I hooked on with a local outfit and the year after that bought the business, which meant a three-room hut with a stove, a van, the name, and the client list. Now I lease two 206s and two 172s on EDO 2130 floats, have two other pilots working under me, and get fourteen to fifteen hundred dollars a load for round-trip flights in the area. Want an Arctic Cat? I can buy one out of petty cash. At least in the high season.

"So are we not going to talk about this?" my wife asked last week after her parents had been over for dinner. We'd had crab and her dad had been in a funk for most of the night, who knew why. We'd said good night and handled the cleanup and now I was lunging around on my knees trying to cover my son in Nerf basketball. He always turns into Game Fanatic at bedtime, so we hung a Nerf hoop over the inside of the back door to accommodate that need. He was taking advantage of my distraction to try and drive the baseline but I funneled him into the doorknob.

"I'm ready to talk," I told her. "Let's talk."

She sat on one of the kitchen chairs with her hands together on her knees, willing to wait for me to stop playing. Her hair wasn't having the best day and it was bothering her. She kept slipping it back behind her ear.

"You can't just stay around the basket," Donald complained, trying to lure me out so he could blow by me. He was a little teary with frustration.

"I was going to talk to Daddy about having another baby," she told him. His mind was pretty intensively elsewhere.

"Do you *want* a baby brother?" she asked.

"Not right now," he said.

"If you're not having fun, you shouldn't play," she told him.

That night in bed she was lying on her back with her hands behind her head. "I love you a lot," she said when I finally got under the covers next to her. "But sometimes you just make it so hard."

"What do I do?" I asked her. This was one of the many times I could have told her. I could have even just mentioned I'd been thinking about making the initial appointment. "What do I do?" I asked again. I sounded mad but I wanted to know.

"What do you do," she said, like I had just proven her point.

"I think about you all the time," I said. "I feel like *you're* losing interest in *me*." Even saying that much was humiliating. The appointment at times like that seemed like a small but hard thing that I could hold on to.

She cleared her throat and pulled a hand from behind her head and wiped her eyes with it.

"I hate making you sad," I told her.

"I hate being made sad," she said.

It was only when she said things like that and I had to deal with them that I realized how much I depended on having made her happy. And how much all of that shook when she whacked at it. *Tell her,* I thought, with enough intensity that I thought she might've heard me.

"I don't *want* another kid," Donald called from his room. The panel doors in our bedrooms weren't that great in terms of privacy.

"Go to sleep," his mother called back.

We lay there waiting for him to go back to sleep. *Tell her you changed your mind,* I thought. *Tell her you want to make a kid, right now. Show her.* I had a hand on her thigh and she had her palm cupped over my crotch, as if that, at least, was on her side. "Shh," she said, and reached her other hand to my forehead and smoothed away my hair.

Set-net fishermen mostly work for families that hold the fishing permits and leases, which are not easy to get. The families sell during the season to vendors who buy fish along the beach. The season runs from mid-June to late July. We fished at Coffee Point on Bristol Bay. Two people lived there: a three-hundred-pound white guy and his mail-order bride. The bride was from the Philippines and didn't seem to know what had hit her. Nobody could pronounce her name. The town nearest the Point had a phone book that was a single mimeographed sheet with thirty-two names and numbers. The road signs were handpainted, but it had a liquor store, a grocery store, and a superhardened airstrip that looked capable of landing 747s, because the bigger companies had started figuring out how much money there was in shipping mass quantities of flash-frozen salmon.

We strung fifty-foot nets perpendicular to the shore just south of the King Salmon River: cork floats on top, lead weights on the bottom. Pickers like me rubber-rafted our way along the cork floats, hauling in a little net, freeing snagged salmon gills and filling the raft at our feet. When we had enough we paddled ashore and emptied the rafts and started over again.

Everybody knew what they were doing but me. And in that water with that much protective gear, people drowned when things went wrong. Learning the ropes meant figuring out what the real fishermen wanted, and the real fishermen never said boo. It was like I was in the land of the deaf and dumb and a million messages were going by. Someone might squint at me, or give me a look, and I'd give him a look back, and finally someone else would say to me, "That's too *tight*." It was nice training on how you could get in the way even when your help was essential.

How could you do such a thing if you love her so much? I think to myself with some regularity, lying there in bed. *Well, that's the question, isn't it?* is usually my next thought. "What's the Saturday before Memorial Day circled for?" my wife asked a week ago, standing near our kitchen calendar. Memorial Day at that point stood two weeks off. The whole extended family would be showing up at Don and Nila's for a cookout. I'd probably be a little hobbled when it came to the annual volleyball game.

"Should you even *have* kids? Should you even have a *wife*?" my wife asked once, after our first real fight. I'd taken a charter all the way up to Dry Bay and stayed a couple of extra nights without calling. I hadn't even called in to the office. She'd been beside herself with worry and then anger. Before I'd left, I'd told her to call me back and then when she hadn't, I'd been like, *Okay, if you don't want to talk, you don't want to talk.* I'd left my cell phone off. *That* I'm not supposed to do. The office even thought about calling Air-Sea Rescue.

"Bad move, Chief," even Doris, our girl working the phones, told me when I got back.

"So I'm wondering if I should go back to work," my wife tells me today. We're eating something she whipped up in her new wok.

It's an off day—nothing scheduled except some maintenance paperwork—and I was slow getting out of the house, and she invited me to lunch. She was distracted during the rinsing the greens part, and every bite reminds me of a trip to the beach. She must notice the grit. She hates stuff like that more than I do.

"They still need someone to help out with the online accounts," she says. She has an expression like every single thing today has gone wrong.

"Do you want to go back to work?" I ask her. "Do you miss it?"

"I don't know if I *miss* it," she says. She adds something in a lower voice that I can't hear because of the crunch of the grit. She seems bothered that I don't respond.

"I think it's more, you know, if we're not going to do the other thing," she says. "Have the baby." She keeps herself from looking away, as if she wants to make clear that I'm not the only one humiliated by talks like this.

I push some spinach around and she pushes some spinach around. "I feel like first we need to talk about us," I finally tell her. I put my fork down and she puts her fork down.

"All right," she says. She turns both her palms up and raises her eyebrows like, *Here I am.*

One time she came and found me in one of the hangars at two o'clock in the afternoon and turned me around by the shoulders and pinned me to one of the workstations with her kiss. A plane two hangars down warmed up, taxied over, and took off while we kissed. She kissed me the way lost people must act when they find water in the desert.

"Do you think about me the way you used to think about me?" I ask her.

She gives me a look. "How did I used to think about you?"

There aren't any particular ways of describing it that occur to me. I imagine myself saying with a pitiful voice, "Remember that time in the hangar?"

She looks at me, waiting. Lately that look has had a quality to it. One time in Ketchikan, one of my pilots and I saw a drunk who'd spilled his Seven and Seven lapping some of it up off the wood of the bar. *That* look: the look we gave each other.

This is ridiculous. I rub my eyes.

"Is this taxing for you?" she wants to know, and her impatience makes me madder too.

"No, it isn't taxing for me," I tell her.

She gets up and dumps her dish in the sink and goes down to the cellar. I can hear her rooting around in our big meat freezer for a Popsicle for dessert.

The phone rings and I don't get up. The answering machine takes over, and Dr. Calvin's office leaves a message reminding me about my Friday appointment. The machine switches off. I don't get to it before my wife comes back upstairs.

She unwraps her Popsicle and slides it into her mouth. It's grape.

"You want one?" she asks.

"No," I tell her. I put my hands on the table and off again. They're not staying still. It's like they're about to go off.

"I should've asked when I was down there," she tells me.

She slurps on it a little, quietly. I push my plate away.

"You going to the doctor?" she asks.

Outside a big terrier that's new to me is taking a dump near our hibachi. He's moving forward in little steps while he's doing it. "Goddamn," I say to myself. I sound like someone who's come home from a twelve-hour shift and still has to shovel his driveway.

"What's wrong with Moser?" she wants to know. Moser's our regular doctor.

"That was Moser," I tell her. "That was his office."

"It was?" she says.

"Yes it was," I tell her.

"Put your dish in the sink," she reminds me.

I put the dish in the sink and head into the living room and drop onto the couch.

"Checkup?" she calls from the kitchen.

"Pilot physical," I tell her. All she has to do is play the message.

She wanders into the living room without the Popsicle. Her lips are darker from it. She waits a minute near the couch and then sinks down next to me. She leans forward, looking at me. Her lips touch mine, and press, and then lift off and stay so close it's hard to know if they're touching or not. Mine are still moist from hers.

"Come upstairs," she whispers. "Come upstairs and show me what you're worried about." She puts three fingers on my erection and rides them along it until she stops on my belly.

"I love you so much," I tell her. That much is true.

"Come upstairs and show me," she tells me back.

That night in 1958, undersea communications cables from Anchorage to Seattle went dead. Boats at sea recorded a shocking hammering on their hulls. In Ketchikan and Anchorage people ran into the streets. In Juneau streetlights toppled and breakfronts emptied their contents. The eastern shore of Disenchantment Bay lifted itself forty-two feet out of the sea, the dead barnacles still visible there, impossibly high up on the rock faces. And at Yakutat, a postmaster in a skiff happened to be watching a cannery operator and his wife pick strawberries on a sandy point near a harbor navigation light, when the entire point with the light pitched into the air and then flushed itself as though driven underwater. The postmaster barely stayed in his skiff, and afterward, paddling around the whirlpools and junk waves, he found only the woman's hat.

"You know, I made some sacrifices here," my wife mentions to me later that same day. We're naked and both on the floor on our backs with our feet still up on the bed. One of hers is twisted in the sheets. The room seems darker and I don't know if that's a change in the weather or if we've just been here forever. One of our kisses was such a submersion that when we finally stopped we needed to lie still for a minute, holding on to each other, to recover.

"You mean as in having married me?" I ask her. Our skin is air-drying but still mostly sticky.

"I mean as in having married you," she says. Then she pulls her foot free of the sheets and rolls over me.

She told me as she was first easing me down onto the bed that she'd gone off the pill but that it was going to take at least a few weeks before she'd be ready. "So you know why I'm doing this?" she asked. She slid both thighs across me, her mouth at my ear. "I'm doing this because it's *amazing*."

We're still sticky and she's looking down into my face with her most serious expression. "I mean, you're a meat cutter," she says, fitting me inside of her again. The next time we do this I'll have had the operation. And despite everything, it's still the most amazing feeling of closeness.

"Why are you *crying*?" she whispers. Then she lowers her mouth to mine and goes, "Shhh. Shhh."

Howard Ulrich and his little boy Sonny entered Lituya Bay at eight the night of the wave, and anchored on the south shore near the entrance. He wrote about it afterward. Their fishing boat had a high bow, a single mast, and a pilothouse the size of a Portosan. Before they turned in, two other boats had followed them in and anchored even nearer the entrance. It was totally quiet. The water was a pane of glass from shore to shore. Small icebergs seemed to just sit in place. The gulls and terns that they usually saw circling Cenotaph Island in the middle of the bay were hunkered down on the shore. Sonny said it looked like they were waiting for something. His dad tucked him in bed at about ten, around sunset. He'd just climbed in himself when the boat started pitching and jerking against its anchor chain. When he ran up on deck in his underwear, he saw the mountains heaving themselves around and avalanching. Clouds of snow and rocks shot up high into the air. It looked like they were being shelled. Sonny came up on deck in his pj's, which had alternating wagon wheels and square-knotted ropes. He rubbed his eyes. Ninety million tons of rock dropped into Gilbert Inlet as a unit. The sonic concussion of the rock hitting the water knocked them both onto their backs on the deck.

It took the wave about two and a half minutes to cover the seven miles to their boat. In that time Sonny's dad tried to weigh anchor and discovered that he couldn't, the anchor stuck fast, so he let out the chain as far as he could, got a life preserver onto Sonny, and managed to turn his bow into the wave. As it passed Cenotaph Island it was still over a hundred feet high, extending from shore to shore, a wave front two miles wide.

The front was unbelievably steep, and when it hit, the anchor chain snapped immediately, whipping around the pilothouse and smashing the windows. The boat arrowed seventy-five feet up into the curl like they were climbing in an elevator, their backs pressed against the pilothouse wall as if they'd been tilted back in barber's chairs. The wave's face was a wall of green taking them up into the sky. They were carried high over the south shore. Sixty-foot trees down below disappeared. Then they were thrown up over the crest and down the back slope, where the backwash spun them off again into the center of the bay.

Another couple, the Swansons, had also turned into the wave and had their boat surfboard a quarter mile out to sea, and when the wave crest broke, the boat pitchpoled and hit bottom. They managed to find and float their emergency skiff in the debris afterward. The third couple, the Wagners, tried to make a run for the harbor entrance and were never seen again.

Four-foot-wide trees were washed away, along with the topsoil and everything else. Slopes were scoured down to bedrock. Bigger trunks were snapped off at ground level. Trees at the edge of the trimline had their bark removed by the water pressure.

Sonny's dad was still in his underwear, teeth chattering, and Sonny was washing around on his side in some icy bilge water, making noises like a jungle bird. The sun was down by this point. Backwash and wavelets twenty feet high were crisscrossing the bay, spinning house-sized chunks of glacier ice that collided against each other. Clean-peeled tree trunks like pickup sticks knitted together and upended, pitching and rolling. Water was still pouring down the slopes on both sides of the bay. The smell was like being facedown in the dirt under an upended tree. And Sonny's dad said the time that passed afterward—when they'd realized they'd survived but still had to navigate through everything pinballing around them in the dark—was worse than riding the wave itself.

A day or two later the geologists started arriving. No one believed the height of the wave at first. People thought any devastation that high on the slopes had to have been caused by landslides. But they came around.

My wife fell asleep beside me, wrapped over me to keep me warm. We're still on the floor and now it really is dark. We've got to be late in terms of picking up Donald from his play date, but if his friend's parents called, I didn't hear the phone.

One of my professors at Saint Mary's had this habit of finishing each class with four or five questions, none of which anyone could answer. It was a class called The Philosophy of Life. I got a C. If I took it now, I'd do even worse. I'd sit there hoping he wouldn't see me and try not to let my mouth hang open while he fired off the questions. What makes us threaten the things we want most? What makes us so devoted to the comfort of the inadvertent? What makes us unwilling to gamble on the noncataclysmic?

Sonny's dad was famous for a while, selling stories with titles like "My Night of Terror" to magazines like *Alaska Sportsman* and *Reader's Digest*. I read one or two of them to Donald, though my wife didn't approve. "Do *you* like these stories?" he asked me that night. In the stories, Sonny's mom never gets mentioned. Whether she was mad or dead or divorced or proud never comes up. In one his dad talks about having jammed a life preserver over Sonny's head and then having forgotten about him entirely. In another he says something like, in that minute before it all happened, he'd never felt so alone. I imagine Sonny reading that a year or two later and going, *Thanks, Dad.* I imagine him looking at his dad later on, at times when his dad doesn't know he's watching, and thinking of all that his dad gave him and all that he didn't. I imagine him never really figuring out what came between them. I imagine years later people saying about him that that was the thing about Sonny: the kid was just like the old man.

The First South Central
Australian Expedition

April 1st, 1840

The three of us traded Christmas tales during our long portage. Hill and Browne both professed shock at my contribution, which seemed less than shocking to me. I had related to them the method by which my father, with what I remember to be the sad-eyed support of our mother, celebrated our Lord's birth each Christmas Day.

Having three sons, myself the eldest, he had resolved, he said, to no longer be tyrannized by the understanding that during this particular season he was obligated as a Christian to provide even more for his family, by way of gifts, than he did in the course of the normal round. Henceforth, then, one and only one child each year would be favored with a lovely gift to commemorate the day. He hoped that the child's siblings would derive the pleasure they should from their compatriot's good fortune. In accordance with his understanding of the general workings of the natural world, the process would proceed by lot. So it was entirely possible that one child would be favored by chance two or even three years in a row. We would all find out only upon coming downstairs on Christmas morning, when we saw what was set about the hearth.

He made this announcement having gathered the family together on Christmas Eve the year I turned five. My brothers, being at the time only three and two, hardly knew what they were being told. His wife and our mother, by all accounts gay and outgoing before her marriage, stood by while he entertained questions about his decision, and then did her best to salvage some measure of wan cheer over the course of those Christmas Days that followed.

My story was greeted with an extended silence. We were having trouble with the horses in the current. Browne announced himself, finally, to have been cudgeled about the head by the damned thing. He meant my story. Hill found it odd that such a father would have shown a willingness to finance a part of the expedition. "I'm sure it's not entirely unusual," I remarked to them, some time later, about my father's notion of gift giving. "I'm sure it is," Browne responded.

April 3rd

My father instilled in me the habit of resolving every day to make a resolution, to be repeated aloud when dressing and undressing. Today's has been: "Think well before giving an answer, and never speak except from strong convictions."

"Are you conversing with yourself?" Browne asked from outside my tent this morning when he overheard.

The rock here is of an oolitic limestone and treacherous with hollows throughout. The surrounding area is beset by stupendous tufts of porcupine grass (spinifex) four to five feet high. The country so far has been stupefyingly consistent. We are now fifteen weeks out and for the last six have continued to wait for some kind of happy transformation in the path ahead.

We stopped at a marshy creek and it came on raining, and Cuppage shot himself. Somehow in stowing his saddle he managed to allow a binding loop to catch the trigger. The ball came out his back under the shoulder.

Our legs are full of the sharp ends of the spinifex. Large numbers of crows are following the baggage train, apparently for the sheep's offals.

April 5th

We have left a note in a bottle as to our progress in the message hollow of the great gum tree at Sadness Creek, per our arrangement, to be collected and carried back to Adelaide by a native sent for that purpose. The bottle is marked with indelible ink *South Central Australian Expedition, R. M. Beadle.*

The animals have been watered and are resting under fair and mild skies. We have been so anxious to proceed at all speed that I have not set down in these pages the full catalog of our expedition. In the matter of personnel, I can state without equivocation that I was given a free hand, and chose a crew of twelve, counting myself, out of over three hundred able-bodied men who applied for positions. Any group of men isolated on a long journey is entirely dependent upon one another, and we will be no exception. Accompanying me on this undertaking are:

> *Officers.*
> *James A. Browne. Second in command.*
> *Richard Scott Hill. Expedition physician.*
> *Philip Mander-Jones. Expedition draftsman and surveyor.*
>
> *Men.*
> *Edgar Beale. In charge of stock.*
> *D. K. Hamilton &*
> *Charles Mabberly. To man the whaleboat.*
> *John Gould. In charge of the horses.*
> *Robert Cuppage. Armorer.*
> *Francis Purdie. Cook.*
> *John Mack &*
> *H. L. Moorhouse. Bullock drivers.*

We carry five tons of provisions and equipment on three bullock drays and two carriages pulled by draft horses. One of the carriages transports the whaleboat. Each of the loaded drays weighs over two thousand pounds. We began with a ton of flour alone, three hundred pounds of bacon, and a quarter ton of sugar. We carry for safety a pairing of sextants, artificial horizons, prismatic compasses, and barometers. A ream of foolscap, this book for journal-keeping, sealing wax, camel's hair brushes, an inkstand, ink, goose quills, colored pencils, and a sketch palette. Five revolvers and two rifles. For ornithological specimens, a shotgun. As well as all the necessary ammunition. Also a trunk of trade and gift items, primarily hats and knives, for the aborigines. In the back of the train are four extra horses, one hundred head of sheep for provision, and four dogs for herding the sheep. Our procession extends more than a quarter of a mile.

We have been empowered to strike north from Mt. Arden into the great interior as far as the 28th parallel of latitude. This in order to determine whether a mountain range or other major height of land exists in that vicinity. The governor and Lord Stanley have to that end approved a budget of two thousand five hundred pounds for an undertaking not to exceed twelve months.

If such a height of land does exist, then everything north of it must necessarily flow into an as yet undiscovered watershed: a vast inland sea.

April 7th

Today's resolution: "Strive, and hold cheap the strain." We have set a guard, and impressed upon the men the necessity of vigilance. And the danger of the journey ahead. Tomorrow we step off into the first truly daunting territory, leaving the southern watershed behind. The aborigines call our resting place Dead Man's Flat. The men in high spirits, the animals in good order. Up late, too agitated for sleep, my mind full of a thousand small tasks, and marveling on this strange, strange country, where even the celestial sphere is the wrong way about.

April 8th

Even as a child, I'd pressed my hand to the map of Australia in my *Boys' Atlas,* palming the blank upon its center. Our biggest cities are but specks perched on the extreme southern and eastern tips of a vast unknown. Men of perseverance and resource have failed to penetrate that remote and oblique vastness. Stowitts set off from the NE coast with the idea of crossing to Perth, and together with his entire expedition was never heard from again. The entire area seems so fearsomely defended by its deserts, one might suppose Nature has intentionally closed it to civilized man.

Browne has pointed out to me in the privacy of my tent that the governor's charge says nothing about an inland sea. My father too tried to strike the boat from the budget list. Browne believes, with them, that the great center is likely to prove in its entirety to be inhospitable desert. But I paid the cost of the whaleboat with my own funds. Explorers have recorded countless westward-flowing streams, none of which empty into the southern ocean. Where do these waters go if not to an immense sea or lake to which there must exist a navigable entrance? I believe the continent to be fashioned like a bowl, with elevated sides and a sunken center, a bowl whose lowest points are likely to be filled with water. "A bowl," Browne said with some unhappiness when I outlined for him my thinking.

And imagine if that sea disembogues into the northern ocean, by way of some strait, I reminded him. "The Beadle Sea," he smiled, as though indulging a child he loved very much. We were together relashing the bundle containing our charter and various maps, such as they were. "The Browne Strait," I added, in order to see him smile again.

April 10th

Browne too has had a vexed relationship with his father, whose unfortunate speculations in corn when Browne was still a child left the family nearly without resource. He admitted during his interview that he had reaped few benefits, emotional or financial, from his parents. He has, nevertheless, turned himself into a young man of no little account. He brings to our group an artist's spirit and a Zouave's resourcefulness. As well as an apostate's skepticism. During a supper gathering of the officers, I listed the altogether beneficial ways in which our various virtues interacted. Hill, I pointed out, besides his skills as a healer, is also a man of refined manners, a genteel disposition, and a sensitive temperament. Mander-Jones has a scientist's exactitude and love of order. Our virtues together, I suggested, comprise one ideal explorer. "Of frustrated ambitions," Browne pointed out. A short while after our discussion, one of the men shot what Mander-Jones informs us is a new sort of butcher-bird, very scarce and wild.

April 13th

Today's resolution: "To love is to be all made of sighs and tears; to be all made of faith and service." Named a dry creek bed of some size Beale Creek, to reward the fellow for the labor of having surveyed it. Sufficient saltbush, which the horses eat readily. Some small, fawn-colored kangaroo, of which the dogs have killed four.

No elevation of any kind breaks the horizon or varies the sea of scrub ahead. At first there will be the appearance of improvement, then barren country again. During our evening meal Browne asked if the governor or Lord Stanley had any knowledge of the whaleboat. I told him that they had made clear to my satisfaction that they had every confidence in myself and my decisions. Cuppage reports that his pain is very bad when he mounts or dismounts. Browne considers it a poor sign that our armorer has managed to shoot himself.

April 14th

All day the sun through heavy clouds, which checked some of its fiery beams. Nothing about but a few coleopterous insects. "Beetles," Browne corrects me, a little peevishly. After encampment we observed four or five signal fires. The aborigines are apparently retreating before our advance.

April 16th

No sign of a previous civilization. Not an arrowhead, not a flint, not even the remains of a cooking fire. Everything suggests an ongoing and immemorial enervation. A kind of trance in the air.

April 17th

Here in this wilderness, we intruded upon an extraordinary gathering: a group of five white men seated upon the ground, weeping. They seemed to have about them ample supplies, and to be without injury. Nothing would make them explain the cause of their grief. In the end we were obliged to continue on our way. Purdie, the cook, in particular, has remained quite upset by the incident.

April 20th

A stretch of better country, over which we have made good progress. Found a native wheat and a rye, and in hollows a purple vetch of which the cattle are very fond. Crossed an entire plain covered with perfectly spherical stones. Formed by the action of water, no doubt, when the plain was—or is—undersea.

At times the land ahead is as flat as a table. The birds are remarkable: ibis with their coral eyes; emus, striding about like enormous indignant chickens on their startling claws; olive green and yellow butcher-birds circling on their updrafts to gain height. Something Mander-Jones calls a "ventriloquist dove," which, with no movement of its throat, makes a sound that seems to come from the distant horizon. We are taking notes and collecting specimens whenever possible. We all feel the exhilaration of putting our other lives behind us. Mack, with Cuppage laid up, has had unusual success shooting pigeons. Today's resolution: "Look round the habitable world! How few know their own good; or knowing it, pursue."

April 21st

A close, humid day which produced an incessant clamminess over the body and called forth innumerable insects. Mander-Jones bitten on the scalp by a centipede in his hat. The dogs killed a fine specimen of something that had been following us, but in the ensuing scuffle they tore off its head. It rained gently in the morning.

April 22nd

When I was less than five years old, I am told, I dragged around behind me on a cord a legless horse to which I was inseparably attached. The poor thing bounced and tumbled along in a most pitiful way, as I remember. No one knew from whence it came. It was a carved lump of pine painted with a blue saddle. It had a mouth but no eyes. I slept with it and named it My Captain, to the puzzlement of those who gave it any thought.

April 23rd

Plagued by the flies, and the rain has brought out the death adders and other snakes. Eight-inch centipedes with ghastly jaws, fearless, mouse-sized scorpions, ubiquitous stinging ants. Men glad of moving on.

Browne at our officers' supper again lodged a complaint concerning the number of water casks we carry (two), which he sees as woefully inadequate. He reminded us all that we're doing what we've been expressly advised by those familiar with the country not to do: travel with no line of communication to our rear and no maps for our forward journey. His reassuring prudence was duly recorded. In order to demonstrate our congruency on this point I cited for him yesterday's resolution, which was "Take care of the minutes, for the hours will take care of themselves."

During heavy winds the dogs shelter in hollows, whining and barking to very little purpose.

April 24th

Finally, some natives. A small group: two men, four women, and a few children. They were camped on a sand hill and sat watching as we approached. The children were in a terrible fright, clinging to their mothers like opossum. The adults are very wiry and strong looking though they tend to be deficient in the front tooth. While we watched they cooked some mice in the hot sand itself and then devoured them entire, fur, entrails, and all, nipping off the tail with their teeth. I had with me a vocabulary of the language of the Murray natives but was unable to make them understand a word of it. We asked, by signs, where they derived their water, and they intimated that they depended on rain. They did so by lifting their hands and then pulling them quickly down while fluttering their fingers. Then they pointed where we were headed and shook their heads vigorously.

They were much taken with our appearance, and some of us do present a sight: Mabberly with his great buccaneer's hat; Beale with his peculiar facial scar. Mander-Jones with his filthy beard. And Hill's spectacles, which are so very small that I constantly wonder how he sees adequately through them. Purdie, the only one of our party to have met aborigines on their home ground before, informed us after we had moved on that they believe Europeans to be black fellows returned from the grave, gone white because of their new status as ghosts.

Tested the water in their water-hole and found it to be 107.8 degrees. Tonight the dogs are barking toward the point from which the wind is coming. One of the horses kicked Moorhouse's gun on the stock and shivered it to pieces. Hill has broken my watch.

April 27th

Dreadful passage. For three days now our road has lain over these abominable and rotten lands on which water has evidently subsided and whose surface the sun has cracked into deep fissures. Whenever the dray wheels drop into the holes it shocks the animals greatly. We are flanked as we proceed by great ridges of basalt and ironstone. Nothing seems tempered by weathering; all edges seem razor-sharp. There is much eurite underfoot. Mysterious columnar formations off to the west. Nearly all we survey seems unsuitable for cultivation. The temperature yesterday rose to 111 Fahrenheit; this morning, it fell to 38. Nights we huddle in flannel pantaloons and greatcoats. Days we suffer in the heat. How it is possible that the natives can withstand such extremes, unprovided as they are against the heat and cold?

Cuppage is now able to lift or carry very little. Hill fears his wound may be infected.

May 1st

Full of accidents today. Moorhouse's dray broke its axle-pole, and Gould's its rear wheel. The country is more open and worse in character. Rents and fissures so tremendous the cart-drivers are thrown from their seats. Mabberly has been admirably careful with the whaleboat, about which, considering the likelihood of her being so soon wanted, I am naturally nervous. Nothing cheering in the prospect to the N and NW.

One of the dogs has been lost—swallowed—in a strange dry salt lagoon comprised of gypsum and black mud. Its compatriots were hysterical with grief and upset. The approaches to the place were most unpleasantly spongy. The wind blows salt from it over the flats behind us like smoke. Old Fitz, our best draft horse, has a swelling on his near hind leg.

May 2nd

Stopped to give the animals a day of rest and to repair the drays. At a dry creek bed, some white mallow, which Gould gave to the horses. Nearer the creek a plant with a striped and bitter fruit. Perhaps some kind of cucumber.

The flies an affliction. Scaled a box tree to consider the path ahead with the telescope. Flies blocked and clogged the eyepiece. Attacked by ants, their bites like a bad sunburn throughout the night.

May 5th

I've directed that the bullocks be fastened by the noses to the carts, so that we might start earlier. The thermometer this morning at half past six stood at 102. Increasingly the only plants we encounter are differing kinds of atriplex with their terrible spines. The only water our advance parties were able to discover today was a shallow puddle so thick with animalcula as to be unfit to drink.

Numerous insects about at night. During the day, the flies. Whether we are out taking bearings or in gullies searching water or in our tents, it is all the same. They watch our movements, and the moment our hands are full, settle in swarms on our faces.

May 12th

A new mortification: we have left behind all scrub and rock to confront gigantic sandy ridges which succeed each other like wave trains, and we climb and descend one just to confront another. Only the smallest, umbrella-shaped shrubs in evidence here and there, the intense surface heat having seared away the lower branches. The ridges are sixty to seventy feet high and as steep as swells in a heavy gale. They appear to extend many miles to the NW. Should we find a body of water in that direction, I am at a loss as to how we would negotiate the dray with the whaleboat that distance.

Even so, the ridges exhibit a regularity that waves alone must have created. What we are struggling with, it follows, was not long ago a submarine position. "Oh, for the love of God," Browne responded when I told him, his hat soaked through with sweat before our day had even begun.

May 19th

A week of stupefying labor. The heavily loaded drays sink deep into the sand, and the overheated bullocks just cease their struggles completely for minutes at a time. The days are scorching hot, and the animals are suffering greatly. Today the sheep came to a dead halt and would not move, while the dogs and horses huddled under and against the drays for such shade as they might provide, remaining there until evening.

Winds and whirlwinds, all oven-hot. The horses are suffering even more than we might have expected. Their legs are pierced in a hundred places by spinifex, which has in the last two days begun to cover the ridges. Both Captain and the chestnut have had a running at the nose which I feared to be glanders, but Gould reports they are better. I have an ugly rash over my back and chest. The men complain of insomnia and sore eyes. This evening at sunset we remarked upon an extended haze of a supernatural blue on the horizon opposite the sun. The effect, we presume, of refraction.

I have had some surprisingly bitter contentions with some of the other officers. More than ever I am convinced that the interior is to be achieved only by careful calculation and that additional headlong rushing about will lead us into further difficulty. As it is now, advance parties, usually captained by Browne, scout twenty to thirty miles ahead of us by horse. Both Browne and Mander-Jones believe we cannot maintain this unhurried pace with summer only four or five months away.

I hope I will not shrink from the trials ahead. The day may come when I must face greater extremes, and I trust I will do so not the less firmly for having only the smallest notion of what I'm likely to encounter.

May 22nd

Cuppage feverish and laid up. A comfortable pallet has been arranged for him in the whaleboat. A few days' inactivity while the advance parties search for water. I have directed that the whaleboat be outfitted and painted.

Hill, who has been working wonders with poor Cuppage's suffering, is really like a young hero from literature: fair-minded, virile, and eager to get on. He articled as a surgeon, which he found not very agreeable. His real passion is for astronomy, and his sense of direction so intuitive he negotiated alone some of the jungles on the northern coast. And few men have less of envy in their disposition.

All of Adelaide, it seemed, approved my choice of Hill for this expedition. And nearly as many lamented my choice of Browne. This man with the instincts and fearlessness of a native in the bush, and of a judgment beyond his station, is in Adelaide a drunkard of the lowest reputation. Hill initially and privately conveyed surprise that I would suffer such a man to be in my party, and my father too expressed violent doubts. But here in the wild there is not a more careful and valuable follower to be found. I believe him to be personally attached to me and nurse the fervent belief that this chance at achievement will have a decisive effect on the rest of his life.

May 28th

Our progress renewed. Today's resolution is "Seek experience joined to common sense, which to mortals is a providence." The ascents are backbreaking and the revelations at the summits unrewarding.

Still little seasonal cooling. The air so rarefied we can hardly breathe. The sun dries everything with such speed that one can almost watch the few pools we do find sink. There is no way of knowing how soon we might be cut off by the loss of water holes behind us. The complete absence of animal life is stark evidence of the dire poverty of what lies all around us and ahead. We are now alone in the wilderness. The wind is blowing from the NE in our faces with the heat of a blacksmith's forge. Despite our exertions, none of us exhibit any moisture on the skin. This is perhaps related to our being now much distressed by violent headaches.

May 29th

Continued all day without knowing whether we were extricating or ensnaring ourselves. We are to all intents and purposes at sea. A carrion kite hovered over us early this morning in befuddlement at our presence.

June 2nd

Recovering in our tents. Supper of a little dried beef. Browne reminded us that we are in a precarious situation, and that the least mistake will be lethal. This is a region in which we have not the leisure to pause. He further pointed out that it wasn't the advance but the retreat that was to be most dreaded.

June 3rd

No travel. Old Fitz now dead lame. The men employed examining the bacon. Today's resolution: "Of comfort, no man speak." Surface heat so great we can't hold stones we pick up with our hand.

June 4th

No travel.

June 5th

Another halt. The men complain of giddiness when they stoop. The bullocks done in. The heat of the sand is so intense that the poor animals paw away the top layers to get to the cooler beneath.

The upper leathers of Hill's shoes are burnt away. Gould's back terribly blistered. The dogs are losing the pads of their feet. The natives could not possibly walk this desert at midsummer. The bullocks' yokes even now are so heated the men cannot handle them. We ride with our feet out of the stirrups because the irons are too hot. Mander-Jones's chronometer has stopped. It is no longer possible to use the quills, the ink dries so rapidly. 139 degrees in the sun.

The monotony of such plodding, hour after hour, and always with the prospect of waking the next morning to more of the same—! We are almost entirely silent during this apathy of motion. This coma of riding. Even a small object becomes an achievement when attained, something on which to focus the mind in so vast a space.

June 9th

I could not more regret the paucity of casks to hold water. I would strongly recommend casks as indispensable on all future expeditions in this country. There is a yellow hue on the horizon each morning which we now understand to be a sure indication of the afternoon's unsupportable heat.

June 12th

We have come upon what can only be called the Stony Desert, the first sight of which caused us to lose our breath. It is more demoralizing than what has gone before. Not a speck of plant life across the horizon. Masses of rock mixed with white quartz split into innumerable fragments. Ruin and desolation, stretching out in an endless plain as far as we can see. Purdie, the cook, whimpered audibly from his seat on one of the drays at the prospect. Some of the men laughed.

The surfaces are diamond-hard and ring under our horses' shoes. The stone is so thick upon the ground that the carts leave no track. Distance traveled fourteen miles.

June 14th

It is as if the earth itself were steel-shod. The horses' hooves are being cut to the quick. We're shaken by detonations to our right and left: great rock masses splitting off in the extremes of temperature. Seven sheep dead from the heat. Distance traveled eleven miles.

Today a new stretch of rock hued with iron oxide, so the plains ahead now have a dark purple cast. The country continues to raise terrible havoc with the horses' shoes, which are wearing away like wax. Gould and Mack report that their headaches have worsened. The men complain of rheumatism, and most of us have violent pains in our hip joints. Hill reports a large ring round the moon last night, most likely indicative of wind. The whaleboat suffered today its first accident: the stern sheets were torn off on a rock. It was not the driver's fault, but mine, for not warning him of its proximity. Each day brings fresh sheaves of anxiety to our already overstuffed bundle.

June 15th

We are all on foot to spare the horses. The stone, in no way rounded, is brutal to the feet. Gould complains incessantly of an excruciating pain in his forehead. Poor Cuppage has not been heard from for days, except to cry out whenever a drop or a crash shakes the whaleboat. Browne's horse has an inflammation of the mucus membrane. The casks are empty. At the first waterless halt, the horses would not eat and instead collected round me, my poor

Captain so much afflicted that he tugged my hat with his teeth to claim attention. Called a halt and asked Moorhouse to reconnoiter the extent of the ridges to our NW from the vantage point of the ridge to our W. His climb provided him, regrettably, with no cover. He returned to pronounce it the most difficult task he had ever performed.

June 20th

Only three miles down a ravine to our E, a kind of natural oasis with a pool thirty to forty feet wide and nearly ten feet deep, situated beneath the shade of large stands of casuarina and mulga trees. Ample feed for the animals. Providence has guided us to the only place where our wants might be supplied for any extended amount of time, but has also here stayed our progress in a region soon to become forbidden ground.

Today completes the sixth month of our absence from Adelaide. How much longer we shall be out it is impossible to say. We still wait for winter rains. I am heartbroken at the delay. I remain of the full conviction that we're fifty miles or less from the Inland Sea. My only consolation is that the present situation is unavoidable.

June 27th

I have been neglecting my resolutions. Today's is "The happy man finds in some part of his soul a drop of patience." I have been trying to chart our position and finding it impossible to put pencil to paper in this superheated tent. Have set the men to digging a chamber deep in the ground from which we might make our calculations.

June 30th

Beale has a pulmonary condition. Was bled yesterday and is better today. Mabberly has had an attack of inflammation of the lungs. Almost everyone is complaining of bleeding at the nose. We are all beset by symptoms of scurvy. My gums are so sore that I cannot take even porridge and have a vile taste of copper in my mouth, intensified by savage headaches. We all trust the symptoms will not increase, because soon we must move despite all risks and under any circumstances. Our diet is unwholesome. We must collect something in the way of a vegetable.

Cuppage is now insensible. We have discussed whether to send him back, but Hill has ventured that he would never survive the journey. Neither would whoever accompanied him, Browne added grimly. He has recently returned, his horse lathered and nearly broken, to report that the water-holes to our rear, at which we not six days ago found ample water, now have no moisture left in their beds. Our retreat is now cut off. We are bound here as fast as though we were on an ice floe in the great Arctic ocean.

July 1st

The barometer remains unyielding. Until it falls we have no hope of rain. I have reduced the allowance of tea and sugar. The men have become as improvident as aborigines. The inactivity is causing between us much vexation and anxiety. About thirty sheep remaining. Have set the men to repacking and inspecting the bacon and biscuit. The bran in which the bacon was packed is now entirely saturated and heavier than the meat. Our wax candles have melted. Our hair has stopped growing.

July 6th

I was born here in Australia, though this is not commonly known. The year of my tenth birthday, my brothers and I were sent to England with my mother's elder sister. We would not see our parents again for more than a decade. We lived with various relatives, always in close proximity to lives of enormous privilege. I began my education at a succession of schools, each of which I detested. Where were my friends? Where was that person for whom my happiness was an outcome to be desired? I led my brothers on a midnight ramble in search of home. They were eight and seven, and complained about neither the distance nor the cold. The younger, Humphrey, was shoeless. I was so moved by their fortitude that I became teary-eyed through the march. We begged milk from a farmer and were rounded up by a constable the following afternoon.

Browne too hated school. He remembered with fierce indignation a headmaster's remark that God had created boys' buttocks in order to facilitate the learning of Latin.

July 12th

I am much concerned about Browne. His behavior has alarmed both Mander-Jones and Hill. He has been refusing water and crouching for stretches out of the shade, hatless. I have tried to provide for him duties that will keep his faculties engaged. A flight of swifts passed over high to the S at twilight. They were beating against the wind.

July 24th

The same sun, morning to night. We might save ourselves the trouble of taking measurements. The ants at sundown swarm under our coverings. The flies intensify at dawn. All manner of crawling and flying insects fill our clothes. There never was a country such as this for stabbing, biting, or stinging things.

Our scurvy is worse. It must be dreadful in its advanced stages for even as it is we are nearly undone. "I have today's resolution," Browne said to me this morning, lying on the floor of our dug-out room. He hadn't spoken for a day. His head rested on Hill's feet. "Always remember that love is the wisdom of the fool and the folly of the wise," he said.

"What on earth are we on about *now*?" Mander-Jones cried out from beside me. I hushed him. "I am traveling with *lunatics*," he said, with great feeling, before lapsing once more into silence.

The men have tipped the whaleboat over to make a shaded lean-to. Today I was the only one willing to leave either shelter to take a reading. The barometer has fallen to a point that would normally suggest rain, but it is impossible to guess what to anticipate here. The water in our oasis is evaporating visibly. It stands now at a depth of only four feet.

August 20th

The eighth month. Midwinter. 112 in the shade, 129 in the sun. The heat has split the unprotected edges of our horses' hooves into fine laminae. Our fingernails are now as brittle as rice paper. The lead falls out of our pencils. Mack and Gould engaged in a fist-fight that was quelled only after Gould threatened to stave in his head. In our dug-out last night, Browne again could not be moved to speak. Hill's voice was a brave croak. Mander-Jones was sullen and uncommunicative, afflicted as he is with sore eyes from the flies getting into them. I told them that it could only have been that our expedition coincided with the most unfortunate season of drought. Even here it could not be that there were only two recorded days of rain in eight months.

Gould reported that grass was now so deficient about the camp that we could no longer tether the horses.

The success or failure of any undertaking is determined by its leader, I reminded them. Browne roused himself in response. He seemed enraged in ways he wasn't fully able to articulate. He most certainly does not look good. He theorized that my choice of bringing extra paint for the boat, rather than adequate casks for water, or lemon or lime juice for scurvy, spoke volumes about the nature of our undertaking. And what *was* the nature of our undertaking, sir? I asked him. Idiotic, sir, he answered. Criminal, sir. Laughable.

August 22nd

Out of sorts from upset and unable to function. Hill, after a discreet hesitation of a few hours, took over the direction of the men in terms of their responsibilities. At sundown the entire horizon to the west was indigo with clouds and heavy rain. Each of us spent the evening absorbed in the spectacle, unwilling to speak.

I dreamed of my father as I saw him on the pier in Adelaide upon my return. When I awoke Browne was kicking the leg of my cot with his heavy boot. He had today's resolution, he announced. He said, "There was an old man in a Marsh, Whose manners were futile and harsh."

"That's not a resolution," I called after him, once I'd found my voice, which was after he'd left.

With what energy we've been able to muster we have been busy all day preparing an excursion to the WNW to try to meet and retrieve some of that rain. This will decide the fate of our expedition. We will take six weeks' provisions, one of the casks, and four or five bullock hides to carry the water back. Browne and I will lead, and Beale, Gould, and Mack will accompany us, along with seven of the horses and one of the drays.

September 12th

Three weeks out. Set out on August 23rd at 4 a.m. The cask is nearly empty. Today we gave our horses as much water as reason would justify before making camp. Their docility under such suffering is heart-rending. They cannot rest and spend the night troublesomely persevering, plodding round the cart and trying to poke their noses into the bung hole. We close our eyes and pretend not to see.

September 16th

A water-hole. A triumph for Browne. The water cloudy and off but purer than any we have for some time seen. Filled the cask and made some tea. The horizon shot through with lightning.

September 21st

Returned to the strictest rationing now that our strength seems somewhat restored. Walking as much as possible to spare the horses. My heels and back lanced with pain. When lying down I feel as though I'm being rolled across a threshing machine. Summer starting to come on. The thermometer between 120 and 133 during the day. Matches held in the hand flare into flame. We must be a sight, I remarked to Browne: burnt by the sun, our clothes in rags, our hats long since shapeless with sweat, covered in insects, each absorbed in his private cell of misery, whether a chafing shoe or an open sore. And almost no quarrels. On this never-ending ribbon of interminable heat. Browne, as if to prove my point, did not answer.

September 30th

This morning we gave Captain, my mount, double breakfast, in hopes it would strengthen him, but it did not. The poor brute staggered rather than walked along. At midnight he fell. We got him up again and, abandoning his saddle, proceeded. At a mile, though, he fell again and could not go on. I sat by him in the night as he expired, after which I felt so desolate I took myself off into the darkness for a while. I had fully intended to purchase him at the sale of the remnants of the expedition, perhaps as a gift for Browne.

October 10th

We have found only a runnel with mud so thick I could not swallow it. Browne managed to drink some of it made into tea. It fell over the lip of his cup like clotted cream, and smeared the horses' noses like clay. They refused it. Browne was then ill all the next day.

October 12th

Some kind of cyclopean boulders now before us. Even the horses regard them with dismay. I dismounted and ascended the first for a bearing. It was no trifling task in our condition and these temperatures. Beale accompanied me with the instruments. "This is more than a Government day's work, sir," he said on the way back down.

I could not respond. Our view had been over as terrible a

region as Man ever saw. Its aspect was so mortifying that it left us with not a tinge of hope. We have to return, with every promise of a better country within reach annihilated. We all stood dumbly in the heat at this understanding, as if concussed by a blow, before eventually retiring to our midday shelter under the dray. Mack and Gould wept. Browne kept up an intermittent continuous hum, like a bush insect. Was it possible to give up, having achieved nothing? I asked myself aloud. One of the horses toppled to its knees as if by way of answer. No one spoke again until sundown, when we turned about and headed back the way we came. We have been defeated, I reminded our little group, by obstacles not to be overcome by human perseverance.

Our bearings record that the farthest point to which we penetrated was to Longitude 138.5.00 and Latitude 24.30.00, and I will in truth affirm that no men ever wandered in a more despairing and hopeless desert. I have no other observations to add on the nature of this country.

November 17th

Made camp yesterday at 6 a.m., nearly done in from lack of food and water. Three of the seven horses lost, the other four nearly useless. All of us are afflicted by a fatigue that seems impossible to overcome. The buttons on our shirts by mid-morning are so heated as to pain us. Few men have ever laid themselves down to rest, if it can be called rest, as bereft as I have been today.

November 20th

Browne has somehow managed another expedition to the south on one of the fresher horses to ascertain how much water remains on our line of retreat. He returned this morning to report that one of the deepest and narrowest channels had long gone dry. With that source lost, there can be no water nearer to us than seventy-eight miles, and perhaps not there.

The horses are at their wits' end. What grass there is flies to powder under their tread. The last ram has taken the staggers and Beale has ordered him killed.

Whirlwinds blowing all morning from the NE increased to a furnacelike gale. The incinerating heat was so withering that I wondered if the very trees would ignite. Everything, animate and inanimate, gave way before it: the horses with their backs to it and noses to the ground, lacking the strength to raise their heads; the sheep and dogs huddled beneath the drays. One of our thermometers, graduated to 157 degrees, burst. Which is a circumstance I believe no traveler on this earth has ever before had to record.

November 24th

A party rebellious to my purposes now intends to strike out to the south in hope of relief. Browne reported this to me. And of whom was this party constituted? I croaked, gazing at him with what I hoped to be severity. Beale, he said. Hamilton and Mabberly. Gould. Cuppage. Purdie. Mack and Moorhouse. And Mander-Jones, to lead.

"That's everyone, besides Hill and yourself," I told him.

He agreed.

"Cuppage is unconscious," I reminded him.

"Mack says he speaks for Cuppage," he told me.

I asked after his own status. Was he going south too?

"I have just been there," he said.

I assembled the group and addressed the assembly without anger. I told them I could only insist upon all I had observed. And that I have always been open to reason. But that I was convinced that at present no hope lay to our south, at least not until the rains returned.

They killed the rest of the bullocks and scraped and sewed their hides to carry water. They will take one cask and leave one. One dray, carrying only Cuppage, the water, and some dried beef and flour. Mander-Jones, who can hardly see from the bites of the flies, is leading nevertheless. He refuses to talk to me at any length. I asked what he wanted done with his specimens and notes and then regretted the meanness of the question.

December 1st

They are gone. The dogs that were left followed them out of camp.

December 2nd

Hill has made a stew of some of the beef. At the last moment Browne tried to arrest the mutineers' departure with a startling display of passion. Now he seems to have withdrawn into himself even more. "Do you think they have any chance?" I overheard Hill murmur some hours later while serving him his stew. Whatever he answered caused poor Hill to weep once he'd returned to his cooking fire.

December 5th

A squall has leveled our remaining tents and torn away the canvas covering of our dug-out. My papers are gone. What's left of our supplies has been scattered. I found a sextant and two goose quills.

The weather remains infernal. A gale unrelentingly blows from the N or E. The flies do not relent. How is human foresight to calculate upon such a climate? We are all suffering from piercing pains in the joints. My gums are now hugely swollen. Hill's lower leg muscles are so contracted he cannot stand.

We sit about with the aimlessness of aborigines, gazing into each others' eyes and preparing for the worst. Only when thinking of my companions do I have regrets. One of my father's favorite resolutions was always that life was worthless save the good that one might do. "We're forced to conclude, then, that for him, life was worthless," Browne remarked during one of our early father discussions.

December 11th

We have pains and do not understand what they are. Browne has become unresponsive, immersed in his own unwinding. He has spoken of starfish and sea ferns. I do not know what we will do if he is laid low. He has always been one of those whom life pushed from one place to another. A useful naysayer, the kind Australians call a "no-hoper."

December 23rd–24th

Hill is unable to walk. Browne and I have resolved to assay one of the unexplored ravines to our E. He speaks of a great flood there, and drowned cattle. Hill looks at him through his tiny spectacles with pity. Hill says he feels no pain while stationary. The skin of his calves and thighs is black and the discoloration is proceeding upwards.

Our horse led us up a draw all night while we dragged along behind it. Daybreak found us in a smallish box canyon of some sort, sheltered, at least, from the sun. Browne then slept while I explored as best I could. It was an extraordinary place, and evidence of our inland sea. There were marine fossils and conglomerate rock that looked like termite mounds. The remains of strange undersea plants and fish fins were clearly evident. Grotesque shapes, and a great silence. I roused Browne to show him. We were both tearful at the sight. "The Beadle Sea," he said to himself when he came around and looked. "No, no, the Browne Sea," I answered, cradling his head, but by then he was again already asleep.

I laid myself beside him, grateful for his presence. He always doubted my judgment but thought my leadership to be worth my blunders. We awoke some hours later to find the horse gone and twilight coming on. More sleep, Browne in a half-conscious state and making small gesticulations. It was as if he had been submerged in a kind of gloaming of the mind, an infant's fatalism. Near daybreak the moon rose in the E and the sun followed, warming us both. It was not possible to tell how long my friend had been dead. I eased my arms from around him and stood, then turned round myself and cried. I squatted beside him. When the sun was full on my head I found a flint and scratched onto the rock face beside where he lay *J. A. BROWNE S.A.E. DEC 25 1840*. I sat with my back to his side for another full day, taking only a little water at sunset. In the blue moonlight the stars seemed to multiply and wheel. I gazed upward full of grievance and self-justification. I called out that we should be done justice to. The canyon walls gave back their response. In the moonlight they became a luminous cerulean. I heard the slosh and slap of water in a great bay. I knew I had had a dream past the wit of man to say what dream it was. The wind picked up. My ears filled with sound. The blackness of a sandstorm dropped over the canyon rim like a cloak. Its force turned my friend onto his side. Its force turned my face to the rock. I saw strange wraiths. Wormlike, coiling figures. Terrible faces. My eyes clogged with grit. I hoped they would fill with everything they needed. While my throat filled with what poured over the canyon rim. And my heart filled with the rest.

My Aeschylus

I am Aeschylus son of Euphorion of Eleusis and I've come this day with my brother to take my place in the line with my tribe to meet the invader where he disembarks and drive him back into the sea. We've rested and waited six days in the Herakleion sanctuary on the plain of Marathon, with the Median fleet filling half the shoreline of the bay, even with their ships anchored eight deep. More men-at-arms are assembling before the Great Marsh than any of us have ever seen. We're told that their word for commander means "Leader of the Hosts."

At the eastern end of the marsh is a lake, which enables them to water their horses. A stream flows out of it to the sea. It's fresh enough to be drunk by cattle where it issues from the lake, but at its mouth turns brackish and fills with saltwater fish.

Who knows me better than my brother Kynegeiros? Who's looked after me with more care? Whom have I disappointed as intensely? Who's been as terrible a household presence?

Who's trained me? Who's pruned my independence? Who's stopped my mouth? Who's set my feet on the path of understanding, and shown that knowledge comes in suffering? Whose hard hand gave me this scar across my scalp, just because it could?

We've spent six days checking and rechecking our kit and avoiding idlers and gossips. He's tried to interest me in his surgeon's packet: here's how you start the needle with the catgut twine; here's how you grip the narrow-nose to extract an arrow-

129

head, as opposed to a sword shard. I don't need to be reminded that battlefield surgery can save a life. Yesterday to please him I sewed up some oxhide as practice.

We marched all night through Pallene, skirting Mount Pelikos to the southeast, and arrived here on the plain at first light. The plain, empty of trees and left fallow for grazing, smells of the wild fennel that gives it its name.

I'm all aches and pains. My brother has a month-old sprain that he aggravated on a gravely downhill track. I'm forty-four and he's forty-nine. We're no longer young men. We have families.

Here is our country's situation as we understand it: the Persian has come in response to our support of the Ionian revolt and the burning of his citadel at Sardis. He has come with the combined nations of Media, Sakai, Ethiopia, Egypt, Dacia, Scythia, Bactria, Illyria, Thessalia, and India. He has come through Rhodes, Kos, Samos, Naxos, Paros, Karystos, and Eretria, subjugating each as he went. Everywhere his fleet has put in, he has demanded and received hostages and men-at-arms. He has come in such numbers that the disembarking alone has taken, according to the local farmers, nine days.

We are of the deme Eleusis and the tribe Aiantis, and when our strategos draws us up in battle order, we will be in the place of honor on the right flank, the sea off our shoulders. We will with our other Attic demes and allies form a rank facing the invader that is sufficiently long but insufficiently deep. Our leaders call it Stretching the Soup. The rest of us call it, with quiet irony, Our Challenge.

I channel the rote and the new and unseen. My head has always been the busiest of crossroads, a festival of happy and unhappy arrivals. In the hours before daybreak when I was a boy, god sent me words as visitors. I told my brother. Back then I was still in his favor. I kept my stylus and wax tablet within reach by my bedside. In the mornings I showed my mother too, examples like *loosed* and *winged.* I remember that *Tartarean* troubled her in ways that I didn't understand.

"Where did you get these words?" she asked. "Who's been speaking to you?"

"Kynegeiros," I always said. Which made her think the words came from him. When he denied it the first time—I was ten, he was fifteen—our father had him beaten. Some of the words were evidently impious.

"Tell *me* about the words," my brother told me later, while I helped him with his back. "Don't tell them." We gathered and crushed in a pestle the foxglove and sorrel, and I applied the paste to the welts he couldn't reach.

What I told him caused him concern. He questioned me about whatever else I may have noticed by way of omens or signs. He talked about how to know if I was speaking only with myself. I became his new responsibility. He gave himself over to it, his resentment plain.

Even so, I didn't stop. In the mornings I'd scratch *Onus* and *Dyad* in the loam of our herb garden. He'd explain their meanings. When our other brother Anacreon or our father happened near, we went about our business, the scratchings our secret.

But when we were alone again, he'd say, "Who's giving you these?" I didn't know, I told him. Where was I hearing them? he'd ask. In my head, I'd tell him. This caused him to hold his forehead with his fingertips.

Once he asked how I felt when they arrived. I didn't know. Did I hear a *voice,* or *see* the words in my head? I didn't know.

So he broke my wax tablet and was angry with me for a week. It scared me. And pleased me. Maybe, I thought, I was headed down the wrong path. Now, words from elsewhere still marshal themselves, rebel or obey me, send their havoc out into the world, and my reward is the laurel wreath. But back then, I spent my time alone in the hills above our house, telling myself that if I couldn't read the meaning of such signs, I could at least learn something about my world.

Anacreon also kept track of my strangeness, but with more hostility. He was the firstborn and eight years older. Usually I told myself that I had one brother who understood and one who didn't, but the week Kynegeiros was angry I wandered around alone, collecting signs to ask him about later, once he'd begun speaking to me again: the wind on a ridge line like a rush of voices, or patterns in a poplar's bark that repeated themselves in one of its taproots. When he finally took me back, I asked him: did my difference mean I was one of the elect, or cast out? He cuffed me for my presumption. I didn't persist, but decided to *act,* and to let the inner spirit follow the outer shadow. I had him cut my hair in what he said was the ancient Doric style: close-cropped at the forehead and long in the back. I modeled as many of his behaviors as I could, the way children learn about the clean hand and dirty hand and which you keep to yourself. Both of my brothers took pleasure in their manners, speaking only when addressed. They were respectful with their gaze, their greetings commendable.

After *matricide* had especially disturbed him, he asked me to remember the first time the words had appeared. Did I remember? I thought I did: a morning when I was three or four, in a powdery season of little rain. I'd had barley dust on my hands. He'd been seated nearby. He must have been eight or nine. He'd been watching Anacreon working a rasp up and down an ash shake for a javelin. As I watched him watch, my heart rose and fell, rose and fell, and no one knew. A word appeared before me: *starfish*. A crow dropped to the ground and both my brothers made note of it and Kynegeiros shooed it away.

I asked if he remembered. He didn't, but held his wrist as if trying to immobilize one hand with the other. When he let go, he said that he did remember the way my expressions, at that age, had been comically severe.

My brothers and their friends played their war games at the edge of our wheat field. When I followed they chased me away.

When I returned they chased me away again. At home I attempted descriptions of the architecture of the stalks, the leaf blades sheathed around the stem or the spikelets' airy intricacy. Just *being* in the field made a force in my chest levitate. But my excitement went too far and somehow upset my family. I tried to confide in Kynegeiros when I caught him alone, but it repulsed and alarmed him that I was so tireless in search of attention, as if he'd found a spider in his soup.

He was already forced to spend time in my company, responsible for ensuring that I arrived, daily, at alphabet lessons and music. When he came of age at sixteen, I marched alone with other boys in ranks from the music master's house to the physical trainer's palaestra. I sang "Pallas, Terrible Stormer of Cities" and "Ajax on His Rock" and played the hedgehog game. I missed him. At home in the afternoon, where I was allowed to watch him play knucklebones or wrestle Anacreon, I sang and resang songs for him. I pretended that I was also sixteen.

That year he commissioned a first helmet like our father's, a variant on the Corinthian design. I was permitted to lift it from its peg and run my palms through the brush of its crest. I coped with the excitement by breathing through my mouth.

And my head was becoming an open gate that the world streamed through. Brothers muscles honey wine stones. Honey brothers muscles stones wine.

He lost patience with me again because of it. In the afternoons they shut me into the outer courtyard, but I followed their games by keeping my eye to the gate latch. They played at quail-tapping. The bird when rapped on its head sometimes stood its ground and sometimes backed out of the ring. They cheered it on or cheated by scaring it, exchanging coins on the basis of its behavior. I watched and sang battlefield paeans and imagined civic crises that would call forth a muster of even the youngest boys.

Anacreon loved the sea and spent his free time assisting the fishing fleet. Kynegeiros helped, but sometimes went his own way. When he did, I followed, reciting lists like *figs, limes, almonds, olives, and lemons* that soothed me and displaced the pressure of other lists that, arrayed in squadrons, so unsettled my brother. To lose me he leapt walls or rushed up high, gravelly hillsides. When he succeeded, my day was ruined. Eventually I'd continue on, miserable. I'd follow flying beetles riding the hot air up those same hillsides, or investigate the drowsings of hornets.

When I found him again, our eyes met like bones jarred in sockets. What did I *want*? he'd demand, and again disappear. I always wondered, by what miracle was the dust and the rock around me transformed into speech? When he talked to me it was like a duet in which the other voice was silent. When I thought of him it was like a sign from god that I wasn't ready to read.

But whenever he talked to Anacreon about me, he'd say, My Aeschylus this, and My Aeschylus that. Anacreon spoke to him of me the same way: Your Aeschylus this, Your Aeschylus that.

Our decision to wait six days was not unanimous. Every knot of two or more citizens has become a discussion group. Hellenes have, after all, made arguing black is white a sport. My brother and I when not engaged in drill have walked the shoreline, both for training and to keep our own counsel. Sometimes we walk until Phosphorus, the morning star and light-bearer, leaves Hesperus, evening and western star, behind. Should we have stayed behind our city walls? Could we continue to wait for the Spartans? Should we have attacked while more of the enemy was disembarking? And why had *they* waited? Concern for their cavalry and its vulnerability to our camp's shelter in the sacred grove? Or were we drawn here, so that our city could be betrayed and given over, like Eretria?

The last three nights there's been a waxing moon above the bay. When it wanes, the Spartans' Karneian festival will end and they'll begin their march to us. We walk every night through the wavelets combing in onto the sand. We walk until the watch fires are banked down. Stretches of the shore are a seafarer's junkyard, with stove-in and disintegrating small boats offering up their salt-eaten and mealy spare parts along the high-tide mark.

Anacreon died of septic misfortune seven years ago following a wound from snapped spears in the campaign against Aigina. He died in our house, a week after having been carried home on a litter. For weeks Kynegeiros seemed enraged at the sight of me. And my own expressions of sadness incited him further.

We groped in the murk of the gods' motives. All we knew was that their directives needed no explanation and had to be obeyed. Artemis is angry: Agamemnon must sacrifice his daughter. Menelaus is favored: Troy must fall. And when a mortal is taken into a god's confidence, that mortal brings everyone bad fortune.

We consulted a local oracle, though our mother hated oracles, with their language tricks and teasing word-mazes. We were told that human life was a nursery in which larger designs were revealed. We were told that we had brought this on ourselves. We were told to look to the youngest. I am the youngest.

Our father for years said with pride that parents live on in their children and that the dead man rises in his offspring. He said, whenever he watched Anacreon on the parade ground, that he was like the gods' medicine, applied with kind intention. He called him the pillar for our roof. Our mother always chided us to remember that we were rich; that heaven's grace had been poured over us.

We drained and washed his wound and packed it with the prescribed herbs. A surgeon bled him. We waited, sitting about as a family through long evenings like the crew of a galley in an onshore wind, sullen and becalmed.

But with him the gods' verdict was suffering followed by death. As if our natural condition were a world without mercy. Our hope dwindled for seven days and then was gone. We were left with our father on his knees and the greasy reek of our brother's infected clothing on a courtyard pyre. Our mother became like Queen Procne, who lost her son and then, transformed into a nightingale, forever sang his name. She went about laureled with misery.

Kynegeiros too went about like a blind man. But my feelings were like chalk drawings, and if my father had known he would have flogged me raw. I cut my hair to crown my brother's tomb. I helped pour the offering. But how could I make my prayers? What words could I pour into his absence? And from which brother did I want forgiveness?

My surviving brother seemed to know. He looked at me as if he understood that in my case, conceit and vanity would never abate. As if he could see now that I was Catastrophe, hand-reared at home.

Why *did* our family act like this? I asked my brother in frustration almost a year ago. Our parents had still not recovered. By then I understood the old saying that grief is a cold hearth.

Others had lives much more filled with grief. Families that had blow after blow rained upon their reeling heads. What was different about ours?

The question has always been an unwise one to ask.

Each night on this plain in front of the invader, sharing with me a sleeping palette damp and cold with dew, my brother lies awake despite his exhaustion, still grieving for our brother and still refusing me forgiveness for having been spared.

Poison sweet waters once and they're poisoned for good. I don't ask him for his thoughts. Calamity is my school, and in it I've learned when to speak and when to keep silent.

By the third watch, it feels as though I'm the only one awake. My cloak, when it covers my feet, doesn't cover my shoulders. Under the wood smoke I can smell marjoram and pine resin. In the distance there's some quiet sentry-stirring in the dark.

When I lie awake on my mat, I compose. I sing about discipline and a good heart, which is not the same as having had either. Though I made my debut at the city Dionysia festival at the age of twenty-two, I did not win the prize until fifteen years later.

Our family belongs to the eupatridae, heir of an aristocratic lineage extending back to the origins of Attica. My brother and I are old enough to remember the tyranny of Hippias and to have voted on Kleisthenes's democratic reforms. We're considered men of some moment, having had a foot in both worlds. My neighbors admire me for what they've seen during the festivals, and they admire my brother for what they know of his spirit. My children hold him up as their model for fiercely applied self-discipline. He doesn't disappoint them. This evening for his supper while I cooked he contented himself with the kind of hard flax seed loaf that's fit mostly for winter boot insulation.

"They'll fight tomorrow," he says from out of the darkness beside me. When I ask him why, he reminds me that the Spartans will arrive the following day.

My brother is always right. Over the morning breakfast fires, we watch the invader's muster. Kynegeiros goes about the business of preparing without acknowledging what's before him. It's a mesmerizing sight and it fills the plain from the mountain to the sea. There doesn't seem to be enough earth to hold all of the activity. Dust kicked up floats slantwise across their ranks in the rear. Their line as it forms looks to have a frontage of about fifteen hundred men. The formations are at least ten to fifteen men deep. The Persians themselves, flanked by the Sakai, form the center. And this is without yet any sign of their cavalry.

Kynegeiros is still refusing to look, like a boy trying to impress me. Finally, we're sixteen together.

We're in the hands of god's justice, one way or the other: the battle pennant, now hoisted, informs us that the command which rotates on a daily basis among the strategoi falls today to Miltiades, who argued the most insistently for our march out to face the invader in the first place. All around us in our tribe we're surrounded by the kind of sons of aristocratic families who give themselves epithets, the way that young people do: nicknames like Sacred Erection or the Self-Abuser. They take courage from one another and from us the way each ship takes courage from its moorings. They present the invader with a version of Hellas bare and lean as a wolf.

Some of us write on small wax tablets or tree bark or potshards scraps of messages for family members or wives. My brother and I each write a line on the disposition of our property. Armorers pass among us with sacks to collect the notes for safekeeping back at the armament wagons with the sacrificial goats.

The squires begin arming citizens from the feet up: bronze greaves prised apart for fitting, then secured by the natural springiness of the metal.

It goes without saying that my brother will handle our private commerce with the gods. He mixes a little of our honey and wine in our grandfather's clay bowl to prepare the drink for Earth, and to give the thirsty dead their sip: libations poured down into Earth's hidden rooms to sweeten dead men's attitudes. Libations for our brother, listening in his buried dark. Soon he'll hear his dirt ceiling groan as it's hammered and scratched open.

Kynegeiros pours the mixture, and a straw-brown mantis with feathery grasping claws walks through the wet when he's finished. On the army's temporary altar nearby, two other goats are kept in reserve in case the bleeding from the first reads inauspiciously.

Even the cynics recognize the usefulness of these rituals: someone's always seeing an eagle when they need to before battle.

When a city falls, the universe is upended, and things are toppled that once climbed to heaven, and bound that should be free. The Persians have upset the natural order of things. As have I.

The final libations have been poured, the omens scrutinized and teased forth. There's that pause, as at a banquet when the tables are cleared and the floors swept of shells and bones. We take our places in the lines, neighbors holding out their hands as they pass, touching fingers like boys sliding palms along fence posts.

Now it's just men waiting in the heat. Squires circulate with water. My brother stands to my right. To my left is a neighbor we call Crayfish because he loves them and because his eyes unmoor from their pairings. The felt of his undercap is already soaked. Clouds like islands of migratory air sail by.

I've prayed. Now I must bring my prayers to flower. My brother beside me marks his place for my father, mother, and brother who died. If I weep my love for the chambered dead, will those tears restore me? The dead's grievances live on and on. I stand shoulder to shoulder with those I love while a flood tide of self-hate beats the prow of my ship. For Kynegeiros, one brother's loss and the other's shame is a grief past bearing, a tether ring that tears against all pulling. We must heal ourselves. Our cure is blood for blood. The ability to live with ourselves must be earned with the spear. We're the corks that lift the nets and the lines that rise from the depths.

He's the man who instructed me in bivouac and foraging, dress and parade rest. He taught me how to balance a pack animal's load. Where in the kit bag to stuff the oil lamp. The usefulness of a hand-mill for grain.

Any contact he's had with me has been a mercy. Orestes after the murder of his mother was given his own table and drank separately from a cup touched by his mouth alone.

After we had carried my brother's body outside the walls of the town, after the pyre, after the ashes and bones had been gathered in his cerecloth and consigned to the urn, after the last libations had been poured, our clothes and house purified with sea water and hyssop, his cult was inaugurated with sacrifice on the third, ninth, and thirtieth days after the funeral, and then on all subsequent anniversaries.

The night after the purification our father, drunk, quoted to us Hesiod's advice about families: "Try, if you can, to have only one son, to care for the family inheritance: that's the way wealth multiplies in one's halls."

He then added that it was a great deal to have been granted even a few years' happiness by the deity.

I found Kynegeiros in the hills above our house some hours later. He was on a slope near a cluster of dead-nettle and mint. He stayed bent-backed, and I stood about. We were like an old man and a soft-boned child. I wanted to say to him: *You will not wear me down. All can still be well.* I wanted to say to him: *How can an infant explain his hunger or thirst or need for his pot? Aren't his insides a law unto themselves?* But I knew better than to voice my self-pity.

The past enters and floods our present while we wait. I've labored to the top of this hill, and it's taken half my life to get here and the other side slopes down. Today once again we'll trust in the way heaven's law compels but not always protects its human allies. Today he'll teach me even more about the war between the self and the world, the self divided into soul and body, the body usually acting as the traitor within the gates. He'll lead me to that magic which we recognize in dreams that make the face of the sleeper relax. He'll show me how my shame could rise like a glad bird and vanish over the shoulder of the hill. I can wish us united in good feeling and in hate, with a cure for every injury, though I know there's no regaining what's gone. We'll act so that something better can be rendered in the days to come.

Medes, Egyptians, Dacians, Illyrians: they're all drawn up now, in full panoply, their marshaling positions invisible against the sheer mass. The marsh behind them is a stretch of searing sun where the air goes hazy with mosquitoes. Nothing moves on the hillside up above them to our left. Braced planks arrest the spill of a wall down the slope in the distance.

They wear trousers. Boots dyed purple or red. Quilted linen tunics. Cuirasses with metalwork like the meshings of a net. Open-faced helmets and animal skin headdresses. Bowcases of leopard skin. Here they come, eager for combat, packed man on man: spear-tamers, horse-breakers, endurance and malice and fear on their faces, in horizon-crowding lines, with their curved Scythian swords and double-ended pig stickers, the flower of the wide world's earth stepping forward while their parents and wives and younger brothers in their cold beds back in Asia count the days they've been gone.

At the signal from our strategos, we hammer our spear shafts on the outer curve of our shields. When we cease, he gives the order to swing down and fit snug the bronze facing of our helmets, and then to advance.

In the sun we will seem an endlessly wide threshing machine of blades and unyielding surfaces. Our paean will be *Zeus Savior, spare us who march into your fire.* They'll hear a roar, a windhowl, our singing together. We will find that bright vibration, that pitch at which the spirit oscillates. We will march through their archers' bolts like covered wagons in a hailstorm. They will see, as we close, the spears of our first four ranks swing down to the horizontal. They will discover how far beyond our shields the blades of those shafts can extend. We will break into a run. We will hit them like a bull. We will savage them of all they have. Our collision with the wood and wicker of their shields will be like the sound of kindling underfoot. After the shock of impact, our ranks behind will seat their shields into our backs, hoist their shoulder bones under the upper rims, and, splaying dust as they scrabble for footing, push and shove with all their force. The invader's wicker will have no purchase against the implacable smoothness of our bowl-shaped bronze. Their front ranks will be left trampled in the gleaning-ground that will spool out behind us as the butchery rolls forward, where they'll meet the spiked clubs and gutting knives and bone-breakers of our light infantry. Our churning feet will continue the push even slipping on their blood, like boys' soles on river rocks. We will hit them like a wave, the wild water seething into seaside homes; we will leave them like a tidal pool after a storm, with its clamor of blasted lives.

All of this is sent to me, or generated in me: visceral shadows instead of words, turning and turning in my imagination. In the cattle-stunning light before we step off, I can see it, my head that

open gate. They will be cut down, body on body. They will endure
being god-overturned in war. Their slaughter will extend all the
way back to their ships at anchor, where we, the right wing, the
tribe of Aiantis, will be like the gods jumping both feet into their
ranks, about to learn the whole reach of pain, our sandals piercing
the shallows and the breakers' roil, our thighs surging back and
forth in the water's wilderness of spumy sand, our bodies wading
in full armor into the surf, our weapons slashing at the back-
watering oars and cable ropes sliding in the waves' retreat, and
gaffing the wounded like fish, and there my brother will lay hands
on the backsliding deck of a trireme, and there, while I watch, a
Persian's boarding axe will chop through one of his wrists, and
there on the beach his life will stream out of him and cover us in
the river mouth of his blood, with his last words to me that their
ships are getting away; their ships are getting away.

They will find out: all that begins well can come to the worst
end. Having done evil, no less will they suffer. And more in the
future. In their pride and self-deception they will have led themselves to the disasters of this day and more coming on. As I am for
my family, with my friends and neighbors I'll be their sorrow, a
sad hollow son born to bring home misfortune, to initiate the roll
of grief.

We can feel our hearts in their bony cages. We're about to
enroll them in the academy of chaos and self-command. We're
about to lead them to that world in which their sons and brothers
are dead and gone. Lost and always there. And they're about to
form for us that jury in which each man reads his own future:
home and hearth, or no home and hearth. Pain, or release from
pain.

Eros 7

14 June 1963 Morning

Though we've been in this cottage for only a day, I got up at first light and set about a housecleaning. Solovyova is still depressed and lay on her bed like a corpse while I worked. When I finished I left. In the chilly air the sun warmed my arms and long blue shadows crossed the roadside weeds and gravel. I walked through the pines to our little river and sat with my toes in the mud. Bream and sturgeon explored the stones on the bottom, flicking their fins.

We are in Kazakhstan, 370 kilometers northeast of a town called Baikonur. Solovyova and I are in one cottage and Korolyov himself is in the other. The cottages were requisitioned for Yuri Gagarin's flight and have been used ever since. Their original owners came by with flowers when we arrived, in honor of our undertaking. The cottage fronts are covered with creepers and face the pine forest. Behind and above them looms the launchpad in all its concrete immensity. It's a kilometer away but looks as if it could be touched with an outstretched hand. The sides of the blast pit resemble the face of a dam. The command bunker alongside is a squat hedgehog with jagged steel spars spiking from its super-hardened roof at all angles, so a malfunctioning first stage falling atop it would break up, thereby diffusing the focus of the blast.

Diary! You are a historic document: my name is Valentina Vladimirovna Tereshkova, and I was born in the Yaroslavl Raion, and I am twenty-four years old, and by 12:30 Moscow time the day after tomorrow I will have put on my orange spacesuit and climbed into my own spacecraft, the *Vostok 6,* to rendezvous with a fellow cosmonaut, Senior Lieutenant Valery Fyodorovich Bykovsky, 150 miles above the Earth. I will become, then, the tenth person, the sixth Russian, and the first woman in space.

But I have more reason to be unable to sit still, as if electrified by joy: the mind that has laid me open to awe and gratitude—the man for whom I'd give whatever I have to give—is already fulfilling his dream, orbiting above us in *Vostok 5.* And I am going to join him.

Technically, of course, that's incorrect. Our mission will be the first step in developing our country's capabilities for orbital rendezvous. Twice daily, during the parabolas of our orbits, we'll approach to within less than two kilometers of each other. But two kilometers is very close. At that range his capsule will be the size of a dried pea at arm's length. Two kilometers, given the slight imprecision of the trajectories, is as near as they dare bring us. As Korolyov put it, the achievement of two cosmonauts orbiting simultaneously would be compromised if they were to kill each other.

Even so, we'll be in space together. In other words, as Solovyova pointed out before she fell asleep last night, the combined efforts of the most diligent minds in the Soviet Union—some one hundred thirty bureaus and thirty factories, employing over seven thousand scientists, designers, and engineers—have come together for however many years of labor in order to indulge my sordid and criminally irresponsible obsession with a Hero of the Soviet Union who bears a spotless reputation. "So that's the best they could do for you: two kilometers?" she asked, reaching to turn off the light.

Bykovsky is married, though he told me he hasn't touched his wife in years.

The plan was to make dual use of the second stage of this group mission to put the first woman in space. And after everything—

the written examinations and the centrifuge, the parachute jumps and the pressure chamber, the psychological prodding and poking and the endless humiliations of the medical testing—Solovyova was judged top of the list. But Korolyov was concerned about her unsteady morals. It was felt she gave improper replies in the final interviews. When asked what she wanted from life, she said she wanted everything that it could offer. She maintained that a woman could smoke and still remain decent. She was unapologetic for having traveled unescorted into town.

When asked what I wanted, I said I wished to support the Komsomol and the Communist Party. I took no trips to town. I do not smoke.

In the end, there were advantages to favoring a farm girl over a teacher's daughter. I was a girl from the backwoods— the way Gagarin and Premier Khrushchev were boys from the backwoods—and our country was telling the world that even we could achieve at the highest level. "The meek shall inherit the earth," Solovyova said when the other women sought to console her after the news had been released.

"When have you *managed* this grand passion?" she wanted to know last night, when I confided in her. "*Where* have you managed it?" She used "grand passion" with an unpleasant emphasis.

The truth is that he hasn't entirely committed to my feelings for him. A week ago we managed for ourselves an hour or so alone by plunging off the trails on a recreational hike, during which we kissed, in the darkness, as though all of our sharing would be accomplished by that alone. I had before those kisses kissed only two other boys: those memories a little keepsake-box of reticence and disappointment. But there in the forest we came together like an immersion, oceanic in its possibilities. The branches above showered us with cold drops shaken off at the breeze. Around his mouth he smelled of sun and beach, with an edge of herbs.

He was shorter but seemed older, and parted his hair on the side in the German manner. He expressed himself so well in our first meeting that I kept glancing at him as though I were doing something wrong. This was the first gathering of the finalists. We'd been asked to mark on mimeographs of a map where our relatives were located. I'd been holding mine upside down, causing the other women to laugh. "I guess *you* won't be navigating," one of them scoffed. But he said with a smile that his was illegible too, and that these were poor mimeographs. And I thought he was kind. And that I wanted some of that kindness inside me.

He's not wildly good-looking. He hoards his green vegetables, whether from superstition or trauma, he won't say. Solovyova thinks his hands are too small. She has a man's hands, like mine.

14 June 1963 Afternoon

Solovyova napping again. In the morning we spent two hours reviewing checklists and two playing badminton for physical conditioning. The badminton was filmed for posterity. Solovyova worked up a sheen of sweat on her golden forearms. Every time she hit a winner she would smack her lips like someone enjoying a sweet. Korolyov watched like a proud father. Afterward he sat with us in the shade. He called us his little swallows. He singled out Solovyova for special praise, reminding her that it was harder to be the backup than the primary pilot. I could detect her inner refusal to tear up.

During our academic examinations all of the finalists scored in the excellent category except me. Korolyov attributed this to my having been too nervous. It was decided that since I would have done better otherwise, there was no need to retest me. On May 14, Solovyova and I were rated Most Ready to Fly, and a week later the selections were announced. We stood before the panel and then she turned to shake my hand. She had a way of inspecting me that reminded me of auctions. She had the characteristics that give Tartar women their reputation for beauty, especially the hair. I asked why she looked sad and she answered so they could hear, "I'm not sad, but serious, as always."

If I've occasionally taken first place in life's races, it's only because of my oxlike perseverance. I've always had to labor at tasks, reiterating them. On school tests, teachers forced me to stop writing, the classroom long since emptied. Eventually I developed the philosophy that everyone could be of use. I grew proud of my diligence. And before Bykovsky, I would have cited calmness as my other virtue.

14 June 1963 Evening

When I was eight, three daredevils risked their lives in a balloon that ascended to a height of 20.8 kilometers. They radioed their achievement, then began their descent. Nothing more was heard from them, though a day later shattered remnants of the gondola were retrieved, along with some body parts, which were described as unrecognizable. I remember my mother's indignation that such a detail would be reported. I remember spending the rest of the day in our chicken coop playing with a small stuffed bear. I remember thinking of them so far up and alone, the slipstream an ocean's roar, the cold an unprecedented affliction. Their bodies coming apart at such unbelievable speeds. My nights were filled with impressions of an inescapable and implacable landscape rushing up at me. Where did I get such images? I never discovered. But at eighteen I was allowed to join a nearby parachute club, and when told that I'd handled my first jump with poise, I answered, "Well, I've been jumping all my life."

"He's a bit of a turnip, isn't he?" Solovyova asked the other day. Bykovsky was consulting a tractor manual while his mates horsed about with a rugby ball. But he appeals to me because of his intelligence: I observe him closely and still feel only occasionally able to predict his next move. Which is rare for me. Also, we're both very good with slide rules.

14 June 1963 Late Night

This evening the movie was *Vostok 1*. The actor who played Gagarin was especially good. Once we were bedded down for the night, it again fell to me to make conversation, Soloyyova having turned to the wall and pulled the summer blanket to her ears. I noted to her that I didn't feel even mildly anxious. Was that normal, did she think? She didn't know what was normal, she answered. Korolyov looked in to wish us good night. "And good luck," she reminded him. Oh, in five years the state'll be subsidizing vacations in space, he told her.

We've been told that strain gauges have been placed under our mattresses to record the quality of our sleep. Wires trail from our bunks to a hole in the wall leading to instruments in a little shed outside the cottage. So we concentrate on lying still. Even now our roles could reverse. A hint of upset in our "sleep" and the doctors could declare the other candidate better rested and more fit for duty. It might come down to who rolls over fewer times during the night.

Her hip under the blanket is a snowy hill in the electric light from outside. Her hair is a glossy cascade. Two hours have passed like this. Who knows what she's been thinking? I've been thinking, *Soon, I'll be with him and not with him.* I've been controlling hours of agitation.

Feelings are unruly. You tell them one thing and they tell you something else. When I was young and read about immaturity in books, I never encountered myself, but when I read about grown-ups, I did. That always left me pleased. Now I seem incapable of contemplation. I'll think the agitation has ended but then from somewhere hope will stir, swelling until it dominates my chest, like that moment when a level ski encounters an unexpectedly steep drop: it's joy, but joy attenuated with dread.

Sometimes I think it's the sacred duty of every mother to

devote her life to her child in order to avoid producing strange iso-
lates like me.

I call him Hawk. He calls me Seagull. Both have been accepted
as the call signs for our flights. The mission patch for *Vostok 5* features two rockets streaking up at a diagonal, side by side.

15 June 1963 Morning

The doctors woke us at 05:30, as they will tomorrow. They wanted
to know how we slept. "As you taught us," Solovyova told them. We
were fed concentrated calories and vitamins in a dark brown paste
followed by a breakfast of meat puree, black currant jam, and
black coffee, and then attended another meeting of the Flight
Committee on the contingency plans for emergency recovery.
There is no realistic chance of our survival if we land at sea. However, plans must be made. Two carrier groups as well as four
Tu-114s would be required to make recovery feasible. These are not
available.

We were eager to hear how Bykovsky's mission was progress-
ing. We were told that all was well and that we'd be able to listen in
on transmissions in an hour. I asked if I might peek in before then.
Kamanin responded that I should worry less about Vostok 5 and
more about my own mission.

"Eros 7, Vostok 5," Solovyova whispered to me in response, as
though relating a football score.

15 June 1963 Morning

The mission calls for the use of a three-stage R-7 rocket that can
lift a mass of 4.6 tons into a circular orbit at 155 miles altitude,
though my altitude will probably be slightly less. The descent and
instrument modules together are only 4.4 meters long; the little

sphere of the descent module, only 2.3 meters in diameter, its size limited by the available volume inside the launch shroud. Two minutes into my flight, the strap-on boosters will shut down and separate by the firing of their explosive bolts. The nose shroud will open a minute later, exposing the *Vostok*. The second stage will continue to burn until it too is depleted and falls away. Then the third will do the same until I've achieved orbit. The spherical shape of the descent module, chosen for its stability, has its center of mass aft so that, protected by its ablative coating, it will assume the correct orientation during reentry, descending along a ballistic trajectory. "In other words, like a bullet, with no attitude control," Solovyova clarified during one of our classroom sessions. Another of those indiscretions that probably counted so decisively against her.

Soft-landing such a mass would have required an enormous parachute and retro-rocket system—a problem considered too time-consuming, given the race with the Americans—so the designers settled on an ejection system initiated by inertial and barometric sensors. Before Gagarin, no one had ever ejected at that altitude or speed. In the event of a trajectory deviation, the ejection could be activated sooner, though no one knew what the result would be. *Sputnik 3* with its two dogs reentered the atmosphere after retrofire at an incorrect angle and burned up. The audio monitors recorded the dogs' cries before the transmission went to static.

We've had to ignore whispers of other disasters, some of them enormous. Bondarenko burned alive in the isolation chamber. A premature ignition of the R-7 that annihilated the launch gantry. Even we knew that mostly what our rockets did, in the early days, was blow up.

So you see, Diary: lovesickness has crowded none of the responsibilities, or apprehensions, from my mind.

15 June 1963 Afternoon

A practice press conference. We're told we both gave incorrect answers about our appetite. Earlier we observed Bykovsky via television. He made no motion while sleeping. "Look at him," I murmured, and even Solovyova was alarmed by my tone. She said all she could make out was his helmet.

Apparently there'd been consternation that they'd kept from us: on orbit 23 he was to communicate with Earth, but no transmissions were received. The Central Committee had been frantic. When he finally did respond, they asked why he'd been silent. He told them he'd had nothing to say. They're still angry.

During our last private moment together I reminded him that when we returned a new life would begin for us, as celebrities and representatives of the Soviet system. His mind was on his launch vehicle. He handled my arms like they were attitude control handgrips. Gagarin and Titov, I told him, dreaming, had been such big stars, afterward; they'd done whatever they dared. We were in a maintenance room of an electrical substation in the basement of the gantry supports. There was nowhere to sit. He entered each of our kisses dutifully, but gave himself over to them once they were initiated. I felt a wash of sadness each time. "Do you want to touch me?" I asked him. "I am touching you," he told me. But then we heard the heavy jingling of wrenches on someone's utility belt down the hall, and we were out of time.

15 June 1963 Afternoon

That first night when the male and female candidates were brought together, I just stood there with my eyes closed, immersed in the different voices. Ponomaryova, an engineer and city girl with some of the starved attractiveness of the old cinema stars, carried on about how much she admired the children of peasants, who got by without adults, the adults laboring in the fields all day while the children became the emperors and explorers of their own world.

I fit in poorly from the very beginning. "Let's go to the cinema!" the other women would say when we had a free moment. "I can't," I'd tell them. But I wanted to so much I could have cried. Why did I do such things? It was hard to watch how much less they came to like me than each other. They were the sort of people who always had stories to tell because something was always happening to them. They looked at me like I was a horse in a stall. Soon we became so petty we stopped handing each other cups during afternoon tea.

And even so, Solovyova had befriended me. We'd taken walks. We found an overgrown pond we christened the Night Witches' Hideout.

But during the mixed gatherings we were more diffident, and I gravitated to Bykovsky. He'd traveled on foreign expeditions and told stories about tropical forests and typhoons. We took our own walks around the grounds. "Did they tell you about city boys, down on the farm?" Ponomaryova asked one night as we lay in our bunks. Solovyova was turned to the wall. The other women simpered. I answered with a joke, telling myself my conscience was clear. But the truth was that a new reality was coming into being for me. Waking up each morning I felt an astonishing absence of emptiness, something I hadn't gotten used to. He was becoming a pressing concern, always present somewhere. Early one morning I gazed at Solovyova's sleeping hand trailing on the floor like a vine and remembered him remarking that he loved my dozing because it seemed such a self-*aware* form of sleep. And I thought I had to have this love so I'd no longer be so endlessly alone. I could feel it making me new.

After Gagarin's flight, the Kremlin had been flooded with letters from women asking to be considered for spaceflight. Soviet women believed they belonged with men in this greatest of all adventures. Because of the ejection requirements, only those who belonged to parachute clubs were part of the initial selection, after which there was further screening for medical fitness, age, size, and weight. Interviews then took that pool from fifty-eight to five. Those who flew would become heroes. Those who didn't would remain unknown.

We were told to inform our families that we'd been selected for a special parachuting team. We were tested for exposure to vibration, noise, pressure, extremes of temperature, and long-term isolation. Various tests exposed various weaknesses. Yerkina was eliminated during an isolation test when she removed her boots and ate only two helpings of rations in three days. Ponomaryova, who'd been so pleased to be the only pilot and engineer, reacted badly to the centrifuge. She complained afterward that we might as well have passenger cosmonauts, since the individual was the insignificant recipient of the collective's work. Sour grapes. I did everything that was asked of me, keeping an eye on Bykovsky advancing through the men's ranks beside me. "Look at the level of your absorption!" Solovyova exclaimed at one point. "It's like a warped version of intellectual activity." I tried to emulate the way he applied his mind to his business, refusing to dwell on the relentless instants that were bearing everything away. Separations were like return visits from nearby desolation, the way my father's death would come to me some minutes after I awoke, even years after it happened. Was something good or bad news? It began to depend on how it influenced my seeing Bykovsky.

"You know, soon *we'll* never see one another again," Solovyova said from the bathroom, apropos of my distress. She pointed out that our menstrual cycles had fallen into synchrony, which happened at times when women lived together. I told her that I felt ready to accept whatever lay ahead. She threw up her hands and left the room.

15 June 1963 Night

Meeting with the Command Staff followed by dinner. Korolyov seemed well pleased with what he calls my preternatural calm. Kamanin remarked upon my appetite. Poor Solovyova: all through the meal I could see her thinking, *If I spill the beans about her, maybe then I could go . . .* But of course she can't. Perhaps none of us could. We've all long since understood that the only accepted way to compete was to outpace one another in cooperation and teamwork.

The R-7 has already begun its departure from the main assembly shed. It runs the length of its hydraulic platform, which is mounted on a rail car. Korolyov is dawdling alongside it in the dark like a nervous suitor. It's nosing along extremely slowly to minimize the vibration damage. Maintenance personnel poke at it, fussing and adjusting. Around dawn it will be brought upright on the pad, the service towers raised, the umbilical connections joined.

There's no question of sleep, though again we're each trying not to move. Solovyova lies on her back, gazing upward in the moonlight as if the ceiling were an affliction.

When I was twelve I told my father I was bored, and he answered, "I hate people who always say, 'I'm bored!' " "Well, you'll never hear me say it again," I told him. And he never did. I took long walks. I spent afternoons jumping over the runoff from storm drains. On dark winter mornings I left for school early, my steps resounding softly in the empty hallways. It was the usual sort of district school: pitiful academic standards, teachers with ungrammatical speech, fistfights between classes. But I preferred it to home. I was beginning to register that I shared many attributes with regular people. Two spirits wrestled inside me: one was the girl who wanted only to please, while the other sought to dedicate her life to something larger. Why couldn't I be someone else? Why shouldn't I imagine myself contented? I resolved to train to become someone I would like. On my thirteenth birthday I told my mother that I would probably become an arctic explorer, and she answered that she always found my conceitedness appealing.

Korolyov like a boy on a first date appeared with flowers and a folded typescript a few minutes before we were scheduled to turn out our lights. Solovyova had just finished her toilet.

"Is this our pep talk, Chief?" she teased. Korolyov smiled to himself, riffling his typescript. "It's an inspirational talk from the Chief Designer himself," he said. We sat, and he stood at the foot of our beds and read what he'd prepared. We were both touched by his awkwardness and care. He reminded us that this was why we had foregone marriage and children. He reminded us that he had asked us to be morally prepared for spaceflight. When it came to this kind of endeavor, woe to the egoists and hedonists, he said. For there was no one so frail and defenseless.

We both waited. "What a strange, strange country we live in," Solovyova remarked. He chose not to respond before going on: this was not so much a culmination as a beginning, he said. He wouldn't sleep a wink tonight, but he was sure that we would. "Thank you, Chief," Solovyova answered.

"I guess I'm finished," he said. "That's the bed Gagarin slept in," he added on the way out, indicating mine.

"I know," Solovyova said. "I told her she should have it."

He turned out the light and left. He'd been rescued from the gulag during the war and put to work in Tupolev's prisoner design bureau, where he'd become a favorite of Khrushchev's for his designs of intercontinental ballistic missiles. But his dream had been spaceflight, and he loved quoting Tsiolkovsky's dictum that the Earth was the cradle of mankind, but one didn't live in the cradle forever.

We could hear him moving about in the other cottage. "He'll be a wreck by tomorrow," I offered, but Solovyova chose not to answer.

During our night in the maintenance room I had told

Bykovsky between kisses that I wanted him to see my old farm—
the far corners overrun with prickly gooseberry bushes and the
pond where one could jab a stick at the green epidermis of algae
and watch an aperture of black water open and close. The creek
with its boulders and the dark yawning overhangs. "What a good
idea," he murmured, distracted. I'd found his mouth again,
remembering a malicious-looking goat roped to a peg, and being
entrusted as a very small girl with a bucket of warm, foamy milk,
my father watching me negotiate it as best I could over a steep and
muddy track.

16 June 1963 Morning

The doctors knocked on our door at 07:00 and inquired how we'd
slept. "As always," Solovyova answered. I was having trouble finding my voice. They supervised calisthenics before breakfast, then
performed a final preflight medical check and administered an
enema. Next, we stood around shirtless while they glued sensor
pads to our torsos. These same doctors would also be analyz-
ing our voice communications for signs of fatigue and stress. As
always, we found their attentions unpleasant but did not want to
be the sort of person who if offered an apple would complain
about its size.

Technicians helped us into our spacesuits and held out paper
for me to sign. One even presented his work pass. Helmets on,
visors open, we boarded the bus, a matching pair of cosmonauts:
me with all the luck, and Solovyova with none. We sat together in
the otherwise empty seats. When the bus pulled up at the gantry's
base, we peered at the infinitely high tower and cavernous flame
trench. Finally Solovyova said, "I wish you all good fortune," her
voice breaking. According to tradition, one should kiss the departing traveler three times on alternate cheeks. We banged against
one another with our helmets, then rose and left the bus.

There we were greeted by Korolyov and Kamanin and the Central Committee. "I'm miserable that I can't be up there with you today," Korolyov said, smiling. He had tears in his eyes.

"Someday we'll fly together to Mars," I told him. We hugged, and I shook hands with the rest of the Committee.

"Everyone's crying today," Kamanin observed.

"That's it, then," Korolyov said. Solovyova climbed back onto the bus, and I stepped up into the gantry lift. I could see her staring through the passenger window in the other direction. Then the lift doors closed and up I went.

When they opened there was blinding sun and horizon all around me. The tiny circular hatch of the Vostok and two technicians broke up the view. I tottered forward. Several kilometers away in the bright sun, some blue spruces surrounded a small white crypt with a gold cupola.

The technicians waited patiently. When I was ready, they hefted my shoulders and I swung my legs over the rim of the hatch and squeezed into the ejection seat. Then they hauled at my straps and connected the life support systems.

I checked my suit pressure and communications line. Through the latter they were piping in American jazz. Above me I could hear the hatch being manhandled into position and the screwdown bolts secured. A palm-sized mirror sewn into the sleeve of my suit allowed me to check its progress. On my right was the radio set, telegraph key and attitude control; on my left, the retro sequence switch panel.

The music stopped, and Korolyov said in my earpiece, "Fifteen minutes." I sealed my gloves and pulled down my visor. The music didn't resume.

I sat. My orbital plane would differ from Bykovsky's by 30 degrees, so we'd approach for only a few minutes twice during each orbit. But during our encounter on the opposite side of the world, we could talk, unmonitored. He'd been in space for forty-five hours. I tried to compose my first words to him but imagined instead Solovyova on her sad trip back to the observation bunker to strip off her suit.

Korolyov announced a delay. I leaned my head back inside my helmet. He said it had to do with a problem with the telemetry. He estimated it at forty minutes, and asked if I wanted the music again. I told him no. I removed my gloves and pulled my notepad from my toiletries box and recorded the above.

17 June 1963 Night

The pen, attached by twine, drifts away when I stop to think, only to be reeled back time after time.

I have now been in space thirty-three hours. Thirty-three hours ago, following the delay, Korolyov announced launch key to *go* position; air purging; idle run; ignition. There was the helicopter whine of the pumps injecting fuel into the combustion chambers and the engines firing up. The rocket shook and caterwauled as the mechanisms adjusted to their inconceivable stresses, and when the gantry's hold-down arms disconnected, I felt a jolt and heard Korolyov report on the ascent. "How are you?" he asked. "How are you?" I asked him back. I was squashed into my seat, shaking like someone on an apple cart, and found it difficult to talk. There was a sharp drop in the g-load as the booster shut down, shoving me forward against my straps, then a bump as it dropped away, the noise resuming with the g-load. When the third stage shut down and fell away, I felt the weightlessness as a buoyancy in my muscles, as if nothing took any effort at all.

The vibrations stopped. The capsule was a marketplace of fans and pumps. It was rotating gently, and through the porthole came a shock of indigo, replaced just as quickly with an ardent black. *Tereshkova,* I thought. *You're in outer space.*

I saw the sun. Clouds. Islands and a coastline. The light blue of the horizon was violet at the edge of its curve. Beyond that were stars. When the sun appeared again, the illumination was so intense I had to turn away.

"Hello, Seagull," Bykovsky called. I leaned forward against my straps and looked out the porthole, as though he were waving.

"Hello, Hawk," I answered. Stars wheeled across my line of vision.

"Did you ask something?" Korolyov wanted to know. He'd heard my weeping. "No," I told him.

Kamanin announced to us both that our greetings were being broadcast around the world. Someone right now was running to my parents' farm to tell them that their little Valentina had just appeared on the television.

We exchanged pleasantries. We told everyone how we were doing. Within minutes we were transferred to Petropavlovsk on Siberia's coast, and then soon after that we swept out over the Pacific and into the vast shadow of the half of Earth that was asleep. Transmissions from below flickered and buzzed and went dead. The fans and pumps were still whirring all around me.

"I've unsnapped," Bykovsky finally said. "Try it. It's wonderful."

"I'm here," I told him. My capsule rotated through two full revolutions. We had only seventeen minutes of privacy on this orbit. "I'm here," I repeated. My earpiece hissed again for a count of fifteen.

"Hello," he finally said, and even in that one word I could hear the forbearance.

What had I expected? I wasn't sure. I still wasn't sure. We hurtled through our planet's shadow. "This is Seagull," I told him, more plaintively than I wished to.

"The slightest push sends you in the opposite direction," he reported, adding that he'd now been unstrapped for nearly ninety minutes.

"Do you have nausea?" he asked.

"Do I have *nausea*?" I said.

"Where are you?" I said.

There was a series of clicks in my ear. "I'm performing one of my procedures," he said.

When I was a small girl, one of my evening chores was retrieving the goat that strayed to browse the garden between two tumbledown houses that frightened me. Each night, my father would say, "Oh, I'll go with you." And then, when I waited: "Go! I'm not going." And every single time, I'd say to myself as I went, *Stupid: you took the bait. But next time you'll be smarter.*

"I'm doing my stretching exercises," Bykovsky informed me, and then his responsibilities absorbed his attention for the rest of the time we were in shadow, and I made no further attempt to distract him.

Our code phrases for communicating our condition, given that the Americans were listening, were as follows: a report of "feeling excellent" signified all was well; "feeling good" conveyed there was some concern; and "feeling satisfactory" meant that the mission might need to be terminated.

"How are you, Seagull?" Korolyov said once radio contact was reestablished. The sun broke around the bottom of the world like the arc from a welder's torch.

"I'm feeling satisfactory," I reported.

"You're what?" he said. "Say again, Seagull?"

But I chose not to answer. There were frantic attempts to reestablish contact.

"Hawk, Hawk, please contact Seagull," Korolyov urged, spinning toward me so far below.

"Seagull, this is Hawk," Bykovsky said after a moment. "Is everything excellent?"

"How are your experiments?" I answered. My gloves seemed steady on the switches before me.

"I think something may be wrong with her receiver, or she may have selected the wrong channel," he told Korolyov.

He also reported periodically that he was continuing to pay close attention to his physical regimen. In that same period of time I failed to activate my biological experiments, failed to participate in my medical experiments, and failed to keep an official log, writing for myself instead. Solovyova tried to raise me, and when she did I reached for my radio but then eased my hand back. My helmet chafed my shoulders. I wished I had toothpaste. I was supposed to photograph the solar corona but the film cassette stuck in the camera and I cracked the inner window with the lens attempting to remove the cartridge.

"Seagull, are you there?" Korolyov pleaded.

"I think she's asleep," Bykovsky finally told him.

18 June 1963 Night

The second-day crisis was that I failed to perform a major goal of the mission: manual control of the spacecraft. Korolyov was frightened that I would be lost should the automatic reentry system fail. Nikolayev and then Gagarin himself were brought in to instruct me from the ground. Gagarin was a gentleman about it. There are two guidance systems for establishing orientation for retrofire: one uses an automatic solar bearing, and the other is manual and visual. My task was to hold the Yzor orientation viewport level with the Earth's horizon for fifteen minutes, but it refused to stop bouncing and slipped out of my crosshairs. "There it goes again," I'd say with equanimity, while below they tried to keep the exasperation out of their responses. My eyes filled with tears and just like that the tears went away.

I had meat mixed with sorrel or oats, and prunes and processed cheese for dinner. The bread was too dry.

19 June 1963 Night

A few minutes ago I passed the lights of Rio within the blackness of Brazil. This morning I was successfully talked through the manual control by Nikolayev. I remember him as a smug and unpleasant person with jowls and the darkest razor stubble I've ever seen. Everyone is much relieved below. They're bringing me back early.

I've often considered what kind of first impression I make. I assume that I initially evoke a measure of intrigue before people get to understand me and become repulsed.

In my most recent exchanges with Bykovsky, I feel as though I've been able to detect with great precision brutality and remorse tinged with diffidence and pity. Some I haven't had the heart to report, even here. None of this should surprise me. Only my loneliness now generates fear. Otherwise I'm an uninteresting and aching surface.

During that first party for the cosmonaut finalists, I found Bykovsky and Ponomaryova holding hands as they touched an exposed wire in her portable radio set. "Come on, you try it," they said.

1 August 1964

What else, that day, did I not do? I still remember. I failed to signal the correct working of the solar orientation system. I remained silent throughout reentry. I did not report retrofire or the separation of the capsule. I was told there was quite the panic down below throughout all of this. I focused instead on the roaring sound of the hot air, the bacon-in-the-pan sound of the thermal cladding in the reentry inferno, and the jouncing which was like a springless cart being galloped down a rutted gully. Then outside the charred porthole I saw white sky and the hatch over my helmet blew away like I'd been shelled and the ejection rockets thundered in a blur of daylight and I saw the burned capsule falling away below as I was separated from my seat.

Against regulations, I opened my visor and looked up, and was struck in the face by a piece of metal. I saw a river and some haystacks. I saw a rail line, with a locomotive. I saw small figures running to where I would land.

At the press conference we faced one hundred and three correspondents. Bykovsky had landed two orbits later. I was asked about the stitches in my face. I told the correspondents that we were proud of what our country had accomplished. I said that I'd felt no fear. Three different correspondents asked if I'd been lonely, and I answered that I'd known my loved ones were even closer than everyone thought, watching me fly. I told them that, descending on my parachute, I'd sung "My Country Hears, My Country Knows." There were ten questions for me for every one for Bykovsky. At one point I turned to him and joked, "Oh, were you up there, too?" and occasioned a roar of laughter. I learned later that Khrushchev had been delighted with my performance.

This was before the contests with the doctors and the inter-views with Korolyov—all devastated disappointment—and the honors, ending with our tour of Bulgaria, Mongolia, Italy, Switzer-land, Mexico, Ghana, and Indonesia. Bykovsky asked that his wife be allowed to accompany us, but Kamanin rejected the request. It was before I received the news of my arranged marriage to Niko-layev, considered the cosmonauts' most eligible bachelor; be-fore the first state wedding in Soviet history, presided over by Khrushchev himself; before the birth, just a few months later, of my little Alyona, a girl who provided proof that space travel inter-fered with neither love nor fertility.

Of course my diary had been found and read immediately upon my return. But before we were separated forever, Seagull and Hawk were allowed their one trip together around the world, chaperoned by the KGB. We had already separated—we had sepa-rated in space—but we still had our walks. On one we traversed a rough track overgrown with honeysuckle and mayweed, leaving our pursuers behind. A wolfhound, very meek and companion-able, had attached herself to us. It was entirely quiet except for her panting and the calls of the KGB. We lay with our heads thrown back. Bykovsky mentioned Solovyova, who'd asked him to contact me when her letters had returned to her unopened. "Why was that, do you suppose?" he asked, when I refused comment. "Though it's none of my business," he added. We talked about how we'd learned about sex. According to my high school friend, it took an hour, and if a couple did it for two hours, they had twins. We kissed for the last time. I asked if he would remove my virginity, and after some reassurances, he did.

I remember how much I'd loved the new teacher who'd arrived to teach physics after the war. He was a gangly and sweet man who could float pins on water and make electricity by combing his hair, which had gone prematurely white. He was so happy we were happy. We were happy because we were grasping those simple things that seemed miraculous. We were happy because at such moments we no longer belonged to only ourselves, but were beginning to experience what other people could see and feel. We were reminded that those sorts of feelings were so brief that it was as if their beginnings touched their ends. And even then I was given a glimpse of how I'd always turn my back to what was offered; how I'd never fully grasp, flailing, at whatever charities the world was able to dispense; how what I thought was my reach was really only my attempt to dismiss, to expel, or to disavow.

Courtesy for Beginners

Summer camp: here's how bad summer camp was. The day I arrived I opened my camp trunk and changed my shirt and just stood there alone and breathing through my mouth in the four-man platform tent, just me and the canvas smell and the daddy longlegs, and then I thought that I was the person who I least wanted to be with, and I stepped out into the cooler air. There was nowhere to unpack anything, and even I wasn't so scared that I could hang around in the tent. It was like 104. Sweat ran down the backs of my knees. The black metal stays on the tent ropes were too hot to touch.

We were in a pine forest. Everything had that baked pine needle smell. My father had just driven away. A squirrel sat up across from me, woozy with the sun. He worked over a nut and then spit it at me. Way off behind him, two kids were sitting on another kid's chest in a clearing. Down the hill to my right, someone was ringing a bell.

I headed down the path toward the noise. I think I was affecting a saunter. I sauntered down to the lean-to where a few kids and some counselors were hanging out. A sign on top said COUN-SELORS LEAN-TO. The counselors were two blond guys, maybe seventeen or eighteen, the kind of guys who seem like nice boys to moms. A fat kid who'd already taken off his shirt was bugging them about something. The fat kid had my glasses. Which was too bad for the fat kid. They were even fixed with electrical tape on the same side that mine were. There was a whine in his voice that I could hear from up where I was, and he kept at it. *You fucking idiot*, I thought the whole time I was walking down to them. I was talking about me. I was always wanting myself to die whenever I found myself in a stupid situation. When I got to the front of the lean-to, I nodded at whoever caught my eye. Nobody nodded back.

"I told you I don't know," one of the blond guys said, watching me fold my arms and stand there. He seemed to be talking to the fat kid. He had both hands on the two-by-four that was the top edge of the lean-to and he was swinging his body a little, keeping his feet in place. He looked dangerously bored. The fat kid said something else. The blond guy ignored him. The fat kid said something after that. The blond guy swung with everything he had and brought his feet up together and caught the fat kid under the chin and up along his face.

The fat kid left the ground a foot and a half and landed on his back. The sound was like when I whacked the sheet on our line with my wiffle bat. We all just stared like now we knew what we were in for, for the next however many weeks. I felt this rush, like I was the blond guy and the fat kid all at once. One of the other kids bent over and found where the glasses had landed.

"How are you?" the guy who'd kicked the fat kid asked me.

"I'm okay," I told him. I didn't know what else to say.

"C'mon. *Talk* to me. Tell me. What's wrong?" my mother said when she got me alone the day before I left. I told her I didn't want to go to camp and she said, *besides* the camp. I told her I guessed I felt bad about my brother and she said, *besides* your brother.

She was asking because she saw what I was like during the day and after school and she wanted to help. She was worried that it would get even worse now that school was over. She said that everyone was worried that everything was taking too much of a toll.

My grades had gone downhill. My friends had stopped coming around. Even the Venus flytrap in my room had died.

She'd also found my list of the World's Deadliest Poisons. I was always ranking them and changing the rankings. I had a notebook with that title written inside on the first page that I kept in my desk. I looked in the encyclopedia and in the library and also under our sink. If it had a skull and crossbones on it, I checked it out.

The blond guys turned out to be Chris and Caleb. Chris was the meaner one and he looked like a guy on TV. Once we all got assembled he started a speech and Caleb finished it. It was a welcome to the camp speech. The fat kid held a dirty hand towel up to his nose while he listened. The bleeding had stopped but his lip and nose were swollen and the kids who'd gotten there late were all clearly wondering about it. He sniffled and kept shooting them looks even though he kept his head down. Chris had found him the towel and told him to suck it up when he handed it over. When he went looking for it, Caleb had helped the fat kid to his feet and had straightened out his glasses and stood next to him with his hands on his thighs, telling him it was all right while the kid got ahold of himself.

There were more counselors than just them, they told us, but the campers were divided into Beaver, Moose, and Fox troops, and they were in charge of Beaver. We were in Beaver.

"You see that?" my new tentmate asked when we were headed up to our tents. It was a stupid question because we'd both been standing there when it happened. The fat kid had landed more or less between us.

I shook my head, a little dazed, as in: *Man: the things I've seen.*

"They can't get away with that shit," my new tentmate said. He sounded like he was worried that they could. He was wearing what looked like his little brother's plain white T-shirt and it was soaked through. I thought I was scrawny but he was so bad you could pass a Dixie cup through his armpit when his hands were at his sides.

Our other new tentmate told us he was horny, first thing. The three of us had our butts on the beds and feet on the floor and were leaning back on our hands. It was still really hot but they'd told us to go to our tents so that's what we'd done. We had some quiet time until the dinner horn, which was apparently going to be a real guy blowing a horn. Somebody had eaten some Hostess somethings and had left the wrappers all over the other bed. Maybe the fourth kid wasn't coming.

The scrawny kid said he was Joyce from upstate. He said "upstate" like that filled in all the gaps, as far as information about him went.

"*Joyce?*" the other kid said. "Hey, there. I'm Wanda."

"You are not," Joyce said. "What's your name?"

"Lulu Belle," the other kid said.

Joyce turned to me. "What's your name?" he asked.

I told him.

"Nice to meet you," Joyce said.

"What happened to the fat kid?" the other kid said.

"Oh, man," Joyce said. "You won't believe it." He told the story. He said, "We were both standing *right there.*"

"That is so fucked up," the other kid said, like he'd just come downstairs on Christmas morning.

"So what *is* your name?" Joyce asked once we were back from dinner. Dinner had sucked. A little piece of metal or something had been in my Salisbury steak, and a kid in line behind me when we were bussing our trays had made fun of my shorts.

"BJ," the other kid said. Now we had more time to piss away before the big Opening Night Campfire.

"What's that short for?" Joyce asked.

"BJ," BJ said.

All through the first part of the campfire my gum was still bleeding from the thing in my food. I could taste it. I kept doing this thing with my face to make it feel better. "What're you, retarded?" BJ asked. I guessed he could see it even though it was getting pretty dark.

I was pressing my hands together really hard. I couldn't keep my feet still. It was interesting, though: being here wasn't any worse than being home, or being anywhere.

There was a big pyramid of wood in front of us. It was like six feet tall. A wire ran from the middle of it to a stepladder set up behind us. Every kid sitting on the grass was thinking *bonfire* and hoping it would maybe get out of control and the state would burn down.

We all had our flashlights with us for the trip back to the tents, though at this point they were supposed to be turned off. Chris pulled three kids from the audience and sat them in front and told them to turn their flashlights on him when he got up onstage. The stage was a plywood sheet on four metal milk crates. One of the kids was still shaking when Chris climbed up there. You could see the light beam jittering. He'd probably been thinking they were going to start things off by kicking three kids in the face.

Instead Chris said hi to us all and then said "I can't *hear* you" four times at what we said back. Finally even I screamed hi. He introduced the Camp Director, who had a beer in his hand. The Camp Director handed him the beer when he climbed up onto the stage. The plywood almost tipped and the Camp Director held his hands out on both sides of him and said, "Whoa, Old Paint." He seemed to think that that should get a laugh.

He told us that Pautapaug was an old Nipmuc Indian name that meant "swampy land." He told us that the camp got started by the Bridgeport Rotary Club in 1919. He said that we were 175 acres from the nearest town. He gave us the schedule: Reveille; Bunk Attack, for kids who slept through Reveille; the Call for Waiters; Breakfast; Sign-Up Events; the Call for Waiters; Lunch; Siesta; Sign-Up Events; Call for Waiters; Dinner; Water Polo or Capture the Flag; Campfire and Taps. He gave it to us again. Then he taught us the camp song.

"Pautapaug, carefree land, Pautapaug, helping hand," the kid next to me sang.

The Camp Director got down and Chris got back up there. The

Camp Director took his beer back. The other counselors were all doing something behind us.

"Fire god of Pautapaug, send down your fire!" Chris screamed.

A coffee can filled with some kind of fire slid down the wire to the pyramid. It bounced when it hit the wood and then sat against it for a minute before the whole thing went up. It must have been totally soaked with gas or something. That was a big hit with the campers.

The kids in the front row had to move back. The toe of one kid's sneaker started to melt.

There was more singing. Then the counselors all went somewhere. We sat there in the dark, looking at the fire.

Was I really going to make it to eighth grade? Did I even *want* to make it to eighth grade? Nothing about the year coming up seemed like anything I wanted to go through.

"So is that it?" BJ said, before the fire was even out.

The counselors came back. They shoved each other around and got each other in headlocks. Campers were dismissed by troops, Beaver first. One kid tripped when we got up to leave and burned his hand. On the way back to the tents everybody had sword fights with the flashlight beams until the counselors told us to cut it out.

Nobody said anything in the tent. I climbed under the covers, already too hot. Mosquitoes buzzed in one ear and then went over to the other one.

They called lights out. We switched off our flashlights. "So, do you beat off?" BJ asked, as soon as they went out.

For some reason I got all teary and rolled my face into the pillow. It already smelled like the bottom of a laundry bag.

"How old are you?" he asked. A light went by outside and I could see his silhouette.

"Who you talkin' to?" Joyce finally asked back.

"*You,*" BJ said. "Anyone."

"I'm eleven," Joyce said.

"Yeah, well I'm twelve," BJ said.

"Huh," Joyce said. In the dark, one of them rolled over and then kicked hard at his sheets.

"What about you?" BJ asked.

"I'm twelve too," I said.

"You are not," BJ scoffed.

"I don't have time for this," I said.

"He is not," he said to Joyce.

"He says he is," Joyce said back.

"Fuckin' liar," BJ said, and rattled something in a box. I could hear him eating.

I was crying, which was the very last thing I wanted to be doing, and trying not to make any noise at all. I was pushing on my eyeballs with my fingertips and I was worried I was going to drive them through my skull. They hurt enough that I stopped. My father had said, "You don't want to go to camp? You don't want to do *any*thing. Times're tough all over. Go up there and force yourself to have a good time. We'll stay down here and deal with your brother." When I tried to bring it up again later on, he told me, "Believe me, you got the better deal."

"I got a boner like an *iron bar*," BJ said. He made a noise on his bed like he was hauling it around.

This is only the *first night*, I kept thinking. And that only made me cry harder, until I stopped.

"What *was* that?" Joyce asked, and he and BJ stopped moving to listen. But then there was nothing else to hear.

At breakfast everybody seemed to know everybody but me. "I *got* you," BJ called to a kid at another table. "I *got* you later on. You're *mine*."

"You know him from back home?" I asked.

"I met him when you did," BJ said. He sawed his fork into some waffles.

I looked at the kid. "When did *I* meet him?" I asked. Nobody answered.

The fat kid and I collided on the way out of the dining hall. He spilled something but I didn't see what. BJ high-fived me on the way down the front steps.

"It's not a crime to *help* somebody," my mother told me once. She was talking about my little brother.

My little brother was going crazy. That was the big worry. I was wound pretty tight and had some issues, which was how my father put it, but my little brother worried everybody. I couldn't tell who was more scared about it, my mother or father. They started going over it one night after school got out for the summer, when they thought we were asleep, and after I listened for a while I sat up in bed and realized he was standing there in the hall in the dark.

"C'mon in here," I told him. He came in and sat on the covers. He was only nine and it felt like he'd been crying since Easter. He had bed head and thick hair and it stuck up like a wing. Even in the dark he seemed sad.

"Waynik, Keough, what's his name, they're all the same," my father said. He was rinsing something at the sink.

"They're trying everything they can think of," my mother told him. "Waynik says to give it some time."

"Waynik sees him one hour a week," my father told her. "Friday afternoon to boot. He's got his clubs by the door. He's ready to hit the first tee."

"You wanna try someone else, we'll try someone else," my mother said.

"We *tried* someone else," he said. "That's how we got *here.*"

My brother had been going along okay until he hit fourth grade. Then it was like everything was fine until it was too hard for him. He'd be shooting baskets and miss three in a row and just go off, tearing down branches and throwing the ball as hard as he could into the street. He broke a new tree my dad planted in half. He pulled his jaw down so hard with his hand he had to go to the emergency room. I caught him hitting himself one night because I heard the wet sound of the blood from his mouth. We were supposed to do our homework at the same time, and I'd hear him stop halfway through and tear it up and then move his arms so spastically that he'd knock over whatever else was on his desk.

That night after they went over things my mother and father were quiet, down in the kitchen. It was pretty bad to think about them down there just looking at each other.

"They think I'm mental," my brother finally said.

"They're worried about you," I told him.

"You think I'm mental?" he said.

"No," I said.

"So why do I do mental things?" he wanted to know.

"I do mental things," I reminded him.

"Not like me," he said.

And I could have told him that I did. I could have told him how weird *I* was. I could've given him a hundred examples. Instead I just sat there with him.

"You're a good brother," he told me before he went back to his room.

"I wish," I told him.

"Are you guys still up?" my father called from downstairs.

Because I was up all night, I got to the sign-up board late and all the good things were taken. All that was left was Trail Policing and the Craft Hut.

"What's Trail Policing?" I asked the kid whose shoulder I was looking over. He didn't answer. He took the pencil hanging on the string and wrote his name under Craft Hut and left.

"What's Trail Policing?" I asked the fat kid. He was sitting in the dirt of the truck turnaround, trying to get something out of the bottom of his foot. The area behind the main dining hall was messed up from all the traffic.

"Picking up garbage," he said.

I wrote my name under Craft Hut. "You know where the Craft Hut is?" I asked him.

"You any good at getting splinters out?" he asked back.

It turned out that the fat kid was there for the entire summer. BJ told us at lunch. It was the talk of the camp. We were there for two weeks, most of us, one kid for three. But this kid was there for the whole summer. His parents were in Europe or Paris or something and had dumped him there. He'd told his tentmates. He'd even had to get there a day early and sleep on the Camp Director's couch.

His parents were probably like, *Oh, I'm sure he'll like it okay. Once he makes some friends . . .*

It ended up that he was in the Craft Hut too. There was one other kid in there who wore an eye patch under his glasses. The kid who'd signed up in front of me wasn't even there. Maybe he was dead.

"You're in my light," the kid with the eye patch said when I sat down.

"Aye-aye," I told him, but I don't think he got it.

He was making an ashtray with clay. The fat kid spent the time scraping at the bottom of his foot with his fingernail. I made one of those lanyards for a keychain.

The other subject at lunch was how much fun everybody else had had. Swimming off the float, doing cannonballs, playing Killer Handbreaker Tetherball.

"I made a lanyard," I told them. People talked about the sign-ups for the Mile Swim. Joyce put his hands on the outside of his arms, like he was already cold. BJ said that he heard that the counselors did a Bunk Attack with the fat kid even though he'd been trying to get up in time. Joyce said he'd heard the same thing. It turned out that Bunk Attack was when they came into your tent and pitched you off the bed so that you fell between the edge of the platform and the canvas wall. "It's *so gross* in there, too," someone said.

My brother's name was Georgie and one of the things he really hated was when I called him Puddin' n' Pie. We'd be riding in the backseat and out of nowhere I'd say it so only he could hear it and he'd go *Stop it!* and scare the shit out of my father and then get yelled at. I hated it as much as he did but I couldn't stop. *Don't do it,* I'd say to myself when it came to pushing him. And then I'd do it. It was like when I did stuff like that at least I had the satisfaction of seeing myself like I really was. He always got mad but he never told them what I was doing.

"How come you never tell on me?" I used to ask him. He told me to stop asking him that.

"You tease your brother?" my mother asked me once. It was after my brother and I had had a huge fight. I'd thrown his record player against his headboard. We'd all gotten calmed down at like midnight. My brother was still making noise in his room. My father had closed all the windows.

I don't know, I said. Sometimes I teased him a little, I thought.

More than that I didn't let him play my record collection. It was the thing he liked to do most but he always scratched everything. We took the bus into Bridgeport with my mother when she went to the bank so we could go to Korvette's afterwards for 45s. We listened to WICC and WMCA. We always asked if we could get two of everything so he could have his own copy and she always said we were lucky to get one. And he'd always like what I got better than what he got. So he'd sit in my room when I was trying to do something and go, "Can we play 'Elusive Butterfly'?" And I'd go, "No." And he'd sit there and hum the music while I tried to keep doing what I was doing. And I'd go, "I'm still not gonna play it." And he'd shrug and keep humming, like that would have to do. Sometimes if he went out in the yard I'd play the song. Before I left for camp he got "98.6" by Keith and I got "Green Tambourine" by the Lemon Pipers. He got a new record player but he wasn't supposed to touch any of my records until I got back. I hid them in the storage space before I left.

"Can I play your records when you're gone?" he asked the morning I was leaving. It was still almost dark but he'd gotten up to see me go.

"I don't care," I told him.

"That was nice of you," my father said in the car on the drive up.

If they called and asked where I'd hid them when I was up there, I'd probably tell them.

I got to the sign-up board earlier the next morning but still too late for the beach. Me and two other kids and the fat kid ended up at Archery. The archery range was a field with three bales of hay and a fiberglass bow. The fat kid said somebody lost the arrows the year before.

"You were here last year?" I asked him.

"I been here three years in a row," he said.

The other two kids had the bow. They were taking turns throwing it at one of the bales.

"Don't your parents know you hate it here?" I asked him.

"Don't yours?" he said.

BJ told us on the hike that afternoon that the fat kid had told on Chris.

"Did he get him in trouble?" Joyce asked. We were spread out along the Widowmaker Trail waiting for lunch. A counselor was on a rock cutting Spam out of the can into fattish cylinders with his Swiss army knife and another one was handing out bread slices. The drink they'd passed around at the beginning had already ruined my canteen. Everybody who had kept their water was being asked by everybody else for a drink.

The fat kid was in the middle of the trail behind us and Chris was kicking and scuffing at his butt like he was trying to get gum off the sidewalk. "Who are you throwing *rocks* at?" Chris said. He'd noticed me pinging pebbles down the trail.

"Both of you," I said.

"Well cut it out," he said.

Before dinner when we got back the fat kid signed out one of the little sailboats and was just getting going when Chris waded out and tipped the boat over with him in it, and then waded back to shore.

"Cut it *out*," the fat kid screamed once he surfaced. "*You* cut it out too," he said when he saw me throwing more little rocks from the shore. They plunked in the water around him.

"Phone call," some kid said to me when we were back in the tents. There was only one phone the campers could use, and it was in the Camp Director's office.

"What's that noise?" I asked my father after he said hello.

"That's your brother," he said.

"What's wrong with him?" I asked.

"He wants to go see the Association in New Haven," my father said.

"The *band* the Association? They're playing in New Haven?" I asked.

"What do you think: he wants to visit their house? *Yes,* they're playing in New Haven," he said.

"How'd he find out about it?" I asked.

"How do I know?" my father said. "He listens to the radio."

"I'm goin'," I heard my brother tell him.

"You're *not* goin'," my father said back. My mother shouted in her two cents from wherever she was.

"Does he want you to go with him?" I said.

"He's nine years old. He's not going to a *rock* concert," he told me.

My brother shouted something I couldn't make out. "*Hey,*" my father shouted back. "How'd you like to not leave your *room* for a few weeks?"

My brother said something else I couldn't hear.

"I told him he could play some of your records instead," he said.

"You talking to me?" I asked him. "My records?"

"No, I'm talking to your mother," he said. "He wants to play our Perry Como. That's why I called you."

"I don't want him playing my records," I said.

"Now don't *you* start too," he said.

"I'm not starting anything," I said.

"Jesus, Mary, and Joseph," he said. "I'm gonna take *all* these fucking records and pitch them out the window."

"Fine," I said. "I don't care what he does. I hope he breaks them all."

"I hope so too," my father said.

"Lend me your flashlight," Chris said to me when I was on my way back to my tent. He'd come from behind me.

"How will *I* get home?" I asked him.

"Lend me your *flashlight*," he said. I handed it over and he veered into the woods and disappeared. I didn't even see it go on.

"Chris has my flashlight," I told my tentmates when I got back. I said it like Godzilla was loose in the city.

It was my father's good one. When we'd been packing he'd been deciding between the crappy plastic one he let us play with and his. My brother had taken his once and had lost it. Even my mother had had to start looking for it. It had been this huge thing. I didn't care which one I had, but his had a better beam. I'd told him I wouldn't lose it and he'd said okay. And now Chris had it and when I tried to get it back he'd beat me to death with it.

As usual I couldn't sleep. I got up when it was still dark and signed up for the beach. I went by the counselors' lean-to but nobody was moving. A raccoon was rooting around in somebody's knapsack in the dirt.

Maybe it was good that I lost it, I thought on the way back to the tent. Maybe when they found out, my parents would be like, *But he knew how much we wanted him to keep an eye on it.*

But I also wanted to be the kid who stayed up when everybody else went under.

The fat kid showed up at the beach too. He said the Camp Director was trying to make it up to him about the Chris stuff.

I cut my hand on the sharp edge of a broken garbage can.

I was worried about the flashlight. The fat kid sat next to me. We were the only ones not in the water. It was so humid you couldn't tell we hadn't been in.

Some kids were having races from the steel dock to the pontoon raft. A few sailboats were crisscrossing, the occasional sail collapsing. One rowboat sat a ways out, trailing a Mile Swimmer. The water over the sand by the reeds where we were was the color of cream soda.

Kids were throwing other kids off the pontoon raft into the lake. There was a lot of shouting, and my hand was still bleeding. I was going to need a better Band-Aid.

"You think BJ stands for Blow Job?" the fat kid said.

I looked at him. I hadn't thought of that.

"Has he asked you yet?" he said.

"Asked me what?" I said.

"He asked *me*," he said. "I told him I would." He looked at my face like he'd gotten the reaction he wanted.

"Why would you say that?" I said, though it was none of my business.

He shrugged, his shoulders up on both sides of his ears.

Someone whacked me on the head with a life preserver. "Camp Director wants you," Chris said when I turned around.

"You finished with my flashlight?" I asked.

He looked at me, trying to figure out who I was. "I don't have your flashlight," he said.

I closed my eyes and when I opened them he hadn't changed his expression. I told him I was the kid who lent him the flashlight.

"I got my own flashlight," he said. "Why would I borrow yours?"

Last night, I told him. On the trail.

"Give him his flashlight," the fat kid told him.

"*What'd* you say to me?" Chris asked.

Then he repeated that I had a call and gave my shoulder a shove while he was still looking at the fat kid. As in *Get going.*

When I looked back, he was standing there over him, the fat kid just looking out over the water like he was alone.

"Where the Christ are the *records*?" my father asked on the phone. When I told him he hung up.

When I got back the fat kid was standing in the water up to his waist, watching the kids on the pontoon raft, and Chris was gone. I got in as far as my knees and the air horn sounded for the end of sign-up events.

"You think BJ stands for Blow Job?" I asked Joyce at lunch.

"*Duh*," he said. He had a quarter-sized strawberry on his forehead, like he'd been dragged facedown across a rug.

"So you think it does," I said.

"It *is* all he ever talks about," he said.

We had our trays and were looking for places to sit. "I haven't heard him say it once," I said.

It turned out that Chris wasn't the only one who was beating on the fat kid. The fat kid's tentmates were too. The night before two of them held him down and one peed all over his face. And his bed. He told me at the Nature Center before dinner. The Nature Center was a two-room cabin that had a stuffed fox on a log and some turtle shells in a glass case. The best things in it were the spiders in the ceiling corners that weren't part of the exhibit. The fat kid said he didn't know where he'd go. He didn't want to sleep with those kids anymore. He didn't want to sleep anywhere anymore.

"I know that feeling," I said. But he looked at me like I was just trying to cheer him up.

When I saw him later that night I thanked him for backing me up with Chris.

"You don't have your flashlight, do you?" he asked.

"No," I said.

"So what good did *I* do?" he said.

We were on our way back from the campfire. "Where're *you* two going?" BJ asked when he saw us walking together. But he sounded worried.

The fat kid ignored me for a while and then he finally said, "I would've left me here too." He was looking down the trail like he could see Paris.

"Your parents go away every summer?" I asked him. That sounded worse than my life.

"I don't have to be this fat, you know," he said. "I eat like all the time."

"Well, stop eating," I told him. "Get some celery sticks."

"That's what I'm gonna do," he said.

We took a wrong turn in the dark and had to double back. He asked me not to say anything about what he said about BJ. "You're not supposed to know," he said. "He asked about ten kids. I think I'm the only one who said yes."

"Don't some kids want to kick his ass when he says something like that?" I asked him.

"Well, *yeah*," he said. Like: Hel-*lo*. "What do you care?" he said when I asked if he was really going to do it. "Guys like it. In case you were wondering. Guys like it when you do it."

We finally found his tent and there was this feeling down inside me like now I'd never sleep. "If you were normal you'd know that," he said.

It was dark and his elbow kept bumping me. One of the kids from inside his tent stuck his head out. "Who're you? His girl-friend? You walk him home?"

"Yeah, I'm his girlfriend," I said. "I walked him home." They all made big noises about that.

"How's your special friend?" BJ said when I got back to our tent.

"Shouldn't you be jerking off?" I told him. And then we both got into our sleeping bags and lay there touching ourselves and trying to think of what to say next. I was still awake when he finally sat up and listened to see if we were asleep and pulled on his shorts and left. I could hear his flip-flops slapping as he went down the trail.

When the first birds started making noise I could see the canvas over my head again. I could feel a breeze and smell something fresh. My eyes were so tired they burned. There were noises in the underbrush up the hill.

I saw Chris three times before lunch and asked him each time about the flashlight. He seemed distracted. "I *don't* have your *flash*light," he said the last time, like he was finally able to focus. I didn't see the fat kid or BJ. For a while nobody knew where they were and then somebody said they were in the Health Center. The nurse who sat in the little front room there said they were both resting and I should come back after lunch. She had a little wooden rack of pamphlets on her desk: *Your Gums and You, Proper Foot Hygiene, Courtesy for Beginners.*

At lunch someone said they both got beaten up, or beat each other up.

There was no one at the desk when I came back so I walked in. They pretended to still be asleep. The fat kid had his hands bandaged with big ice bags on them and had a bandage on his ear too. BJ had two black eyes and an ice bag wrapped in a towel on his head. His cheek was swollen.

Outside, Chris was sitting on the steps of the Health Center with his head in his hands. His knuckles were scabby with dried blood. Two of the other counselors were trying to cheer him up. He was saying he was 1-A and his lottery number was five. Unless he took off for Canada he was going over. His brother didn't have a deferment either. He was over there already.

"That's the least of your worries at this point," the Camp Director said. "Come with me." And he got Chris up and they went to the Camp Director's office.

"What're *you* lookin' at?" one of the counselors said when he saw me.

I stuck my head in the Health Center's back window. BJ closed his eyes when he saw me, but the fat kid looked back, like he finally had something he could tell his parents.

I spent the rest of the day in bed. Daddy longlegs and flies came and went. Joyce looked in and then left. The next morning I missed breakfast but somebody got me out of bed because there was another phone call. When I got to the phone both my mother and father said hello. They were both on the line. I guessed somebody was upstairs and somebody was downstairs. "We had another episode with your brother," my father said. I was just listening. My mother said he was going to have to go away. She started crying. She said that Doctor Waynik told them he was a danger to himself.

"Because he couldn't play my records?" I said.

That seemed to surprise them. "He has your records. It's not your records," my father said.

I stood there holding the phone. He was nine. The year before he'd been playing with his toy trucks.

"Can I talk to him?" I said.

"I got some more 45s," he said when he got on the line. "Dad took me."

"What'd you get?" I asked. He told me. I raked my fingernails across my neck. "Those're good," I told him.

"You like them?" he said.

I told him I did. Especially the MacArthur Park one.

He seemed happy about that. "You can play them when you get back," he said.

"You all right?" the Camp Director asked me. He'd come out of his inner office, where he had Chris. He looked at my neck. He didn't leave until I nodded.

I was holding the dial part of the phone in front of me. I'd lifted it off the desk but there wasn't much reach on the cord. "You there?" my brother said.

"Yeah," I said. "You gonna be okay?"

He started crying. "They're gonna put me somewhere," he said. "I'm scared."

"Oh, Georgie," I said.

And what I could have said then was: I'll come home and we'll talk and you'll feel like somebody understands and you won't have to hit yourself or throw everything you have around the room. Or you can come up and see me, come up and visit, come up and be a part of the worst camp anybody's ever seen. Or let's keep our records together. Let's keep them in your room. Let's make a list of all the ones we've got. Or I'm sorry I make it harder and I have trouble too and maybe if we take walks or get a hobby we can figure out how to get through this. Or put Daddy on, you can't go away, you have to stay, we have to stay together. But what I did was the kind of thing you'd do and the kind of thing you've done: I felt bad for him and for myself and I went on with my week and then with my summer and I started telling my story to whoever would listen. And my story was: *I survived camp. I survived my brother. I survived my own bad feelings. Love me for being so sad about it. Love me for knowing what I did. Love me for being in the lifeboat after everyone else went under.* And my story made me feel better and it made me feel worse. And it worked.

Sans Farine

My father, Jean-Baptiste Sanson, had christened in the church of Saint-Laurent two children: a daughter, who married Pierre Hérisson, executioner of Melun, and a son, myself. After my mother's death he remarried, his second wife from a family of executioners in the province of Touraine. Together they produced twelve children, eight of whom survived, six of whom were boys. All six eventually registered in the public rolls as executioners, my half brothers beginning their careers by assisting their father and then myself in the city of Paris.

My name is Charles-Henri Sanson, known to many throughout this city as the Keystone of the Revolution, and known to the rabble as Sans Farine, in reference to my use of emptied bran sacks to hold the severed heads. I was named for Charles Sanson, former adventurer and soldier of the King and until 1668 executioner of Cherbourg and Caudebec-en-Caux. My father claimed he was descended from Sanson de Longval and that our family coat of arms derived from either the First or Second Crusade. Its escutcheon represents another play on our name: a cracked bell and the motto *San son:* without sound.

You want to know—all France wants to know—what takes place in the executioner's mind: the figure who before the Revolution wielded the double-bladed axe and double-handed sword and who branded, burned, and broke on the wheel all who came before him. The figure who now slides heads through what they call the Republican Window on the guillotine. Does he eat? Does he sleep? Do his smiles freeze the blood? Is he kind to those he kills? Does he touch his wife on days he works? Does he reach for you with blood-rimmed fingernails? Did he spring full-blown from a black pit to send batch after batch through the guillotine?

Becoming shrill, my wife calls it, whenever I get too agitated in my own defense.

"What struck people's minds above all else," Livy, the great Roman, wrote in his *History* on Brutus's sacrifice of his own sons for the good of the Republic, "is that his function as consul imposed on the father the task of punishing his sons, and that his unbendingness compelled him personally to order the execution, the very sight of which was not spared him." In Guérin's rendering of the scene, the hero turns away but does not blanch. Standing before it in the old Royal Academy with Anne-Marie, I told her that perhaps this is the way we attain the sublime: by our fierce devotion to the required. She was not able to agree.

I am a good Catholic. The people's judges hand out their sentences, and mine is the task of insuring that their words become incarnate. I am the instrument, and it is justice that strikes. I feel the same remorse as anyone required to be present at an execution.

Before the Revolution, justice was apportioned and discharged in the name of the King, who ruled by divine right as one of God's implements. Punishment of malefactors was God's will and therefore earned for his sovereign minister God's grace and esteem. But in the eyes of most, that grace and esteem did not extend as far as the sovereign's handservant. Before the Revolution, daughters of executioners were forbidden to marry outside the profession. When their girls came of age, such families had to display on their doors a yellow affidavit clarifying the family's trade, and acknowledging the taint in their bloodline. Letters of commission and payments were not passed into their hands but dropped before them. They were required to live at the southern ends of towns, and their houses had to be painted red.

Before the Revolution, a woman with whom I dined at an inn

demanded I be made to appear in court to apologize for having shared with her a dinner table. She petitioned that executioners be directed to wear a particular badge or color upon their coats or singlets so that all would know their profession. Before the Revolution, our children were allowed no playmates but one another.

For lunch today there was egg soup with lemon juice and broth, cock's comb, a marrowbone, chicken fried in bread crumbs, jelly, apricots, bread, and fennel comfits. Clearing the table, Anne-Marie reminisced about a holiday we took when the children were small. When she speaks to me, she holds the family before us like a pleasing little stove. At first she was able to treat this terrible time as a brigand unable to trespass upon the better world she bore within.

With children, everything and nothing registers. My earliest memory is of the house outside Paris, and the height of the manure pile, and the muck dropped by the household geese. I remember flies whenever one went outside. I remember my mother's calm voice and associate it with needlework. She was fond of saying that I had no ideas of grandeur and that she would wish that to continue. My grandmother always chided me for losing even a crumb of my bread, since, as she put it, I couldn't make for myself even that. My father was a quiet man who, when it came to my understanding the world, resolved that his little boy should become a person capable of self-sufficiency, so he allowed me to negotiate my own passage through that household. I was perceived to be headstrong but inhibited. I was sent away at an early age and then pitched from school to school, since the moment my classmates uncovered my family's profession, life became unbearable again. I wrote my mother a series of supplications outlining my misery and pleading for a response. In a cheerless chapel in a school in Rouen—my fourth in as many years—I received my father's letter informing me of her death.

He remarried; the house was repopulated with half brothers

and sisters; I stayed away at my schools. I matured into a beanstalk whose expressions excited pity on the street. My teachers knew me as dutiful, alert, frugal, and friendless: a nonentity with ambitions. I was often cold and known for my petitions to sit nearer the room's hearth. I volunteered for small errands so that in solitude I might gather the strength to face the rest of the day. I wrote to myself in my notebooks that I felt my bleak present within me and ached to my bones with wondering if loneliness would always be the measure of my days.

Anne-Marie was a market gardener's daughter in Montmartre, her father's establishment a luncheon stop on my infrequent visits home from school. She was his eldest, born the same day as myself, and when we first conversed I imagined that we had loved each other from that date, unawares.

Her first act in my presence was to scratch at a rash on her foot until chided by her father entering the room with the roast. She visited the water closet, and back at the table returned my gaze as if examining a distant coastline. She was still chewing a bit of carrot. From that first meeting I have perched perpetually, in a kind of dreamy distress, on the very edge of relieving my longings. Her lovely large mouth and deep-set eyes with their veiled expression, and her child's posture have been my harbor and receding horizon. Her seat, that first luncheon, was in the sun, and her skin was so fine I could see the circulation of her blood. When she blushed, I could feel the warmth.

I contrived to visit more often. She confided her various sadnesses, her mother having led a life regulated by an intricate and dispiriting routine, much of which centered itself on the needs of her younger sister. Her father's health and general cheerlessness prevented him from finding solace in anything. But even in that company, she found the resources to engage, with animation, in any society offered her, as if the seas that swamped other shipping beat upon her little boat in vain.

With her I tended toward passionate recollection of my own imagined virtues. Without her my private life had been a record of uninterrupted emptiness and misery. Her first letter to me upon my return to school concluded, "I seem to have written you a newspaper instead of a note, as was my intention. My conduct is most mysterious. Well. Until later—"

She saw in me a perceptive enough boy, self-educated in a variety of disciplines, from astronomy to law, from medicine to agronomy. I was tall. I was charitable, and kind to the poor. I played the cello, and seemed someone with whom a good home could be constructed. Her family was poor enough that an executioner's son was still a possibility, but respected enough that she was as good a match as my family would find. For her, marriage to someone like me meant renouncing vanities she had never possessed, and for which she had no desire.

Soon after our marriage I related to her the story of my first execution, a story designed to elicit her pity. From the age of eleven, whenever I was home from school, I had been my father's assistant. When I was sixteen he retired and left me alone on the scaffold with a few of his assistants, now mine. A man named Mongeot was to be bludgeoned and then broken on the wheel for having murdered his mistress's husband. His mistress was to be held under guard and made to witness what transpired. A snowstorm had enveloped the scaffold, coating it in a kind of sleet, and I stood in the wind clutching my collar against the wet while my mulatto did the bludgeoning. The man's mistress shrieked and clawed at her guards' faces and tore at her hair. It took Mongeot two hours to die. I'd worn the wrong boots, and my feet were soaked through and freezing. I could not see for my weeping and misheld the lever when we were in the act of breaking his legs. My grandmother, bundled in robes and representing the family, lost patience and shouted at me. The crowd hissed and showered me with contempt.

Anne-Marie pitied me for such stories but after an expression of sympathy maintained a wary silence. Our newlyweds' happiness was then colored by a kind of quiet. There were other stories I didn't share with her. After Mongeot, a man named Damiens who had tried to stab the King was sentenced to be drawn and quartered. No one had been quartered in France since Ravaillac, more than a century before. I went to my father, who said he had no advice to give. I offered to resign my commission, but my grandmother summoned my uncle, executioner of Reims, to steady me. Our assistants were to handle the preliminaries, and on the appointed day drank until they could barely stand. They tottered between the instruments while the crowd jeered at their fumblings and shouted abuse. The hand that had held the knife was severed and boiling oil and lead were poured into the wound. The man's screams were such that we could not hear each others' instructions. Then the horses only dislocated his limbs without separating them from the trunk. The executioner's sword lodged in one of his shoulder joints. I had to run and find an axe.

Some three months after the fall of the Bastille, the National Assembly took up the issue of renovating the penal code, and in the middle of those proceedings, Dr. Joseph-Ignace Guillotin, deputy from Paris and professor of anatomy on the Faculty of Medicine, set forth his argument favoring a fixed punishment for the same crimes, regardless of the convicted's rank and estate. He reminded the Assembly of the infamies of the unenlightened past and proposed a less barbaric method of capital punishment: automatic decapitation by a mechanism yet to be developed. A Jesuit, he'd left the order, choosing a ministry of the body over that of the soul. He wanted the machinery of execution to be fearful but the death to be easy. There was enthusiasm for his proposal among the revolutionaries: a capital punishment that was mercifully quick and democratic would mark another step toward the regeneration of society. It was pointed out that while the executioner's sword might require two or three strokes, with a machine the condemned man would not be kept waiting. Lally-Tollendal's name was resurrected: some years before, I'd proven unable to dispatch him, requiring my father to take over the blade.

After the usual delay the measure was adopted in the new penal code, and the next challenge became how to cut off all those heads. I was invited to submit a memorandum sharing my views, in which I explained that in any multiple execution, the sword is not fit to perform after the first, but must be either reground and sharpened or replaced by an impractical succession of swords, depending on the number condemned. I also pointed out that for an execution by sword to arrive at the result prescribed by the law, the executioner must be consistently skillful and the condemned at least momentarily steadfast, and that in the event of multiple executions, there would be the issue of blood in such quantities that it would affect even the most intrepid of those to be executed, so that it would be indispensable to find some means by which the condemned could be secured for the blow, and the public order protected.

Dr. Guillotin had begun to lose interest in his idea, but Dr. Antoine Louis, secretary of the Academy of Surgeons, engaged a German pianomaker to build the prototype. There was some diffi-culty finding men to do the job. They had to be made exempt from signing the usual working papers so that their identities could remain a secret.

The result is what my assistants call the Great Machine. At the heart of its design are two uprights five meters high and fifty cen-timeters apart, which flank a blade weighing seven kilos. Bolted to the top of the blade is a thirty-kilogram iron bar to heighten the force of its descent. The assembly falls from top to bottom in three quarters of a second. The cutting edge is slanted so that the blow, as it penetrates into the parts it divides, acts as a saw of lightning efficiency. The blade lands at the head of a narrow tablelike arrangement for the condemned. From a distance the whole thing has the austerity of a diagram. The grooves are rubbed down with soap before each use. Disassembled, it's stored in a shed known as the Widow's House.

My sons and I supervised its first test at the Bicêtre Hospital on the outskirts of Paris. Before us and the assembled dignitaries Dr.

Louis beheaded a bundle of straw, a live sheep, and several corpses, the last of which required three tries, so it was decided the height of the uprights would be extended, and weight added to the blade. At that very first demonstration, I was heard to wonder aloud whether the machine's very efficiency would prove to be a source of regret.

So on the 22nd of March in the year 1792, the Abbé Chappe bestowed his invention, the telegraph, upon the Assembly. And on the 25th, Dr. Guillotin and Dr. Louis's machine was inaugurated. The culprit was strapped facedown to the plank, which was then tilted to the horizontal and run forward on grooves until his neck slid onto the lunette, a semicircular block. The block was not struck by the falling blade but grazed at high speed, so that the head was planed off. In an eye-blink it leapt seventeen or eighteen inches from the trunk. For some the head was gone before the eye could trace the blow. It became clear that the minimum size for the basket must be that of an infant's bathtub. The executioner's role in the proceedings consisted of giving a little tug on a lever. The crowd saw the blade but not the hand that moved it. Much time was consumed afterward with the mess. Four buckets of water alone were used on the grooves and block.

I used to have a constitution able to endure labor that might have hamstrung a team of oxen. Now my complaints include dizziness, inflammation of the eyes, colic, and rheumatic pains.

What talk I have with Anne-Marie occurs in the early morning before the workday begins. On the way out of our little courtyard I'll pass her hanging laundry to dry, if it's warm enough, or plucking salad herbs into a basket. Across from us a shop sells brushes of every manner and use. Its proprietor is a drunk and in all weather slumps beside its door in an old wreck of an iron chair. We can hear the knife grinder's bell as he makes his rounds.

For the last three months I've approached her heartbroken

with the misfortune I helped author, because in August at the execution of three men accused of forging promissory notes, our youngest boy, Gabriel, fell when exhibiting one of the heads, fracturing his skull and dying before my eyes. He was twenty-one. There'd always been in our family puzzled concern about him, since he'd kept hidden his aspirations and inner life. All we knew was that he was great for peeling oranges when they were in season. In response to interrogatives he stroked his upper lip with his forefinger and seemed to wait for the intelligent part of the question to emerge. He'd wanted to try his hand at another profession, and Anne-Marie had wished the same for him. But I'd reminded her of his cousin's experience of having apprenticed himself to a locksmith only to find that no one would patronize their shop. The subject had been dropped. Then Gabriel had offered to join the National Guard, to which his older brother had responded by asking if he thought himself too refined for the family business. His uncles hadn't been even that kind. I had done my best to comfort him but had also requested that he remain a realist about his future.

That morning the clouds had poured forth rain, the sky churning as if with empyrean seas. The wood up on the scaffold was slick and the cobblestones below greasy with mud. Our hair was whipped by the wind. There'd been the usual silence as the executioner had walked about the platform, while each assistant tended to a special task, one assistant handling the strapping to the plank, one seeing to the remaining condemned, one adjusting the heads on the lunette while wearing a waxed ankle-length apron. Each assistant is given a chance at one point or another to display one of the heads.

Gabriel I usually assigned to the remaining condemned. He moved about his responsibilities like a child resignedly attending a new school. The third head pitched from its lost shoulders. It was his turn to reach his arm down into the basket. I could not see from where I stood whether his expression as he held it up by the hair was one of fascinated horror or queasy forbearance or distracted indifference. The rain and the three men's blood made the front of the scaffold slick as soap. There was no rail.

Perseus hoisted Medusa's head. Judith, Holofernes's. David, Goliath's. The head warns of the consequences of violating the sovereign peace. Held by the hair and presented at the scaffold, it represents the government's discharge of its promise to maintain order. An executioner's reputation depends to a large extent upon his efficiency and elan with that display. Doing his best to manifest the head to as much of the crowd as he could, and failing to look where he put his feet, our Gabriel slipped and split his head open on the cobblestones. The head he'd been holding scattered the crowd. We carried him back to the house in the cart that had brought the condemned.

It's said that, losing his wife and crazed with grief, Robespierre's father abandoned his four children, the eldest being only seven, and traveled in turn through England and the German states, eventually dying in Munich. And so young Robespierre became at seven the implacable and unhappy figure he remains today. All through the early morning hours of that terrible night, Anne-Marie lay like one of the Furies on her bed and would not be consoled. I was not allowed into the room.

A week passed before she addressed me. Her misery was a well from which her spirit refused to surface. I saw only stiffness and mistrust when I got too near. All her gestures seemed devitalized, as if viewed in dim candlelight. If not for her capacity for work, she would have seemed imprisoned in a perpetual exhaustion.

It was a busy time for the executioner. She observed without comment my unimpaired predilection for order, my consistency of demeanor, and my undiminished capacities of concentration.

We both remembered a time, after the imprisonment of the King, when I'd been of a sudden possessed by an ungovernable rage with all of those in power who had brought our nation to her present catastrophe, and had resolved to leave Paris. Gabriel in particular had loved the idea. But my passion had subsided, and

I'd understood just a bit of what such a decision would involve. Was everyone to abandon his post every time the country took a turn for the worse? Was it left to each servant of the state to decide which laws he would carry out, and which he would not? Did anyone but the highest ministers have sufficient information on which to base their opinions?

Yesterday there was a hard frost and we woke to discover the waste plug had burst and covered the corridor in filth. Some of it had already frozen, and we scraped and chipped at it in the early morning darkness. The smell from what hadn't frozen drove us back. It was unclear to me, working beside my wife, which in me was stronger: hatred of my profession or hatred of myself. I asked her opinion and she didn't answer until later when making her toilet, when she remarked that she found my self-contempt understandable, given the minuteness of my self-examinations.

Even with my family, she told me as she served my supper before leaving the room, I craved the advantage of invisibility. My supper turned out to be beef and cabbage and runner beans.

I eat alone. I sit alone. Without her I have no intimate friend. No affectionate relations. For three months she's remained close-buttoned and oblique, her expressions lawyers' expressions. Some nights I sleep, when Heaven has pity on me.

The night before the waste plug, she woke to my weeping. She remained on her back and addressed the ceiling. She told it she'd overheard a boy on the rue de Rennes tell his wet-nurse that he'd gone to see a guillotining, and oh, how the poor executioner had suffered. Her tone prevented any response.

She knows that the exclusion of our profession from society is not founded on prejudice alone. The law requires executions, but compels no one to become an executioner.

So now I carry an emptiness with me like the grief of a home-sick child. I understood my wife's misery and, under the compulsion of duty, added to it. Each night I take a little brandy, hot

lemonade, and toast. My belly is in constant ferment. I'm a pio-
neer in a Great New Age in which I don't believe. My profession
has grown over us like a malevolent wood.

Another frost this morning. In our window box, frozen daisies.

The executioner has the uncontested title to all clothing and jew-
elry found on the men and women put to death. He pays no taxes.
The condemned are subcontracted to him by the nation. The
trade in cadavers with the medical profession brings in some additional revenue. But in terms of expenses there's all household costs
plus salaries and repairs to the carriages and feed for the horses
and any number of other constant vexations. And of course the
expectation that the machine will be maintained and housed. My
father wore on execution days a brocaded red singlet with the gal-
lows embroidered across his chest in black and gold thread. In
bright sun onlookers could make out a heavily worked panel of
darker red satin along his spine. His culottes were of the finest silk.
What do I own? A coat of black cloth, a satin waistcoat from an
old-clothes shop, a pair of black breeches, a pair of serge breeches,
two clothes brushes, four shirts, four cravats, four handkerchiefs.
Two pairs of stockings, two pairs of shoes, and a hat.

This morning in the courtyard, Anne-Marie was doing no
work at all. The sun was out but it was very cold. Clouds issued
from the mouth of our sleeping neighbor in his iron chair. She sat
with her back to the plaster, wrapping and rewrapping a shawl. I
tucked it behind her and she thanked me. We sat for half an hour.
Sometimes when addressed she seemed as if she were alone. I told
her that I had stopped for wine on the way home the previous
evening, and had overindulged. She responded that it was probably a part of my unconquerable rejection of anything that might
cause me to think. And what was it I should be thinking about? I
wanted to know. The world and my place in it, she said. And what
was my place in it? I asked, and touched her cheek. She stood,
composing her carriage. Around me now she carries herself like

the Holy Sacrament. She returned to the house. We've had two weeks of her working in silence, the Austere Isolate, while the rest of us come and go, playing off one another like members of a mournful choral trio.

Perhaps, I told her at dinner, my curse from God was that I lacked that stone tabernacle within the soul in which I could treasure absolute truths. We were having soup, skate, and artichokes. She answered, after some thought, that I was killing her, but that I was also teaching her how to die.

We kept to ourselves the rest of the evening. At one point we had to consult over the household's ledger books.

Ask any soldier what his profession entails. He'll answer that he kills men. No one flees his company for that reason. No one refuses to eat with him. And whom does he kill? Innocent people who are only serving their country.

Together Anne-Marie and I have negotiated, like wood chips in a waterfall, the Revolution itself, with its shocks and transformations; the trial and condemnation of the King; his execution; and all the deprivations of the war with the allied powers. We covered our heads and hurried past each disaster, sometimes speaking of it afterward, sometimes not. The poor King's troubles began when he was dragged into the unhappy affair with America. Advantage was taken of his youth. In financing his support of America's revolution, he fell victim to that belief of monarchs that expenditure should not be governed by revenue, but revenue instead by expenditure. Then nature provided its additional burden: the summer of 1788 and its unprecedented drought. We saw starvation in our own neighborhood. Suddenly everyone was busy holding forth on the subject of just which radical changes needed to be made, each to his own attentive audience.

So events took their course, thanks to that crowd of minor clerks and lawyers and unknown writers who went about rabble-rousing in clubs and cafés. From such crumbling mortar was the Edifice of Freedom built. After the Bastille's fall de Launay was decapitated by a pocketknife used to saw through his neck.

Foulon, accused of plotting the famine, had the mouth of his severed head stuffed with grass. It was proclaimed that the great skittle row of privilege and royalism had been struck to maximum effect, revealing a newly cleared space for civic responsibility. The treasury was refilling, the corn mills turning, the traitors in full flight, the priests trampled, the aristocracy extinct, the patriots triumphant. The King did nothing, apparently believing the more extreme sentiments to be a fever that had to run its course.

Anne-Marie took up needlework, then abandoned it as unsatisfying.

The National Assembly had announced only the abolition of royalty. Everyone saw clearly what needed to be razed or pillaged, but no one agreed on what to erect in its place. Not a man near the wheels of power was equal to the task at hand, with ever greater tasks impending. The more radical, sensing conspiracies, wanted evermore surveillance, evermore wide-ranging arrests, evermore extremity. The maintenance of civic virtue, they insisted, was impossible without bloodshed. They learned the hard way that *government* was impossible if the bloodshed was not monopolized and managed.

First the King's Swiss Guards were slaughtered defending him at the Hôtel de Ville. Some were thrown living into a bonfire. Others from windows onto a forest of pikes. My assistant Legros, passing the Tuileries, saw furniture together with corpses being pitched from the upper stories into the courtyard. He met us on our way home, and Anne-Marie and I had to wait at each city gate so he could shout "Vive la nation!" like a good sansculotte, thereby diffusing the murderousness of those roaming the streets around us. Four times we were stopped and made to swear an oath to the new regime. At the entrance to our courtyard we found half a corpse, which I dragged out of the archway by the feet.

Then in September it was deemed necessary to weed out royalist sympathizers after the Prussians had enjoyed some success against our armies, and people's tribunals, set up in each of the prisons, began handing prisoners over to crowds gathered outside with butchers' implements and bludgeons. In four days thirteen hundred—one half of all the prisoners in Paris—were massacred, including the Mme de Lamballe, whose body was dragged behind a wagon by two cords tied to her feet while her head was carried on a pike to where the royal family was imprisoned, so that it might be made to bow to the Queen. One of the killers was said to have used a carpenter's saw. Each neighborhood seemed to have its own mob of National Guards and sansculottes, a few of them mounted, on their horses bearing fishwives and bacchantes, filthy and bloody and drunken, their clothes all at sea. At the Quai d'Orsay hung a whole row of men mangled and lanterned, their feet continually set in motion by people brushing past. Garden terraces were ashine each morning with smashed bottles in the sunlight. It was said that Mme de Lamballe's head was found wedged upside down on a cabaret bar and surrounded by glasses, as if serving as a carafe. She'd been famous for her fragile nerves and her penchant for fainting at the slightest unpleasantness.

As was the King. We followed his trial through the newspapers and broadsheets. Talking with Henri-François, our eldest, was like conversing with a rock garden, so Anne-Marie was left with me. During meals we were circumspect because Legros shared our table, but at night in bed some of our old intimacy returned. She argued the King's side: perhaps the mildest monarch to ever fill the throne had been precipitated from it because of his refusal to adopt the harshness of his predecessors. Throughout the proceedings the Jacobins—men and women alike—ate ices and bawled from the galleries for the death penalty. Legendre proposed to divide the accused into as many pieces as there were departments, so as to mail a bit of him to each. My wife was at a loss, reading such news: where did such ferocity originate? I had no answer for her. Just as the King had no ally in the Assembly willing to risk his own life on his sovereign's behalf. Having refused to become the patron of any one side, our helpless monarch had become the object of hatred for all.

Robespierre finally doomed him with the argument that if the

King was absolved, what became of the Revolution? If he was innocent, then the defenders of liberty were malefactors, the royalists the true inheritors of France. To those who said that the state had no right to execute the King, he countered that the Revolution had been "illegal" from the outset. Did the deputies want a Revolution without a revolution?

We were both awake the entire night before the execution. The day before, I'd been authorized to oversee the digging of a trench ten feet deep, along with the procurement of three fifty-pound sacks of quicklime. The machine was moved to the Place de la Révolution, near the pedestal from which the bronze equestrian statue of the King's father had been hacked down.

I had asked the prosecutor to relieve me of my responsibilities in the King's case. That request had been denied. I then asked for more detailed instructions: would the King require a special carriage? Would I accompany him alone, or with my assistants? I was informed that there would be a special, closed carriage, and that I was to await the King on the scaffold. The latter instruction I understood to suggest that I myself was suspected of royalist tendencies.

I asked Legros to rouse me at five, the same hour that the King's valet, Clery, would be waking him. I heard his step outside my door and called that I was awake before he could knock. "Please don't do this," Anne-Marie whispered from her side of the bed. Her fist pounded lightly on my rib. But knowing the danger in which we already found ourselves, she only held the pillow over her face while I began to dress.

Clery reported to me later that the King's children had been rocking in agony as he'd prepared to depart under guard. For the previous hour they had consoled themselves with the time they had left together, the little Dauphin with his head between his father's knees.

Would the population rise in revolt against such an act? Had the allies planted agents in order to effect a rescue? These questions and more terrified the deputies, who ordered each of the city's gates barricaded and manned, and an escort of twelve hundred guards provided for the King's coach. The streets along the route to the scaffold were lined with army regulars. The windows were shuttered on pain of death.

The crowd throughout was mostly quiet. The King when he arrived seemed to derive much consolation from the company of his confessor. A heavy snowfall muffled the accoutrements of the carriage.

Before mounting the steps, he asked that his hands be kept free. I looked to Santerre, commander of the Guard, who denied the request. The King's collar was unfastened, his shirt opened, and his hair cut away from his neck. In the icy air he looked at me and then out at the citizenry, where the vast majority, because of weakness, became implicated in a crime that they would forever attribute to others.

I was assisted by my eldest son and Legros. That morning I had received absolution from a nonjuring priest—the new term for one who has not yet forsworn his allegiance to the church. I had checked and rechecked the sliding supports on the uprights, and resharpened the blade. The King tried to address the people over the drum roll but was stopped by Santerre, who told him they'd brought him here to die, not to harangue the populace. Henri-François strapped him to the plank. Legros slid him forward. He died in the Catholic faith in which he had been raised. In accordance with the custom, the executor of justice then found the head in the basket and displayed it to the people. He lifted it by the hair, raising it above shoulder height. He circled the scaffold twice. The head sprinkled the wood below as it was swung around. There was an extended silence followed by a few scattered cries of "Long live the Republic."

The executioner did not accompany the wicker basket to the cemetery. He was told that it fell from the cart near the trench, where the crowd had then torn it to pieces. He ordered more expiatory Masses said on his own behalf. He made certain that the King's blade was never used again.

And he also made certain that his wife never discovered his trade in packets of the King's hair: his eldest son's idea. Though for months afterward she saw the broadsheets of his hand holding the King's severed head over the caption *May this impure blood water our fields.*

Thereafter there seemed to be no space anywhere in the country for moderation. All dangers and all proposals conceived to counter them partook of the dire, the drastic, and the headlong. The nation was in peril, and what constitutional safeguards remained had to make way for emergency measures. Danton claimed that if a sufficiently severe Revolutionary tribunal had been constituted that September, there would have been no massacres. The government's discipline had to be terrible or the people themselves would again spread terror. A tribunal empanelled to punish with death all assaults on the indivisibility of the Republic could operate, as he put it, with an irreducible minimum of evil.

Anne-Marie by then was a wraith, disappearing from rooms, a cough the only evidence of her presence in the house. One night she didn't come to table at all. Legros had to fetch our dinner from the kitchen. Henri-François informed me that she'd had an altercation with another woman at the bakery about her place in the breadline. He was no help with details. I waited while together we watched the shoveling motion of his spoon. Finally I asked if she'd been hurt, and he shrugged, saying, "Well, she got the bread."

I found her sorting through potatoes in our root cellar. Many had already sprouted. The skin under her eyes was blue.

"Are you well?" I asked.

"I'm unable to eat," she told me. "I'm sure it will pass."

"Are you injured?" I asked.

"I'm sound in body and mind," she answered. As if to prove her point, she showed me a potato. We could hear someone above us who'd returned to the kitchen for a second helping from the pot.

We said nothing for some minutes, sharing the close darkness. The damp smell of the dirt was pleasant. I sorted potatoes with her.

"It's not assumed that the wife of the Executor of State Judgments will be found brawling in the street," I joked, gently.

"You thought you married a lady," she said.

"I only meant that this was not a time for public demonstrations," I told her.

"They know you by now," she said. "You're as suited to take a hand in political faction as you are to arrive on the moon."

But she underestimated me. I attended commune sessions when I saw fit, ready to speak if the occasion warranted it. The Law of Suspects was promulgated that September to speed the work of terrorizing foes of the Revolution. Suspects of any sort could now be denounced and detained by local committees formed on the spot and unfettered by the sorts of legal concerns that had no doubt already allowed too many culprits in league with our enemies to escape. This category of suspects extended first to all foreigners residing in France; then to those who speculated in any way with foreign currencies; next to those who spoke too coldly of their enthusiasm for the Revolution; and finally to those who, while having done nothing in particular against the cause, hadn't seemed to do much for it, either. A prisoner might be accused at nine, find himself in court at ten, receive sentencing at two, and lose his life at four. Anyone's neighbor might be the allied agent already at work to engineer famine or defeat. The Law of Suspects was a reminder to the populace that a nation at war might have to exterminate liberty in order to save it. Prisons like the Conciergerie tripled their detainees. In some rooms the sewage fumes were so strong that torches brought into them went out.

By such measures idlers and thugs had now become the People. Histrionic patriotism was the only requisite for public speaking, so those especially compromised by shameful pasts rushed to demonstrate their worthiness by addressing their Popular Societies, agitating in all corners, disrupting the courts and trials, searching homes themselves, denouncing and condemning and turning France into one boundless parade ground of calumny. The solution for all national troubles was understood to be an unflagging austerity of purpose in the form of an evermore passionate embrace of ruthlessness. There've been mass cannonadings in Lyon. Carrier, the Revolutionary representative at Nantes, sealed hundreds into the holds of barges and sank them in the Loire in what he called "vertical deportations." Saint-Just announced that the Republic consisted of the extermination of everything that opposed it. The Marquis de Bry offered to organize a force he called the Tyrannicides: freedom fighters dispatched to foreign capitals to assassinate heads of state or anyone else the Committee might stipulate.

"The People make their demands," Henri-François remarked one night at dinner, apropos of our ever-increasing workload. His hair fell across his forehead like a scrubbing mat. He always seemed to be nursing a grim new resentment against his mother.

"Their inner lives have been made bestial," Anne-Marie said to him, after having been silent the entire meal.

"That's not entirely what she means," I told Legros, who observed her as though she were a mouse in the grain supply.

"That's exactly what she means," he answered, with some affability, and then went on with his meal.

I drove my assistants day and night, but we could not master our burden. Lethal misadventures and irregularities compounded daily as batch after batch moved out of the tumbrils and into the baskets. One Tuesday we dispatched twenty-two condemned in twenty-nine minutes. Pastry merchants divided their attention between the scaffold and their customers. Friends asked friends in the crowd if they were staying and were told, no, not today—they had things to do. So much blood ran down the front of the platform supports that boots there sank into the supersaturated earth as if into a mire. One woman in line among the condemned told me that the lunette's wet wood looked like it would be unpleasant on the front of her neck. When the blade dropped, her body jerked in the straps, as if abruptly trying to find a more comfortable position.

In our home, with Legros and Henri-François sent away on an errand, we received the Sacrament from our nonjuring priest.

"They're putting the Queen on trial," Anne-Marie told me one morning, once the priest had left. She said that he had confirmed the rumor. In one stroke she seemed to have resuscitated all of her old intensities. She crossed and recrossed the room. She wrung her hands in a series of nervous contractions. She was beside herself with certainty that the Queen would be condemned.

"Not necessarily," I told her, trying to get my bearings.

"You have to resign. You have to withdraw. You have to refuse to have any part in this," she said.

"There's nothing to refuse, yet," I told her.

"You have to refuse," she cried.

I told her I would attend as much of the trial as I could. On those days I did attend, she demanded a full recounting. I spared her very little. In those chambers, the Queen was the Austrian she-wolf, the arch-tigress, the cannibal who wanted to roast alive all the poor Parisians. It was claimed she'd bitten open the cartridges for the Swiss Guards in their defense of the royal family to help speed their slaughter of the oncharging patriots. She sat alone in the dock, a childlike figure further diminished by her incarceration. Her eyesight had begun to weaken and her hair to turn white. She looked twenty years beyond her age. She'd been made to reply to accusations of incestuous relations with the Dauphin. The poor boy had been made to parrot unspeakable things, and his testimony was read back to her.

Everything about the Dauphin injured Anne-Marie. She knew a wife of the assistant jailer and learned the boy had just passed his eighth birthday alone. Apparently he was chronically ill and had been ministered to by his mother with unceasing tenderness until he'd been made a ward of the Republic and dragged to a cell immediately beneath hers, from which she could hear him shrieking in his terror and loneliness. He was left to himself for weeks at a time. The shoemaker appointed to be his personal jailer looked in only every so often. Even he found the boy's cries hard to take. But he also made him wear the red bonnet and sing the carmagnole and the Marseillaise and to blaspheme God from his windows.

My wife lay awake nights, mute with suffering as she considered various aspects of his plight, until she burst out with wailing, jolting me from my half drowse. When I embraced her she demanded a promise that I wouldn't be a part of this. She needed to be sure that I wouldn't be a part of this. I wouldn't be a part of this, I assured her, and reapplied my embrace.

Only weeks after the inauguration of the machine, the medical community found itself grappling with the controversy concerning the survival of feeling and consciousness in the separated head. Did the head hear the voices of the crowd? Did it feel itself dying in the basket? Could it see the light of day above it?

The question became more urgent following Charlotte Corday's execution for the assassination of Marat, when Legros, apparently communing with his inner brute, saw fit to slap the severed head while he was displaying it. And the face, hanging by the hair, showed the most unequivocal signs of anger and indignation in response. There was an uproar from those in front of the scaffold who could see it, and afterward many medical eminences were interviewed on the phenomenon for the newspapers.

Eventually I was asked to assist a Dr. Seguret, professor of anatomy, who'd been commissioned to study the problem. He set up an atelier on the same square as the machine and my assistants delivered to it a total of forty heads. We exposed two—a man's and a woman's—to the sun's rays in his back courtyard. Their eyelids immediately closed of their own accord, and their faces convulsed in agony. One head's tongue, pricked with a lancet, withdrew, the face contorting. Another's eyes turned in the direction of our voices. One head, a juring priest's named Gardien, dumped into the same sack with the head of one of his enemies, had bitten it with such ferocity that it took us both to separate them.

Other faces were inert. Seguret pinched them on the cheeks, inserted brushes soaked in ammonia into their nostrils, and held lighted candles to their staring eyes without generating movement or contractions of any sort.

His report was suppressed, and he refused to have any more to do with such experiments, or with me.

"What have you decided?" Anne-Marie took to asking each day as the Queen's trial dragged itself on. In addition to all of the other charges, there were the letters abroad, many of which had been intercepted. All military defeats were being blamed on her treachery. Her son's illness on her sexual demands. As proof of the latter, his hernia was displayed.

In bed with my weeping Anne-Marie, I tell her I see no way out: the letters demonstrate conspiracy, and for all other charges, the accusers invent the evidence they lack. We must be resigned to God's will and summon the strength to prepare ourselves to endure the terrible stroke.

"*Your* terrible stroke," she responds. "You *must not* do this. You *understand* that."

But she knows, I tell her, that God alone can alter the course of events at this point. It's His mercy for which we must ask, even as we submit to His decrees.

"I'm not appealing to you to save her," she answers. "You know what I'm requesting."

A few nights later, lying beside me in the darkness, she palms my cheeks and moves her face so close that her lips graze mine.

"Listen to me," she says. "Don't dismiss me like this." She moves our bodies to their newlyweds' position. But then she says nothing else.

Henri-François brings us the news as we're sitting down to some pigeon, red currants, apricots, and wine: the tribunal, according to the declaration of the jury, and in compliance with the indictment of the public prosecutor, has condemned the said Marie Antoinette, called Lorraine d'Autriche, widow of Louis Capet, to the pain of death, the judgment to be carried out in the Place de la Révolution, its dictates printed and exhibited throughout the Republic.

On the appointed day, my wife is missing when I awake. Our drunken neighbor across the courtyard claims not to have seen her. She's nowhere to be found when I return. The Queen flinches upon seeing the open cart in which she'll ride. She explains she'd been hoping for the enclosed carriage that carried her husband. She apologizes for treading on my foot as she climbs the steps.

My wife does not return that evening, or the next. Henri-François notes a missing trunk but mentions nothing else, contemptuous of my agony. Legros takes over the cooking. In the wee hours I occupy my fireside chair, swigging wine. The future unfolds in the flames like a gameboard dotted with opponents' pieces. I envision new laws abolishing the accused's right to any defense; the frightened seeking to outpace one another with the zeal and homicidal efficiency of their patriotism; and prisoners condemned in groups, identities muddled in the confusion, as sons die in the name of fathers, alongside entire families decimated by misspellings and clerical errors. At the scaffold, a nightmarish constancy, with only the actors changing. Chemists. Street singers. Fifteen-year-old servants. An abbé who founded and ran the orphanage for the city's chimney sweeps, most as young as five or six. Carmelite nuns. Peasant women from the Vivarais, unintelligible in their patois and bewildered at their arrest. One boy in a forgeman's cap. One in a hat of otter skin. One already bloodied and bareheaded. One with little guillotines on his suspenders. One who'd drawn in ink on his neck: *Cut on the dotted line.* The executions proceeding at such a pace that the heads tip from the filled baskets and roll from the scaffold's lip. Never enough in the way of carts, straps, bran, hay, nails, soap for the grooves, or tips for the gravediggers. Baskets changed every two weeks, the bottoms rotted through, the sides chewed by teeth. The machine frequently moved as a menace to sanitation. An old man taking in the great pile of clothing discarded by his predecessors and extending me his compliments, and noting that I must have the most extensive wardrobe of anyone in France.

A man climbs the stairs. He's strapped to the plank. The plank slides forward. The half-moon is brought over his neck. There's a frightful second. His open eyes see the basketful below.

And when the blade comes down, a fiery mist explodes about his eyes. It's radiant with reflected light. The light converts to pain. The pain saturates all that follows. The head suffers for three days and nights, its spark finally extinguished beside its body in the lime pit.

Sulla said he stood before all of Rome and dared to declare: "I am ready to answer for all of the blood I have poured out on behalf of the Republic. I will render an exact account to anyone who comes to plead for a father, son, or brother." And he said that all Rome was silent at his offer.

What a creature is Sanson! Impassive, standing with his slightly timorous look beside his sinister friend, the black heart of the Revolution. He chops off whatever is brought to him. Does he fear being alone? He eats. He gazes at others. Their heads elude him, as his eludes theirs. Will he in his dotage have visitors, each wanting to touch the blade, peer inside the baskets, lie upon the plank? Will he become the town eccentric who plays the cello badly but remains a good neighbor, puttering with his tulips and relating anecdotes to the curious?

Through years of vigils and crises and alarms that kept men

from sleeping, he was never seen unshaven. Insignificance, silence, and dissimulation were his most powerful tools. His machine was a celebration of geometry formally applied, and geometry is the language of reason.

Who presented Pompey's head to Caesar in Egypt? Who presented Cicero's to Antony? History records only whose head was presented to whom. Who did the chopping? Those impossible beings. That species unto themselves.

From his chair Sanson tends the fire and coddles the past. The past for him is his wife. On their first walks their conversation was like the exhilaration of learning itself. When he spoke with her, she lowered her eyes. When he stopped, she lingered until he continued. He blurted during one of their partings that without her he'd be his broken cello, all tunes lost. She smiled when he was in particular need of indulgence. And when her mouth touched him, she smelled like a linen sheet in the sunshine.

In a day or so he knows he'll receive a letter, its hand uneven as though composed on a knee or post: a letter in which she advises him not to be anxious on her behalf, but to honor her steadfastness, which he should have no trouble imagining. A letter in which she tells him she has no counsel to give, and that he should follow those he needs to follow. In which she informs him that she wants nothing in the way of a settlement. In which she confides to him that the time will come when he'll be able to judge the effort she has made to write this. In which she closes by noting that she has no more paper, and that the misfortune that she's awaited has arrived, and that she claps him to her heart.

And even then he'll understand the implication that he could still renounce this life and find her where she suffers. But instead he'll sit in his house, with the face of an absconding debtor. His father told him that if he offered to carry the basket, he shouldn't complain of the weight. His grandmother told him that the tears of strangers were only water. He himself was given a miracle and threw it away. Let his society perish, then, through the ferocity of its factions. Let his city return to its original state of forest. Let his neighbors relapse into the primitive, from which they could one day start again. Let it all go on without him. He was already that head without its body, jolted with the consciousness of its own death. He was already a tiny, bat-winged machine fluttering over a wave of corpses. He was already that empty narrow space between the raised blade and its destination: that opportunity, gone in a tenth of a second, which would never return again.

ALSO BY JIM SHEPARD

PROJECT X

In the wilderness of junior high, Edwin Hanratty is at the bottom of the food chain. His teachers find him a nuisance. His fellow students consider him prey. And although his parents are not oblivious to his troubles, they can't quite bring themselves to fathom the ruthless forces that demoralize him daily. Sharing in these schoolyard indignities is his only friend, Flake. Branded together as misfits, their fury simmers quietly in the hallways, classrooms, and at home, until an unthinkable idea offers them a spectacular and terrifying release. From Jim Shepard, one of the most enduring and influential novelists writing today, comes an unflinching look into the heart and soul of adolescence. Tender and horrifying, prescient and moving, *Project X* will not easily be forgotten.

Fiction/978-1-4000-3348-5

LOVE AND HYDROGEN

The stories in this dazzling array of work in short fiction from a master of the form encompass in theme and compassion what an ordinary writer would take several lifetimes to imagine. A frustrated wife makes use of an enterprising illegal-gun salesman to hold her husband hostage; two hapless adult-education students botch their attempts at rudimentary piano but succeed in a halting, awkward romance; a fascinated and murderous Creature welcomes the first human visitors to his Black Lagoon; and in the title story, the stupefyingly huge airship Hindenburg flies to its doom, representing in 1937 mankind's greatest yearning as well as its titanic failure. Generous in scope and astonishing in ambition, Shepard's voice never falters; the virtuosity of *Love and Hydrogen* cements his reputation as, in the words of Rick Bass, "a passionate writer with a razor-sharp wit and an elephantine heart"—in short, one of the most powerful talents at work today.

Fiction/Short Stories/978-1-4000-3349-2

VINTAGE BOOKS
Available at your local bookstore, or
visit www.randomhouse.com